WHEN ONE
DOOR OPENS
JD RUSKIN

Dreamspinner Press

Published by
Dreamspinner Press
5032 Capital Circle SW
Ste 2, PMB# 279
Tallahassee, FL 32305-7886
USA
http://www.dreamspinnerpress.com/

When One Door Opens

Cover Art by Justin James
dare.empire@gmail.com

ISBN: 978-1-62380-252-3

Printed in the United States of America
First Edition
December 2012

eBook edition available
eBook ISBN: 978-1-62380-253-0

For Brit and Kristen.
Thank you for your support and encouragement.

CHAPTER ONE

LOGAN SELLERS grabbed another box off the truck trailer and placed it on the conveyor belt, sending it down the line to the mail sorting station. He was only an hour into his shift, but his back and thighs burned from the repetitive motion. He was glad the company's dress policy allowed him to wear shorts and a tank top. He couldn't imagine surviving the heat otherwise. The industrial fans positioned throughout the warehouse were more likely to render a guy deaf than fend off the roasting temperatures of Chicago in July. Swiping a bead of sweat from his forehead, he reached for another package. The boxes and mailers of various sizes filled the truck bed. Being six feet seven inches was coming in handy for once; he spent less time climbing in and out. The work was hard, fast-paced, and monotonous, leaving no time for idle thoughts. It was the perfect job for him. Idle thoughts had caused him enough problems. He'd been lucky to apply during a time when they were short on package handlers. While he was still considered part-time, according to his supervisor, he would be needed for at least five hours most days. He earned only enough to scrape by, but the early-morning shift meant he could hopefully find another job during the day.

"Hey, Logan!"

Logan turned toward his supervisor, still holding a box that had to weigh at least seventy pounds. He'd hold the box all day if it meant not dealing with the obnoxious redhead. She wore a pair of hip-hugging jeans and a T-shirt so tight you could ski down her cleavage. "What can I do for you, Ms. Foster?"

"I thought we agreed you'd call me Karen." As she ran her eyes over him in appreciation, Logan resisted the urge to roll his in return. She pouted her too-red lips at him when he didn't comment. "The boss wants to see you," she said before twirling away and sashaying her ass down the line.

Logan sighed, slipping the box onto the conveyor belt. Only one week on the job and already being called into the boss's office was not a good sign. He made his way through the warehouse toward the back offices, passing a long line of workers pulling boxes from trucks and depositing them on the conveyor belt that ran the length of the warehouse. Rounding the corner, he found the floor manager, Harrison Klass, hovering outside his office. When he caught sight of Logan, Klass's eyes widened like those of a raccoon facing down a semi. Logan's height and build meant Logan was used to seeing the look, but now people had a new reason to be skittish around him. Ex-con. He'd been honest when he filled out the job application, but he wondered if the bigwigs had changed their minds about letting someone with a record work here. He hoped not. A steady job was a condition of his parole.

Klass ushered him into the office with a wave of his hand. "Have a seat, Mr. Sellers," Klass said, sounding calmer than he looked. He was on the short side and sixtyish, with a narrow, lined face. Behind an uncluttered mahogany desk, Klass manhandled a black leather swivel chair into position and lowered himself into it with a sigh. The bookshelves on the wall behind him held binders, books, and folders, all arranged with enough precision to make a drill sergeant smile. "I asked to speak with you to see if you're interested in making a special delivery for me."

Logan frowned in confusion. Drivers made deliveries, and as he understood it, it would take a year before he was eligible to apply to the drivers program.

"It would be a—" Klass cleared his throat. "Personal off-the-books delivery."

Logan had just gotten out of prison. He had no intention of doing anything to get his ass put back. He folded his arms across his broad chest, flexing his biceps just a bit. "I don't get involved in drugs, not for nothing."

"Oh, no," Klass stammered, his eyes skittering between Logan's face and the hard muscle of his arms. "It's not what you think." He rubbed his beak of a nose. "I need your help with my sister's kid. He's housebound and needs someone to help him out. You'd be paid a hundred dollars a week plus travel expenses."

Logan dropped his arms to his sides, thinking over the offer. An extra hundred would make life easier until he could find a better job or another part-time one. He didn't mind the idea of helping a guy out, but he wasn't cut out to be anybody's nurse. "What would I be doing exactly?"

Klass smiled and settled back into his chair as if he'd been sure Logan would ask that question. "Twice a week after your shift, you'll retrieve mail from his PO box and take back any he gives you. He prefers Monday and Friday, but he can be flexible if needed. Every couple of weeks, you'll also need to get his order from the grocery near his apartment."

"That's it?"

Klass started fidgeting, twisting the sleeve of his button-down shirt in his hands and looking everywhere but at Logan. "I'd also like you to spend a little time with him just to make sure he's doing okay." He scratched his snow-white hair. "Caleb's an agoraphobic—gets that from his mother, she was a worrier, God rest her soul—and because of his condition, he doesn't leave the apartment. Are you interested?"

Logan hesitated, wondering why his boss would want an ex-con to take care of his nephew. *Maybe he doesn't like his nephew?* If the job turned out to be a nightmare, he'd have a hell of a time getting out of it.

Seeming to pluck the thought from Logan's head, Klass said, "Give it a try and if you decide it's not for you, I'll understand. The last package handler, Marco Rodriguez, did it for over a year before he moved to Florida."

If the last guy did it for that long, how bad could it be? "Okay."

AFTER giving the cab driver the address, Logan looked at the innocuous mailer with the name Caleb Klass scrawled on it. *The guy goes by his uncle's last name.* He realized Klass hadn't mentioned Caleb's dad. *Maybe he's dead or a complete bastard.* He hoped that wasn't the reason the guy never left the apartment. When the cab hauled to a stop, Logan paid the driver and climbed out of the car with the envelope mailer tucked under his arm. After unlocking the door with the front entrance key Klass had given him, he made his way into the medium-sized brick apartment building. He considered himself a fit guy, but climbing in and out of a truck bed for the past five hours had left his calves feeling like jelly. The place was in a decent neighborhood, a far better one than the rathole he lived in. No blood on the walls or stench of urine on the stairs was always a good sign.

He got to Caleb's floor and found his apartment. Number 401. He knocked. And waited. Just when he was about to knock again, he heard a muffled voice through the door: "You're not Marco."

Logan peered at the peephole. "Marco moved to Florida and I'm the new delivery guy," he said, wondering why Caleb didn't already know this. He heard the lock unlatch, and the door slid open, catching on the still attached chain.

"S-shove the p-package through the gap, please."

Logan looked at the instruction sheet Klass had given him. Feeling ridiculous, he said, "It says you've gotta let me in before I can give it to ya." He thought he heard a mumbled curse before the door closed and he heard the slide of the chain lock.

The door reopened enough to allow a pale arm to poke through. "My uncle has a twisted sense of humor and loves screwing with the new guy. P-please, just hand over the p-package and we can both get back to our lives."

Logan hesitated. It had been a long, hot day, and he'd like nothing better than to get out of here. His plans for the weekend included parking his ass in front of the fan and not moving until Monday. He sighed, looking at the sheet of paper again. *Watch out, he's sneaky,* was the second instruction. "You're not getting this package 'til ya let me in."

The arm disappeared, and the door opened far enough for Logan to make his way inside. His eyes took a few seconds to adjust to the dim interior. Floor-length black curtains covered the right wall completely, blocking out the natural light. The main room was spacious, but it had been crammed so full of mahogany and leather that the effect would have been stifling if not for the air conditioner set to arctic. Logan took a moment to savor the icy air on his heated skin before continuing to look around. An L-shaped leather couch, a massive mahogany desk that looked just like his uncle's, and a wall of bookshelves dominated the room. Unlike his uncle, Caleb's books appeared shoved into all available space and filled with everything from paperbacks to leather tomes to cookbooks. A black entertainment center with a flat-screen TV and a shelf filled with DVDs gave Logan a pang of longing. He couldn't afford a radio, let alone a flat screen.

Drawing his gaze away, Logan noticed the man hovering in the kitchen that opened into the main room. He was as far away as he could get without climbing onto the back countertop. Caleb had his back pressed against a stainless steel fridge that matched the rest of the appliances in the kitchen. A light sheen of sweat dampened the hairline of his blond hair.

Logan held out his hands, still holding the mailer. "Don't freak out."

Caleb's green eyes narrowed, and he put his hands on his hips. "Is that supposed to be funny?"

Logan winced. "Didn't mean it like that." He ran a hand over his shaved head. "People tend to get jumpy when they first meet me."

Caleb attempted a smirk, but it came across strained. "That's because you're a giant." He took a step forward, keeping the kitchen island between them. "I wouldn't be surprised to learn you eat angry villagers for breakfast." He had his uncle's talent for sounding calmer than he looked, but his body language screamed "scared rabbit."

Logan noticed the kitchen was spotless, not a dirty dish, half-open cabinet, or food stain to be seen. He remembered Klass mentioning he needed to take out the trash once a week too. He couldn't imagine being so afraid that a trip to the dumpster seemed impossible. Looking around the kitchen, he didn't spot a garbage can. Or smell one for that matter. *What does the little neat freak do? Wash his trash before hiding it away in a cabinet?*

Hoping to put the man at ease, Logan said, "I only eat villagers when I run out of maple oatmeal." That got him a fleeting smile that looked more genuine and drew Logan's attention to the rest of Caleb's face. His hair was shaggy, not like a rock star, but like a woman's hair gets when she's growing out a short style, awkward angles of blond locks. *Guess there aren't many barbers who make house calls.*

"Now that we've bonded over breakfast food," Caleb said, stepping around the island, "how about you hand over the package?"

Logan eyed his boss's nephew head to toe, taking in his form-fitting sweatpants and Chicago Cubs T-shirt. According to Klass, they were the same age, but Caleb looked closer to sixteen than twenty-six. Glancing at his watch, he said, "Not for eight more minutes."

Caleb rolled his eyes, giving Logan a ridiculous craving for the lime Jell-O they served in prison.

"Marco never stayed for the whole ten minutes." He licked his lips, his gaze drifting down and back up again. "He just came in, asked the three Hs, and left."

Logan squinted at the paper. "How are you?"

"I'm agoraphobic. How are you?"

"I'm an ex-drunk," Logan answered automatically. His jaw dropped, and he heard his brain spin in the awkward silence that followed. *What the hell?*

Seeming to take pity on him, Caleb said, "I once offered to host an agoraphobic group meeting, but nobody showed up."

Logan snorted, glad the guy could laugh about his condition. He himself had covered his minifridge with every tasteless joke and cartoon he could find about AA and being an alcoholic. Laughing about it made it somehow easier to deal with. He had the bizarre urge to tell Caleb about his fridge decorations, which made no sense. It wasn't like him to want to share something like that, especially with a man he'd just met. Reading the next question, he raised his brow. "How's your sex life?" he asked. He stared incredulously at the paper. "Why the hell would your *uncle* want to know that?"

"I try not to think about it," Caleb deadpanned.

Suddenly, Logan could think of nothing else. Caleb was the perfect combination of wholesome appeal, with his big green eyes, and sexiness, with the type of lips that made Logan's dick twitch. High cheekbones and a narrow chin gave him a boyish appearance, making Logan wonder if he tasted as sweet as he looked. His thoughts derailed when he read the last question. "Have you left the apartment?"

"No," Caleb said, his cheeks flushing bright against his pallid skin.

"How long has it been since you left?"

"That's n-not on the l-list."

Logan looked away. "Sorry, not my business."

Caleb surprised him by answering. "I sometimes go into the apartment across from me when Mrs. Simon needs something, but I haven't done that for a couple of weeks." He looked at his clutched hands before continuing. "I haven't left the building in almost three years."

Logan glanced at Caleb's pale face, noticing the dark shadows beneath his eyes. He felt like apologizing again, but he held his tongue. He doubted Caleb would appreciate pity from a total stranger. He wouldn't in the same circumstances. Glancing at his watch, he struggled to think of something else to talk about; small talk wasn't one of his strengths, especially not while sober. "Do you have any mailers for me to take back?"

Caleb sighed as if relieved to have a question to answer. "Not today." He crossed his arms over his chest. "I run a small web design and editing business... from home." He winced. "Obviously."

Logan had wondered how a guy who never left his apartment could afford the rent. Caleb had to be pretty good if companies hired him without even meeting him. Given the jumpiness, he doubted Caleb entertained clients here. A trained monkey knew more about computers than Logan did, so the conversation stalled once again. It had been a long time since he'd been so tongue-tied around someone as attractive as Caleb. But setting his sights on a hot guy and making a move wasn't the same as making chitchat. No wonder Marco usually bailed in the first few minutes.

"You'll need me on Mondays and Fridays, right?"

"Yes, and I'm hoping you can pick up my grocery order this coming Monday from Meng's Market." He walked over to the desk, giving Logan a nice view of his tight ass. "Meng's is just three blocks south from here." He brought back a store flyer and handed it to Logan. "If you need to switch days, just let me know. I listed my number." Shifting his weight from side to side, he continued. "Leave a message on my voice mail if I don't answer."

Logan blinked. "Because you might be with your neighbor?"

"Right." Sighing, Caleb rubbed the back of his neck. "Or, I don't always do well on the phone." He looked straight at Logan, his eyes verging on desperate. "Please tell me it's been ten minutes. I swear I'm not normally such a freak. I just have trouble with first-time meetings."

"You're no worse at it than I am," Logan muttered. He didn't have the excuse of a severe phobia. He'd never been much of a conversationalist, but he didn't remember being this bad before prison.

"Do you want something to drink?" Caleb's eyes widened in realization at the implication. When he continued, the words poured from his mouth. "Water, water to drink. I don't have alcohol, and I never do, or coffee or pop because the caffeine makes me hyper, or more hyper and—"

"Water'd be great."

"Right, sure." He headed for the kitchen. "Oh, the part about me not being a freak. Total lie." He pulled out two bottles of water and handed one to Logan.

Grinning, Logan accepted the bottle. "At least you're an honest freak."

"Only when forced," Caleb said.

LOGAN unlocked the door to his studio apartment and made his way inside. After securing it, he stood in the middle of the dank room, his mind going back to the conversation with Caleb. *Three years!* This place wasn't much bigger than the cell he'd lived in for the past year. He'd been sentenced to three years, but lucky enough to get out in one. Caleb was as much a prisoner. Except he hadn't done anything wrong and had no guarantee of ever being released. *That's a fucking depressing thought.*

Logan walked over to his kitchen, which consisted of a wheezing minifridge covered in cut-out comics, a microwave, and a coffee machine. He opened the fridge and pulled out a bottle of water. It wasn't the drink he wanted, but he unscrewed the top and downed the contents. Needing to rein in that train of thought, he dropped to the floor and did twenty push-ups. He alternated between sit-ups and push-ups until all thoughts of oblivion in a bottle fled his mind.

Recovering, he lay back with his arms folded and cupped behind his head, looking at the water-stained ceiling. He'd considered himself lucky when he'd gotten the "no deposit necessary" lease even though twenty-five ex-druggie, ex-crazy, or ex-con residents also called it home. It seemed like a bad idea to have that many unstable individuals in one place, but choices had been limited to say the least. He needed to open the windows and get the fan blowing. Not that it would do much to stifle the oppressive heat. Catching a whiff of himself, he cringed. He was ripe before the workout; now he smelled like a dead skunk. *Maybe that was the real reason Caleb was standing on the other side of the room.* The thought made him smile, and he hauled himself to his feet.

After opening the windows and starting up a white, plastic fan, Logan entered the cramped bathroom, turned on the shower, and adjusted the spray to just above lukewarm. Removing his clothes, he got into the stall. He slid the glass shower door shut and let the water wash over his face and body. Even after a week of being on the outside, the luxury of showering without an audience and taking as much time as he wanted was still a heady feeling. He toyed with the idea of a cold shower to get relief from the heat, but his calf muscles whimpered at the thought.

He ran a washrag over his broad chest. He'd always kept in shape, but he had packed on more muscle after his conviction. There hadn't been much else in the way of entertainment in prison. The weight room became his main escape from tediousness. There were other reasons to want a hard, strong build in prison, but he didn't like to think about them. He'd closed the door on that life. After he lathered his shaved head, he squatted and turned to try to get the spray to hit the top of his head. *The world was built by midgets.* Ridiculously, the thought made him think of Caleb. Caleb was probably just shy of six feet, which made him tiny in comparison to Logan, but hardly short.

Logan closed his eyes and leaned forward, resting his hand on the shower wall in front of him as tepid water poured over his back. Thinking about Caleb was a bad idea. He knew it, but he couldn't seem to stop himself. The subtle once-over Caleb gave him after he'd calmed down had sent a thrill running through Logan that he hadn't felt in a long time. Picturing Caleb's face as Caleb licked his full lips, Logan slid his hand to his hardening shaft. Caleb's long fingers would be satin-smooth but firm as he gripped Logan's cock. For a guy that never left home, Caleb had the lean build of a runner. Logan figured he'd find pale skin rippling with tight muscles under the clingy T-shirt and sweatpants Caleb wore. He squeezed the base of his shaft once before pulling away and applying soap to his hand. He imagined what it would be like to feel that lean body under his, hot and eager to be stroked. *Had it been years since Caleb had been touched?* He let his hand slide up and down in a slow and steady rhythm over his cock.

As the pressure built, Logan started moving his hips, thrusting into his tight grip. Feeling himself about to explode, he leaned forward, resting his head against the cool tile. As his body rushed toward release, he couldn't help imagining Caleb's face, his green eyes turned dark with desire. Logan's breath caught in his throat, and he dropped his other hand to fondle his balls. One touch was all it took. He threw his head back and shot his load against the tiled wall. Knees wobbling, he made a halfhearted attempt to clean off the tile before shutting off the shower.

As he reached for a towel to dry off, Logan wondered how Caleb would feel if he knew that Logan had just jacked off thinking of him. He cringed. *The guy isn't freaked enough? He's got to worry about an ex-con wanting to bend him over and fuck him against the countertop?* He didn't know why his libido had suddenly gone into overdrive, but considering Caleb was his boss's nephew, he needed to get a handle on the feelings.

THE sound of the phone startled Caleb, causing him to spill chamomile tea on the kitchen countertop. With a sigh, he put the kettle back on the stove and snagged a dishcloth from the drawer. He didn't need to look at the caller ID to know who was calling. Uncle Harrison had been phoning every half hour for the past four hours in an attempt to badger Caleb into talking to him. *Why didn't he tell me he had found a replacement for Marco?* Picking up the mug, he cleaned up the spill. *Does he expect me to forget to be phobic if I'm surprised?* Caleb knew he could answer the phone and ask his uncle directly, but he stubbornly refused to do so.

After the voice mail kicked in, he picked up the kettle again and filled the mug with the fragrant brew. He needed the soothing properties of the tea to untangle his jangled nerves. Taking a deep swallow, he let his thoughts shift to the new package handler. He didn't know what to think of Logan other than he was huge and hot. There was something strangely vulnerable about the way Logan had sat with his broad shoulders hunched as his secret spilled from his tongue. Shock had been plain on his face when he admitted to being an alcoholic. The look was quickly replaced with resignation. *He expected me to be afraid of him.* For some reason, Caleb had felt compelled to show Logan otherwise.

When the phone began ringing again, Caleb was tempted to disconnect it. But he wasn't sure if his uncle would follow through on his threat. Uncle Harrison had found a behavioral therapist that was willing to come to the apartment. He said he would show up at the apartment with the therapist in tow if Caleb disabled the phone again. Caleb couldn't take the risk. What if the therapist declared him unfit? Would they force him to leave his apartment? A tingling shiver raced up Caleb's arm, chasing away the warmth of the tea. He snatched the phone from the charger and hit the Talk button. "I'm fine."

"You're angry with me. Is that why you refused to answer? I've been worried sick."

Caleb wanted to ask him why he had called instead of coming over and knocking on the door if he was so concerned. Hell, he had a spare key. He could walk right in. Caleb hadn't bothered to get the lock changed after the last time his uncle showed up unannounced six months ago. "It would've been nice if you had told me Logan was coming today. What if I had been out?"

"You're deflecting."

Caleb bit down on the urge to say *am not* like a recalcitrant child. He'd be listening to his uncle spout pop psychology proverbs all night if he didn't get a better handle on his emotions. "Like I said, I'm fine."

"Do you want me to try to find someone else to deliver your mail? Did Logan upset you?"

"Logan didn't do anything to upset me. I'm fine with him coming over," Caleb said, surprised to realize it was the truth.

"If you are sure," his uncle said, sounding doubtful.

"I am. Good night, Uncle Harrison."

He sighed. "Goodnight, Caleb."

CHAPTER
TWO

ON MONDAY morning, Klass had Foster fetch him a couple of hours into his shift. Logan knew he should tell Klass he wasn't interested in the job. He should make up an excuse about being too tired or not knowing if his parole officer, John Dabb, would approve the job. Both were true, just not the reason. He'd cleaned the reason off the shower wall on Saturday morning.

Sitting behind his impeccably neat desk, Klass asked, "How did it go?"

"It went fine. I followed your instructions," Logan said, silently hoping his boss didn't expect a report on his nephew's sex life. He really needed to stop thinking about sex and Caleb in the same sentence.

Klass sighed. "I know he's a grown man and I've no right to pry into his life." He straightened an already straight stapler before continuing. "I loved my sister, Mr. Sellers. And she *loved* that boy. I just want to do right by her. Since she died three years ago, he's been slipping further and further away."

Logan swallowed hard. *The guy's worried and I'm perving over his nephew.* "He looked okay, a bit on the skinny side. I don't think I would've noticed if you hadn't told me he was phobic."

Klass nodded. "Let me know if anything changes."

This was the opportunity to get out of the job and just walk away. Let someone else help Caleb. Logan sighed. Who was he kidding? The money was too good to pass on. His dick would just have to get with the program. "Sure thing, boss."

Klass hunched forward, dropping his chin to his chest. "Also, please tell Caleb to fill you in on the details about the radiator."

Logan returned to his work station, wondering what would be up with the radiator in July. It was busy, so the rest of his shift passed quickly. When he saw the clock and realized it was almost time to go, it came as a pleasant surprise. He wiped his forearm over his sweating forehead and wondered if he ought to go home for a quick shower before picking up Caleb's groceries. In the end, he decided not to. For all he knew, Caleb might not have any food in the apartment and was quietly starving. The guy was skinny enough already.

The end of his shift rolled around, and Logan walked out into the sunshine, temporarily a free man. Oh, except for the fact that he now had to find a place called Meng's Market and pick up a grocery order for the boss's nephew. The thought of groceries made him remember how inadequate his hasty breakfast had been several hours earlier. Hopefully this delivery wouldn't take too long and he would be able to go home and grab a bite.

LOGAN stepped through the sliding door at Meng's Market. The place featured high-quality meats and locally grown produce, making it worlds away from the 7-Eleven convenience store he shopped at. He walked past the aisles, ignoring his grumbling stomach, and made his way to the service counter next to the produce. He stopped when he spotted an advertisement for instant oatmeal. After grabbing a box of maple flavor, he continued to the back.

At the counter, a short, wiry Asian man scowled at a computer screen as if it had insulted his mother. Logan could relate. They had kicked him out of the technology course in prison after his third computer committed suicide. When the old man smacked the side of the monitor, a sweet-faced Asian woman with glossy black hair down to her hips appeared at his side.

"Let me do it, Grandfather." She adjusted her thick black glasses and set to work, fingers flying over the keys.

The man grumbled and turned his attention to Logan. His bald head gleamed in the fluorescent lighting. "How I help you?"

"I'm here for Caleb Klass's order."

The man traded a look with his granddaughter, and they began having a heated conversation in a language Logan couldn't understand. He thought it might be Korean, but that could be his stomach talking. Korean barbecued pork was on the list of things he'd longed for in prison. That the list mostly consisted of food and liquor was a bit disconcerting.

"Is there a problem?"

The little guy straightened his shoulders. "Mister Klass good customer." He pointed a finger at Logan. "He... e-mail order."

Logan looked at the girl, but she just covered her mouth with her hand. Her olive-black eyes held amusement and affection. After a moment she said, "You must be Logan. I'm Min." Her voice was bright and cheery with no trace of her grandfather's thick accent.

He shook hands with Min, her strong grip in contrast with her delicate frame. She said something else to the man before grabbing a partially filled box. "I'll go get the perishables, Grandfather."

The man waved her off. "I only give what Mister Klass order."

Logan looked at the box of oatmeal in his hand, finally understanding. "I can buy my own oatmeal." Barely, but he hadn't planned on sticking Caleb with the bill. He pulled a five-dollar bill from his wallet and tossed it on the counter.

The man spent an insulting amount of time examining the money before he rang up the order and placed the box in a plastic bag. Who would use counterfeit money to buy oatmeal?

Min reappeared, carrying the box. "I'm sorry about that." She placed the now filled box on the counter. "Grandfather's a bit protective of Caleb." The glint in her eyes said Mr. Meng wasn't the only one. "He's a long time customer and he's helping us set up a website."

"Not a problem," Logan said, thinking there was probably a reason for the caution. The thought pissed him off. Some asshole must have tried to get Caleb to pay for his booze or cigarettes. It was no wonder if Klass was hiring ex-cons to help his nephew.

Looking at the grocery bag, an idea occurred. "Can I borrow a marker?" He pried open the box of oatmeal and pulled out one of the brown packets. *Maple, the preferred flavor for giants.* After accepting the marker, he scribbled "in case of emergencies" on the packet and dropped it into the box. Min's lips quirked as she took back the marker but she didn't comment.

When an uncomfortably familiar female voice called out his name, Logan stifled a groan, not wanting to turn and face the hundred and ten pounds of hairspray and cheap perfume heading for him. *This day just keeps gettin' better and better.* As he turned, he schooled his expression, thinking neutral preferable to irritated when dealing with his supervisor, if he wanted to keep getting a paycheck. "What's up?"

"I had no idea you shopped here," Ms. Foster said. "After the shift, I had a *craving* I just had to fulfill." She tilted the plastic handbasket, drawing Logan's eyes to the contents: a bag of limes, a jumbo-sized box of condoms, and a bottle of tequila so cheap even the college kids wouldn't touch it. She tossed her too-red-to-be-natural hair over her shoulder and he felt a pang of sympathy for her boyfriend. He'd heard the man used to work at the warehouse. Logan hoped never to meet the guy, but not because he feared his reaction to his girlfriend's obvious interest in another man. The guy *had* to know Foster slept with every man she could sink her claws into even if he wasn't around to see her blatant flirting.

Ms. Foster's hand on his chest drew his thoughts back to her. "It must be fate us meeting here. I normally never settle for shopping at a place like this," she said, her nose wrinkling in disgust.

Logan heard Min mutter something that he guessed meant bitch in possibly Korean. He looked over his shoulder and mouthed the word "sorry," feeling responsible for subjecting them to his supervisor. Min gave him a brief, sympathetic smile.

A manicured hand on his chin had Logan turning back toward Ms. Foster. She gave an annoyed huff. "As I was saying, it must be fate that I stopped here today. How about we get out of here and toss back a few?" By the sour smell of her breath, she'd already started with beer.

Logan had always been a working drunk, putting in his hours at the construction site before heading out to get plastered. He'd placed five different alarm clocks around his apartment that were loud enough to drag his ass out of a drunken stupor. He'd always made it to work on time, even if it meant hacking his guts into a garbage bag before getting out of his truck. Just a few beers to relax after work, a shot or three to forget about the asshole foreman. Rinse and repeat until he stumbled home. He saved the weekends for the real hard stuff, waking on Sunday morning smelling of booze and sex with no memory of how he'd gotten home or who he'd fucked. He was damn lucky not to have gotten seriously hurt, or caught a disease from one of the nameless people he'd slept with while trashed. With all those turbulent memories tumbling through his brain at the first whiff of alcohol, a quiet voice in the back of his head still whispered to him. Tequila was rough stuff, but a couple of beers wouldn't be so bad. A six-pack of Corona would go great with the limes. He'd worked hard. Didn't he deserve to kick back and relax? He could just take the night off and then get back on the program tomorrow. He shook his head, stepping back until his body jammed against the counter. "I can't do that."

"You better get those groceries home," Min said, ignoring the scowl on Ms. Foster's face. "It isn't good for them to be out in this heat."

Ms. Foster shoved her basket on top of a pile of oranges and walked away, stepping around the falling produce. When Logan could breathe again, he opened his wallet and pulled out a business card, handing it to Min as he turned around. "You see me buying liquor, I want you to call this guy, John Dabb, and let him know."

She looked at his parole officer's business card, her brows puckered. "Won't you get in trouble?"

"Yeah." Logan grabbed the box. "But not as much trouble as I'll cause if you don't." He left before she could comment.

AS HE lumbered up the stairs with the groceries, Logan wished Caleb's building had an elevator. He'd worked his own shift and half of another guy's today. He shook his head and gave himself a mental note to start using the stairs at his third-floor apartment to avoid sounding like such a pussy in his own head.

Caleb looked surprised when he opened the door, wearing another pair of obscenely tight sweatpants and a different Chicago Cubs T-shirt. The chilly air was enough to make his nipples as perky as a cheerleader during homecoming. "I wasn't sure if you'd be back." Caleb took the box from Logan and walked into the kitchen, setting it on the counter. "I went through half a dozen guys before Marco."

Logan did not need that image in his head as he avoided looking at Caleb's ass. "The money's good and the job's not hard."

"Oh," Caleb said, throwing up his hands. "I forgot last time." Opening a breadbox, he pulled a twenty from a stack of bills in a bank envelope. Logan resisted the urge to roll his eyes. Caleb obviously had no common sense. *Why don't you hand over your wallet while you're at it?*

Handing the money to Logan, he said, "This is for travel expenses for today and last time."

On Friday, Logan had been kicking himself for not remembering to get a receipt from the cab driver. He'd assumed Klass would make him track everything if he wanted to get reimbursed. "It didn't cost me this much to get here," he felt compelled to point out.

Caleb flapped a hand as if this were an insignificant detail. "Consider it hazard pay." Before Logan could ask him what he meant by *that*, Caleb handed him a folded note.

After unfolding the paper, Logan said, "I didn't realize instruction writing was genetic."

"Ha, ha. What do they do in your family? Devour villagers?"

Logan smirked. "It's not my fault you come from a family of midgets." When Caleb scoffed, he added, "Sorry, I meant vertically challenged." While Caleb grumbled about finding an axe, Logan read the note. In bold print, Caleb had written *Panic Attack*. Below the words was a list of instructions. *1. Don't Freak Out.* Looking up, Logan said, "I'm never going to live that down, am I?"

"Nope." Caleb started to unpack the box of groceries. "I'm thinking of putting it on a T-shirt."

Logan read the next instruction rather than stare at Caleb's chest again. *2. Don't try to help.* He felt a pang of relief and a stab of guilt seeing the words. He'd seen new fish in the pen melt down when the reality of prison life beat them over the head their first night. Many of them yelled at the injustice, some even cried, and a few just got real quiet, retreating into themselves. The quiet ones rarely lasted long, either taking their own life or by pushing someone else into doing it for them. Shaking off the memory, he read the last instruction. *3. Close the door on your way out.* "That's it? I'm just supposed to walk out and leave? You don't need me to call a doctor or nothing?"

"Trust me, it's better that way. It'll be over quicker if I don't have someone around to see it. And there isn't much a paramedic can do other than drug me up and tell me to stop breathing like a pregnant lady in labor." His gaze grew distant and his voice sounded distracted. "It won't kill me. It just feels that way." He turned toward the fridge, placing a few items inside before returning to the box.

Logan didn't like the idea of leaving him alone, but he didn't argue. He didn't have any experience with this sort of thing. "Can I ask what the panic attack is like?"

Caleb was quiet long enough to make Logan think he wouldn't answer before he spoke. "It's like walking through a haunted house. You know some college student in a cheap costume is going to jump out and try to scare you." He shook his head. "You know it isn't real and that you're not in any danger. But when that arm reaches out and grabs you, your body reacts. You flinch away from the touch, your breathing quickens, and your heart races. You can't stop it. No amount of logic or reason can stop it."

Logan froze. He knew that feeling. When a seemingly uncontrollable urge took over and made him crave booze that he knew he shouldn't drink. He hated that feeling, the absolute helplessness it evoked. He cleared his throat. "I'm supposed to ask you about the radiator."

Something flashed and then disappeared in an instant on Caleb's face, something Logan couldn't identify. His voice sounded wooden when he spoke again. "What's the penalty for not telling you?"

"He didn't mention nothing. Just said to ask."

"I swear he gets off on making me look like a freak."

"Then blow him off. You don't need him to get mail or groceries delivered. Why let him bully you?" He didn't like being Klass's weapon of choice, but he disliked Caleb passively letting it happen even more.

"I wouldn't have my business if he hadn't lent me the startup money." Caleb said the words grudgingly, his bitterness palpable. "I owe him and he takes full advantage of it in the name of curing me of my little problem." He shook his head. "I don't know why I'm telling you these things."

Logan wasn't sure why either, but he didn't want the conversation to end. "I don't know anything about your uncle, but he acts like he's worried about you. Like maybe he wants to help you and don't know how."

When Caleb spoke again, he turned away, facing the stove as if he didn't want Logan to see his face. "Two winters ago the radiator broke." His words were clear and methodical like he'd recited them many times before. "I knew I needed to contact the apartment manager to get it fixed. Even on a Saturday, they would've sent someone what with the weather being so cold. All I had to do was p-pick up the ph-phone."

Caleb paused, taking a slow, deep breath. When he continued, his voice showed no sign of distress, but his shoulders trembled. "I started to call, but then my brain started What If-ing. What if they try to make me leave the apartment or evict me? What if the maintenance guy can't fix it? What if I go crazy while he's here? Or I freak the guy out so he rushes the job and the radiator ends up exploding and burning down the apartment complex? I got more and more upset until all I could do was crawl under the covers and bury my head like a little kid afraid of the boogeyman."

The idea of agoraphobia being potentially deadly wasn't something Logan had considered. What if there was a fire? Would Caleb refuse to leave his apartment? Moving around the island, Logan brought his hand to Caleb's shoulder and rested it there, noticing how red and puckered the skin above his too-tight T-shirt collar looked. There was no flinch, no nervous reaction, just a softly exhaled breath before Caleb continued. "I don't remember anything else before waking up in the hospital four days later. My uncle told me that I was clutching the phone and mumbling *need help* over and over when he found me. I figure I calmed enough to realize I needed help just in time for the hypothermia to completely muddle my brain and make it impossible." Seeming to shake the dark thoughts off easily, Caleb asked, "Are you hungry?"

Logan's stomach answered for him while he was still brooding over what Caleb had told him.

Caleb chuckled and began pulling more items from the box of groceries. "I'll take that as a yes."

Logan walked back to the other side of the island. "I can get something on the way home." He didn't sound convincing even to himself. He was so sick of eating fast food he was actually missing prison slop.

Caleb pulled out a grill pan from a bottom cabinet and set the burner to medium. "It's no bother and this way you can report you saw me eat." He pulled a loaf of crusty Italian bread from the box and began slicing it. The fresh-baked aroma had been torturing Logan since he'd retrieved the order. His stomach gave another gurgling grumble. Last night's dinner had consisted of stale crackers, peanut butter, and water. At least in prison, he got a carton of milk. *God, I'm pathetic.* Realizing what Caleb had said, Logan replied, "He don't ask for specifics, just wants to know if you're okay."

Opening a jar of red roasted peppers with more force than necessary, Caleb said, "Marco said he wasn't allowed to tell me." He pulled out two peppers and placed them on a cutting board with a splat. He started chopping them with enough force to make Logan concerned for his fingers.

Hoping to distract the man from his thoughts, Logan asked, "Was Marco an ex-con like me?"

Caleb froze, the knife poised over the peppers.

Logan blinked. "Your uncle didn't tell you? What the hell was the guy thinking?"

Caleb shook his head, his green eyes wide. "But he did call me right after you left."

The sudden anger this answer evoked was almost overwhelming, and Logan couldn't stop himself from saying, "That ain't good enough. He should have told you I had a record. For all he knew, I could've forced you to say everything was okay."

Seeing Caleb's distressed face, Logan willed the anger from his voice and asked, "Why would he pick me of all people?" *Why trust me with you?* was his unspoken thought. Klass had to know what a vulnerable position his nephew was in, or he was a complete moron. A guy too afraid to call a maintenance worker wouldn't be likely to call the cops either.

Caleb's cheeks flushed, and he ducked his head. He started assembling the sandwiches, layering the bread with slices of ham, some sort of white cheese, and the peppers. "I can guess why," he said, sneaking a peek at Logan before lowering his head again, "but you probably don't want to know."

"Tell me."

He lowered his long gold lashes. "Um… I told you my uncle has a twisted sense of humor." Turning his back to Logan, he placed the sandwiches on the grill. He then grabbed a cast-iron skillet and placed it on top of them for some reason before he spoke again. "Well, I have a type and… you're pretty much it."

Logan raised his eyebrows. "So you and Marco…."

Caleb spun around. "No," he said, holding out his hands. "Marco is married and even if he hadn't been, I wouldn't have been interested." He grabbed a sponge from the sink and wiped the cutting board before putting it away. He then went to work on the counter, keeping his eyes cast down as if the cleaning needed his full attention.

Ignoring the alarm sirens hammering Logan's skull, he asked, "Why not?"

Caleb didn't say anything at first, turning back toward the stove. He flipped over the sandwiches and replaced the skillet. "Marco's a good guy—even if he has the annoying view I should be more obedient toward my uncle." He shrugged. "It's not something I've done… or wanted to do since I stopped going out."

After moving around the island, Logan pulled on Caleb's arm, encouraging him to turn back around. "I know the feeling," he said, keeping his voice low and serious. "Guys named Spike and Bubba were just dying to date me in the pen." When Caleb's eyes widened and his mouth dropped open, Logan couldn't maintain the façade. He laughed, and then laughed harder when Caleb swatted his arm in indignation.

"Let's eat, Romeo." Removing a set of plates from the cabinet, Caleb directed Logan to sit on a stool in front of the island while he placed the sandwiches on plates and added a handful of tortilla chips.

As Logan bit into his sandwich, he lifted his eyebrows in surprise. "Oh, man, that's good." The saltiness of the ham and cheese mixed with the smoky tang of the peppers blended perfectly.

Caleb smiled. "I'm glad you like it." He handed Logan a bottle of water from the fridge. "Marco was too chicken to eat the crazy gringo's cooking."

"He's an idiot," Logan said around a mouthful of sandwich. "I should be paying you for this."

Caleb concentrated on his own sandwich, a hint of a blush touching his cheeks. They finished the meal in companionable silence. After clearing away the dishes, Caleb flipped over the box, causing the oatmeal packet to plop to the floor. He bent over to retrieve it, and Logan bit his tongue to keep from groaning. Logan watched Caleb break into laughter when he read the package. It seemed to light his entire face. He hoped he would see that light again.

Caleb walked Logan to the door. As it opened, a woman's shrill voice called out to them.

"Hello, Mrs. Simon," Caleb said, poking his head through the opening. Logan observed the white-knuckled grip Caleb had on the doorframe. He peered over the top of Caleb's head to see an elderly woman in a white blouse and a long, flower-patterned skirt standing in front of the apartment across the hall.

"Who's that strapping young man you've got with you?"

"Come on," Logan whispered, grabbing Caleb under the armpits and hauling him into the hall. He ignored Caleb's yelp and continued, "Introduce me to the old bird before she starts beating us with her twenty pound purse."

Moisture dotted Caleb's forehead, but there was a ghost of a smile on his face.

"Hello, ma'am. I'm Logan Sellers."

The old woman shuffled across the hall. Her thick silvery-white hair was pulled back in a long braid from a fine-boned face. She was so tiny that Logan thought he'd have to kneel just to shake her hand. She saved him the trouble by squeezing his elbow in greeting. "Glad to meet you, sonny."

She looked at Caleb and dished out the kind of embarrassment only the ancient can get away with. "Is he your boyfriend?" She tilted her head back to look Logan over and said, "He's quite a big fella."

Caleb looked down, and spots of high color appeared over his cheekbones. "He's Marco's replacement, not my… uh… boyfriend."

A twinkle shined in Mrs. Simon's eyes as she pursed her lips. "Caleb, dear," she said, laying a delicate hand on his arm. "Could you give me a hand with some boxes?"

Not looking the old woman in the eye, Caleb said, "Actually, I really need to work." He looked at Logan, his eyes wild. "Could you help her?"

"Sure thing."

Caleb nodded his head vigorously. "Great. That's great. Thanks." He scurried back into his apartment and secured the door. Sneaky bastard.

The old bird's affable demeanor disappeared with the slide of the lock. "You," she said, pointing a bony finger against Logan's stomach. "Come with me." She turned toward her door, not bothering to see whether he followed. He did the only thing he could. He followed.

Logan took in the apartment. It mirrored Caleb's, but it couldn't be more different. Lacy cream curtains let the light soak the room. A sparse collection of antique and uncomfortable-looking furniture populated the main area. Doilies and crocheted blankets covered every available surface. He rubbed his nose as the smell of potpourri and cat hair invaded his nostrils. An enormous orange cat groomed itself on the pillow-piled sofa.

Mrs. Simon settled herself primly on the couch, smoothing her skirt. "Have a seat, sonny."

Logan eyed the little paisley couch dubiously before taking a seat. The springs squealed in protest when he settled into place.

She folded her hands in her lap. "I have a hard enough time getting that boy to come over here without you offering to do it for him. He's too scared unless he thinks I need his help."

"Maybe he just don't like cats," Logan grumbled when the tabby came over to investigate him. He didn't cringe away from its polka-dotted nose sniffing his arm, but it was a near thing.

"Do you know about what happened with the radiator?" Mrs. Simon asked, reaching for the orange cat, and cuddling him in her arms. Logan was surprised she could lift the thing. It had to be part tiger.

"Yeah, Caleb told me."

"Before that, his uncle used to try harder to get Caleb help, but realizing that Caleb would rather die than leave his apartment shook him to the core." The monster in her lap began to purr like a Harley when she rubbed behind its ear. "But what his uncle doesn't understand is it wasn't about choice. Do you know why so many old folks die when the weather turns really hot?"

When Logan shook his head, she continued, her voice somber. "The frailty of the body as we age is part of it but not all of it. They die because they are too afraid to open the windows. They know how dangerous the heat can be, but they are more terrified of a robber coming into their homes than they are of dying from the high temperatures. Caleb didn't choose to die. He was just more afraid of the alternative."

Logan hadn't thought of it like that, but it made a twisted sort of sense. Caleb chose to risk freezing to death instead of the possibility of burning if the radiator exploded. It would be damn terrifying to believe those his only options.

"Someone has to help that child, and that uncle of his sure as heckfire doesn't know how."

Logan snorted. "Ain't that the truth." It bothered him more than it should. He knew there were professionals who checked on housebound people. *Maybe they're more expensive and Klass's a cheap bastard.* Except Caleb ran his own business and, by the look of his apartment, was doing good. Whatever the reason, Caleb needed to know who his uncle was bringing in to help him. Logan wouldn't do anything to hurt Caleb, but Klass didn't know that.

"Caleb's a nice young man and would have a lot to offer someone." She paused, giving Logan a pointed look that made his ears burn. "I imagine it won't be long before he's snatched up." The unspoken challenge was clear in her voice. He stifled the urge to tell her to mind her own damn business. The idea of her working her matchmaking skills on Caleb irked him irrationally. He'd give her credit; she was a perceptive old lady. Most people were too busy gawking at his height to wonder about his orientation. She'd figured it out in a matter of seconds. That she thought he might be a potential match for Caleb surprised him, but it wasn't like he wore a name tag reading "alcoholic ex-con." If she knew his background, she'd likely never consider him as boyfriend material. Shaking off the thought, he offered his hand and said good-bye before heading out.

ON THURSDAY, about a dozen people waited on the platform for the Red Line L train as Logan climbed the stairs. A double shift at the warehouse and then an hour-long anger management class had left him with a less than cheery disposition. The potent smell of piss and coffee wasn't helping his mood. Today, the speaker had lectured them in her condescending baby voice about the body's biochemical response to anger. It was pretty clear her idea of anger management was not yelling at the Starbucks server who'd screwed up her soy mocha latte. It was hard to worry about the threat of heart attack or stroke from chronic anger when there were more immediate dangers. Like three to five years for an assault conviction.

Logan made his way under the wooden canopy and leaned against a metal pillar. The AA meeting he was headed for now was also court ordered like the class, but he knew he needed to go to it. That hadn't been the case when he'd started the program in prison. He'd been thinking about making himself a better parole candidate, not about recovery. It wasn't until he'd listened to the other cons tell their stories that he realized how close he'd come to making the pen his permanent address.

A rumbling vibration that shook the whole platform signaled the arrival of the train. After the train ground to a halt and the doors slid open, Logan ducked his head and made his way inside. The train wasn't packed, but there weren't any open seats. Moving away from the doors, he latched on to a metal rail. An old man in tattered clothes grumbling in the back corner made Logan think about the cantankerous priest who had run the AA meetings in prison. Father Murphy had been in AA for more years than Logan had been alive. His direct, honest approach could slice a man to pieces, but he'd be there to help put him back together.

The train screeched and rattled like an old-time wooden roller coaster as it pulled away from the station. Father Murphy had been the first to introduce Logan to the idea of a "higher power." Logan hadn't been religious growing up. He could remember his mom going to church alone, because his old man said he wouldn't let the pompous hypocrites infect his son. Logan had supported any belief that had him eating cereal and watching cartoons on Sunday mornings instead of spending two hours in a stuffy church. A hazy blur clouded his memories of the night he was arrested. He couldn't say he believed in God any more now than as a kid, but he liked to think that some intangible thing had stepped in and stopped him from killing that night. The train lurched to a halt, and the conductor announced Logan's stop.

As Logan exited the station and headed toward Belmont Avenue, he wondered whether Stacy would be at the meeting tonight. She'd been too busy at work to make the 6:00 p.m. start time last week. He'd first met Stacy a few weeks ago at an AA meeting hosted by the prison, where volunteers agreed to help inmates transition from jail meetings to local AA meetings. She had moved to the area recently, having transferred to her company's Chicago office, but was a veteran of AA for the past seven years. The meeting chair had prattled endlessly about the importance of selecting the right sponsor once the inmate was released. After the inmate joined a meeting, the guy recommended they find a sponsor of the same gender and socioeconomic level. He'd then called a five-minute cookie break...

A striking woman in a power suit and four-inch heels had strutted across the room, heading straight for Logan. Without preamble she said, "I'm a lesbian and don't want to sponsor a chick." She then gave

Logan a feral grin, her straight, white teeth gleaming. "But if you call me your fag-hag, I'll rip your balls off."

Logan stared slack-jawed at her as she gave him her contact information and demanded the details of his release. She claimed him like a momma cat taking in a wild cub. No amount of arguing with the woman could convince her she'd be better off helping someone else...

While Logan completed the inmate reentry program, Stacy went scouting, explaining it was important to find the right meeting. Eventually, she settled on a gay/lesbian closed-session group that required people apply rather than just show up and that had about twenty members. Logan had followed Stacy like a good little cub.

New Town Club hosted the AA meeting. The non-profit organization supported LGBT individuals with just about every anonymous recovery there was, from overeaters to sexual compulsives to drugs. As Logan entered the reception area, he gave the decorators credit for picking a theme and sticking to it. There were bright blue walls, a fire-red couch, a huge rainbow banner on the wall, and a dozen colorful framed pictures. He greeted the receptionist with a nod before heading for the front meeting room.

The yellow walls of the meeting room were near blinding in their intensity. More colorful pictures decorated the walls, along with poster-sized versions of the AA "Twelve Steps" and "Twelve Traditions." Logan turned as he heard his name called out. Stacy stepped into the room, dressed to kill as usual in a short black skirt, a snug top that enhanced her bosom, and high heels. Her dark hair was pinned in an elaborate up-do.

The heels brought Stacy to nearly six feet. Logan bent over so Stacy could air-kiss his cheek. Lipstick lesbian. Not that Logan was stupid enough to say the words aloud. He had liked her from their first meeting and in spite of their very different backgrounds, they were well on their way to becoming friends after only a month of acquaintance. There was something about having a shared history, knowing each other's bullshit and excuses because you'd lived them.

Logan noticed Stacy scowling at the only other woman in the room, Kathy. A pixie blonde in her thirties, dressed in a trendy tracksuit, she was dragging blue folding chairs into place to form a circle.

Stacy crossed her arms across her ample chest. "I don't think I can stay if Soccer Mom is chairing."

Logan sighed. Members took turns running the meetings, and tonight was apparently Soccer Mom's night. "My PO, Dabb, will be pissed if I switch groups again."

"She's not even a real lesbian, but a closet-case that does nothing but whine about how her husband and forty kids don't understand her. No shit. They don't even know she's in AA let alone that she prefers pussy to penises. How *can* they understand her?"

Logan clenched his jaw to avoid laughing. Wagging a finger at her, he said, "No judgment," parroting one of the meeting's unofficial rules.

Stacy looked stricken. "You're right. I'm being judgmental."

Giving Stacy's shoulder a squeeze, Logan said, "Hard to blame you after she spent twenty minutes talking last week about how the cat throwing up on the carpet made her want to get wasted. It sure in the hell made me want to drink after having to listen about it."

Stacy giggled. "It was bad, but everybody's stressors are different. I have to remember that." Turning toward the door she whispered, "Your boyfriend is here."

Jeffrey entered the room, eyes scanning until he zeroed in on Logan. He smiled as he walked, and he had one hell of a smile. He had an attractive face with big blue eyes and streaked, shoulder-length light brown hair. He was dressed in jeans and a black T-shirt, which clearly outlined the muscles of his chest and stomach. He had the kind of body that showed he worked at it.

Jeffrey bounced on his toes, plainly waiting for Logan to say something. He kept smiling, but his expression held something that looked too much like longing to be comfortable. If he hadn't been a recovering alcoholic, Logan might have been tempted to go for him, but combining vices was never a good idea. That and Dabb really would be pissed if Logan was thrown out of the group because the fling turned sour.

"How's it going, man?" Logan asked.

"It's great to see you," Jeffrey said like he'd been mainlining caffeine. "Both of you."

He was always in perpetual motion. Hands fluttering, toes tapping, mouth masticating a piece of gum. Logan had been shocked to learn Jeffrey wasn't a current or ex-smoker like so many of the members. Jeffrey was just a bundle of nervous energy. Booze had been the only thing to tame his constant jitters.

Jeffrey hadn't propositioned him, but he'd made his interest clear and Logan wondered what it would be like to be the focus of that much energy. Father Murphy had told Logan not to fuck anything but his right hand for the first year after prison, which had been seriously disturbing coming out of an eighty-year-old priest's mouth. Messy relationships ranked as one of the top reasons alkies ended up going back to the bottle. *Maybe I should go for it*, Logan thought as he watched Jeffrey make the rounds, greeting arriving members and looking over his shoulder at Logan every few steps. *I'd be less likely to hit on Caleb that way.*

More guys, mostly in their forties and fifties entered the meeting room and took a seat in the circle of chairs. Soccer Mom stood at the podium, arranging sheets of paper and encouraging people to enjoy the cookies on the snack table.

"He wants you bad," Stacy said as they both watched Jeffrey take a seat across from where they stood.

"How do you know that? Did he pass you a note during study hall?" Logan pulled Stacy over to the chairs and took a seat. "I'm not looking for a boyfriend. I got enough shit to deal with."

"He's just looking for some fun, not to get you in a tux." Stacy gave him an assessing look. "You got someone else wanting to rock your world?"

Logan felt his face flush. Against his will, the memory surfaced like a burst of sunlight in his head: Caleb's sweet smile and bright green eyes.

Stacy's blue eyes widened as if drawing the story from Logan's head telepathically. "You do! Who is it? Someone from work?"

Ignoring her, Logan leaned back on his chair as Soccer Mom recited the opening prayer with about half the members saying it with her. Another member took over and started reciting the "Twelve Traditions and Promises." Logan let the now familiar words soak in, trying to get into the inner headspace he'd heard so much about.

A bony elbow to his ribs interrupted his attempt at enlightenment.

"I'm your sponsor. You have to confide in me," Stacy whined.

"I'm not talking to you about Caleb, so you can forget it."

Soccer Mom gave Logan the stink-eye, making him feel like he was back in high school. He snuck a peek at the suddenly quiet Stacy. Her grin was blinding. "So the guy you're dating has a name. Caleb," she said, drawing out the syllables like a snotty teenager.

"I'm not dating him. He's housebound and I deliver stuff to his apartment a couple a times a week."

Her grin faltered. "Is he disabled?"

Logan didn't like thinking of Caleb like that. "No, he's real smart and he makes web pages."

Stacy bit her bottom lip. "Not porn sites, right? He hasn't asked to take your picture?"

"What?"

Her grin reappearing, she said, "You don't want to end up on Jerkme.com."

Logan realized the rest of the room had gone quiet. Too quiet. Reluctantly, he looked away from Stacy and at the rest of the members.

A grizzled man in his sixties said, "I'd pay to see that."

"Now I'm not judging," said a preppy-looking guy Logan thought was named Mark. "But there's a lot of substance abuse in the porn industry. Aren't you worried being in that environment will affect your recovery?"

Stacy muttered, "Sorry."

Logan took a deep breath. Soccer Mom would never sign his court voucher if he strangled Mark with his too-skinny tie. "I'm not a porn star." He ignored several murmurs of disappointment. "I just work for a guy who makes websites."

"Is he also the star of the site?" That was Jeffrey. The asshole.

"No, dammit. He…." Logan's brain overloaded as an image of Caleb looking sweet and coy in front of his laptop as he trailed his fingers down his too-tight shirt pushed its way into his head. Shifting in his chair, he continued, "He makes normal sites for local businesses like Meng's Market."

"I love that place," someone said as if it freaking mattered.

Logan was saved by Kathy, and he resolved to never think of her as Soccer Mom again. "I think we should get started with tonight's discussion. Hopefully, you completed your regret, resentments, and… uh… sex inventories for tonight."

Stacy smothered a giggle.

Leaning over, Logan whispered, "Worst. Sponsor. Ever."

Stacy nodded vigorously. "I really am sorry."

Logan snorted and pulled three folded sheets of paper from his pocket. Their homework this week had been to reflect on their current and past actions to acknowledge what they'd done, why they'd done it, who they'd hurt, and how it made them feel. It hadn't been a fun exercise.

"Does anyone have any experience, strength, or hope relating to the inventories, which they would like to share?" Kathy's gaze flickered to Logan before she looked away. She looked relieved a moment later when Jeffrey raised his hand.

"Hello, my name is Jeffrey and I'm an alcoholic."

A chorus of "Hello, Jeffrey" rang out.

"As I was filling out the inventory, I realized it's so much easier to flirt when drunk. To be charming and confident, because I'm too trashed to know the difference. I can go for any guy I want," Jeffrey said, his eyes drifting to Logan. "And if I get rejected, it doesn't hurt. Nothing hurts." He looked at the sheets of paper in his hands, folding and unfolding them several times. "But nothing feels good either. Not really. I can fuck or be fucked, but that numbness never goes away."

Kathy's nose wrinkled in disgust, from either Jeffrey's admission or his language. She opened her mouth to speak, but Stacy beat her to it. "When was the last time you were with someone while sober?"

Jeffrey's eyes darted back and forth several times. It was painfully obvious he couldn't remember. After a pregnant pause, his face crumpled and he bent at the waist, covering his face with his hands. Members on either side of him put their hands on his head and back, murmuring words of comfort.

Logan knew *his* answer to the question. Never. He'd never had so much as a hand job while sober. He'd been a monk in prison, refusing the guys who were willing to go down on their knees to have Logan protect them and keep them from being anybody's meat who wanted them. He'd been too worried about ruining his chances at parole to help them. Snagging a pen from Stacy, Logan added another entry to his regret inventory.

"Maybe you should consider making that a goal for this week," Kathy said.

Face flushed and eyes too bright, Jeffrey said, "To fuck sober?"

Kathy winced and folded her hands in her lap. "To flirt sober."

Several members offered to help Jeffrey practice, making him smile and roll his eyes. The rest of the meeting went by in a blur. Some of the members shared stories while others remained quiet. A lot of the same themes were repeated over and over again. The damage the addiction caused was hard to recognize in the moment. Hindsight was a bitch, but hopefully they could avoid repeating the same mistakes.

As Kathy called the meeting to a close, Stacy said, "I gotta run. Give me a call next week and we'll go to lunch."

Logan said good-bye and rose. As the members exited the room, he noticed Jeffrey lingering behind as he took his court voucher over for Kathy to sign.

"Can I buy you a cup of coffee," Jeffrey asked, batting his eyelashes enough to make a diva proud.

Logan barked a laugh. "An A+ effort."

"In that case, you'll have to say yes."

There was one fact Logan hadn't shared yet with anyone in the group but Stacy. Glancing at the paper in his hand, he said, "Court voucher is because I just got out of prison a few weeks ago."

"DUI?" Jeffrey asked, sounding hopeful.

"A bar fight that turned ugly and I ended up doing a year in the pen."

Jeffrey swallowed visibly. "I'm sorry." He looked away. "I feel like a hypocrite but that's scary stuff."

"No, that's your common sense stomping on your libido. It's making you think."

Jeffrey didn't look convinced.

"Mixing two ex-drunks is like drinking that cheap Milwaukee brew and tequila in the same night. The result is bound to be messy."

Jeffrey smiled weakly. "I'll see you next week."

LOGAN rapped his knuckles against the door and heard a muffled "It's open." Open? Had they been transported to the burbs? After opening the door, he paused in the threshold. He saw Caleb sitting behind the massive desk, typing away on a sleek-looking laptop. His annoyance nearly faltered at the sight, but he stayed frozen in place until Caleb finally dragged his attention away from the computer and looked up. Caleb blinked several times and cocked his head like a floppy-haired retriever.

"Is there a reason this door is unlocked?" More blinking. Logan secured the door and chain with more force than necessary. *I'm not his freaking babysitter*, he reminded himself. This was the second time in the past two weeks he had found the door either unlocked or unchained. Today, both had been true. When he turned around, he found Caleb standing in front of the desk looking like a kid who'd been caught smoking his first cigarette.

"I opened the door when Mrs. Simon brought me her garbage." Caleb paused, as if only then realizing how strange that sounded. "Marco used to take her trash once a week too since the dumpster cover weighs more than she does." He licked his lips. "I must've forgotten to lock the door again after talking to her."

"Your uncle might've put up the money, but it's your big brain bringing in the customers. If you can do all that fancy programming stuff, why can't you remember to lock the door?"

Caleb's cheeks flushed, and his eyes got all skittery again. "Normally, I lock the door right away, but then I started thinking about you coming by and it must have slipped my mind."

Logan felt both flattered and horrified by the sentiment. The effect left him a little dizzy. He liked the idea of Caleb trusting him and wanting to see him, probably more than he should. But he was supposed to be helping Caleb, not making it easier for some asshole to walk in and rob the place. "Even in this neighborhood, you need to know who you're letting inside."

Caleb nodded distractedly and turned back toward the desk. "Since it looks like you're keeping the job, I need you to fill out a tax document." He grabbed a manila folder and directed Logan to take a seat.

Logan sat on the butter-soft leather couch, angling his body toward Caleb when he joined him. "Your uncle said this was off the books."

"Tax evasion is a federal offense." Caleb said, his voice filled with reproach. "You can't afford to take that risk."

The tone rather than the words catapulted Logan back to his life before prison. *He sounds like Michael.* He shook off the thought, refusing to go there. He needed to focus on the here and now. He certainly didn't want to do anything to violate his parole agreement, but he was barely getting by now. He paid supervision fees to the state in addition to his living expenses. They had taken his truck and his savings when he'd been convicted in order to pay restitution. *God help me if Uncle Sam takes another cut.* "Can't I put it off until April? It's not like I'm bringing in six figures." In six months, he'd likely have a permanent full-time shift if he managed to avoid doing something stupid. *Like jump his boss's nephew.*

Caleb handed him a half-sheet of paper. "All I need you to do is fill out this W4 form. My uncle promised you a hundred a week. I'll cover the taxes."

"More hazard pay?" Logan wasn't sure how he felt about that. It seemed too much like charity. He doubted Caleb had paid Marco's taxes, since Klass hadn't mentioned it.

"It's not your fault my uncle didn't think about the tax implications. I also want to give you this." Caleb handed Logan a sealed envelope with his signature written across the back. "This is a statement of employment for your parole officer." He handed Logan a sheet of paper. "Here's your copy. It lets them know you work for me on a part-time basis."

Logan hadn't even thought about how he'd explain the job to his PO. His parole agreement required he disclose his job information, but Logan had been reluctant to tell Dabb about it, hoping to put it off until his monthly review. But his PO would likely know the package handler job wasn't enough to survive on. *Jesus.* He could have screwed himself if Dabb thought he was bringing in money on the side. *He'd think it was drugs. No doubt about it.* Dabb had said to think of him as a stalker. He'd be watching Logan to make sure he followed the conditions of the parole. He could be lurking nearby right now. Logan cleared his throat. "My PO, John Dabb, might want to meet with you. I know he's planning on seeing Klass this week."

Caleb's eyes widened, and he started chewing on a fingernail. "I c-could do that. I l-listed my c-contact information."

Logan hated hearing how distressed Caleb sounded, knowing he was the cause. A guy trapped in his apartment 24/7 felt sorry enough for him to swallow his own fear. Damned if that didn't sting. The thought threw him for a moment. He hadn't realized his pride had survived prison. He hadn't gotten a spotless record without sacrificing it on a daily basis. His pride was a big part of why he'd ended up there in the first place, refusing to ask for help when he needed it and pretending he had everything under control. He didn't want to be that man again, but he also didn't want to be anybody's charity case, and least of all Caleb's. The man in question had gone real quiet, likely confused by why his generous offer had been met with brooding. "Appreciate the offer, but I don't want to owe what I can't repay."

"Oh!" Caleb's arms flew up. "A favor. You could do me a favor, so we'd be even."

"What favor?"

"Pizza," he said breathlessly.

"You're paying my taxes and vouching for me with my PO and a pizza is supposed to make us even?"

Caleb's stomach grumbled loud enough for the neighbors to hear. "Not just pizza, but a pie from Nick's." He smiled wistfully, likely remembering a past greasy encounter. "My uncle refuses to pick one up for me. Says I have to leave to get it."

That comment gave Logan pause. He didn't want to do anything to get in the way of Caleb getting better. *Especially since he's only doing it to help me.* Klass might have the right idea, seeing how much Caleb seemed to love the food at Nick's. "Then maybe I shouldn't either."

"Oh," Caleb said, his whole body slumping.

"Here." Logan held out the envelope.

Caleb pushed the envelope toward Logan. "Keep it."

Logan opened his mouth to object, but Caleb beat him to it. "I'm sure there's something else you can help me with...." Logan could hear the wheels squealing in Caleb's head as he struggled to find a way to soothe his wounded pride. It was painful to watch. Even more so because Caleb had so obviously abandoned his own disappointment, seeming to care more about figuring out a way to help Logan. He was pretty sure a puppy kicker would be giving him reproachful looks right about now. He didn't know how the hell Klass had resisted.

"Couldn't hurt to get pizza this one time."

Caleb gave him a dazzling smile, leaving Logan feeling breathless.

Logan cleared his throat. "Nick's, you said?" The name sounded familiar. "That the place where the pizza makers' shirts are covered in sauce?"

Caleb bounced in his seat like a kid on Christmas morning. "That's the one!"

Logan remembered going there years ago. He'd been vaguely disturbed by the place. He recalled the food being good, but the flamboyant pizza makers were a little freaky. They looked like they were murdering the pizzas instead of baking them. Of course, he had been smashed at the time, so that might have been it. "Plenty of places around here that deliver." He wasn't surprised when Caleb scoffed at the idea. Caleb knew his food and wouldn't settle for what he'd deemed mediocre pizza. He pulled an advertisement from a drawer on the coffee table and Logan punched in the number.

"What do you want?"

"A large—no, make that an extra-large pepperoni pizza." He tugged Logan's arm. "Do you like pepperoni?"

Logan grinned in response. The restaurant answered the call, and he placed Caleb's order. He snapped the phone closed. "It'll be ready in half an hour."

"Thank you." Caleb looked at his lap. "I know my uncle means well, but he acts like I can just flip a switch and turn the panic off." He removed a piece of lint off his sweatpants. "Like I'm just being stubborn or something. I know I'm not doing as much as I should to get better, but I can't just snap my fingers and make the fear disappear."

"Do they really have agoraphobic group meetings?"

Caleb looked puzzled for a moment and then gave a sad smile. "I don't actually know, but I'm guessing they do. Most people with the phobia have trouble going out or to certain places alone, but refusing to go out at all is pretty rare."

Logan sometimes forgot Caleb never went out. Stupid, considering it was why he had a job. Caleb acted normal for the most part, but staying inside for three years wasn't normal. The glassy-eyed head cases that lived in Logan's complex seemed to have more obvious problems, but he wondered if that was true. They, at least, were trying to recover as a condition of living at the halfway house.

"Can I ask what an AA meeting is like?"

"There's different formats, but the one I go to is about twenty people, all guys except for my sponsor, Stacy, and this perky soccer mom I never woulda pegged as an alky. We sit in a big circle and the leader has us go through the AA literature. Then people take turns talking about what's going on in their lives. The successes and the stumbles."

"Does everybody talk?"

"You don't have to, but it helps. They understand in a way no one else can. You ever talk to another agoraphobic before?"

Caleb shook his head. "I've gone to an online bulletin board a few times, but never posted." He looked at his clenched hands. "I didn't know what to say."

"In AA, they always want to know your story. Can you tell me how it started? Or would that freak you out?" When Caleb narrowed his eyes, Logan covered his face with his hands. "Sorry, I'm an idiot."

Pulling his hands from his face, Caleb said, "You really are," but his voice was light and teasing.

"You don't have to tell me."

Caleb made his way into the kitchen and pulled two bottles of water from the fridge. He settled back on the couch and handed Logan a drink. "The first time it happened was during my freshman year at college. I'd been marathon studying, guzzling coffee, and stressing out about final exams. One minute I was sitting in the library with a calculus book on my lap and in the next, I was huddled under a desk, feeling more afraid than I had in my whole life." He unscrewed the top of his bottle and took a sip of water. "My heart felt like someone had taken a blowtorch to it. I clung to that book, thinking that if I started going crazy, I'd hit myself over the head to knock myself out. Somehow that was a comforting thought because it meant I might be able to stop those awful feelings." He looked at the bottle and started peeling off the label. "I shook off the experience and the concerned library aide, telling her and myself I wouldn't put my body through that kind of physical stress again. A month later, it happened again. I stopped going to the library."

"Did you get any help?"

"Not until my junior year." His eyes grew distant like he was being sucked back to that time. "I'd go to the cafeteria and see students standing in line and sitting at tables and I just couldn't bring myself to go inside. I tried going during off times and that helped sometimes but not enough. I couldn't afford to buy my own food, so I started losing weight." His hand moved to his stomach, rubbing back and forth seemingly unconsciously. The ill-fitting sweats and T-shirts were starting to make sense. The thought of Caleb being skinny enough for them to fit made Logan's gut clench.

"One of the lunch ladies followed me back to my dorm room after an aborted attempt to go into the cafeteria. This old lady in a hairnet muscled her way into my room and started talking about how anorexia wasn't just for girls." He rolled his eyes, but his expression was fond. "She was the first person I told and she was really great about it. She arranged to have meals bagged for me and I could pick them up at the back entrance to the cafeteria. She slipped in pamphlets from the campus wellness center. It was a while before I could bring myself to see the counselors. They sent me straight to the hospital when they learned my mother had had heart problems all her life. When the tests all came back normal, I almost didn't go back to the wellness center, but I knew I needed help if I was going to graduate. I couldn't face the idea of telling my mom I'd failed because I was too afraid to go to class. They helped me enough to graduate."

Logan wanted to say something comforting, something that would chase the haunted look from Caleb's eyes, but words failed him. He swallowed hard. "It's probably time for me to head over to Nick's." It wasn't, but if he didn't get out of here, he'd do something drastic like hug Caleb.

Caleb nodded as if he'd expected Logan to react like an asshole and wasn't bothered by it.

Logan got up and headed for the door. "I'll stop off at Foremost and get some Coke. You need anything?"

Caleb leaped from the couch and crossed the room rapidly. He grabbed onto Logan's arm and said in a strangled sounding voice, "I don't need it and neither do you."

Logan stood baffled at the reaction for several seconds until the reason slotted into place. He'd said Foremost, a liquor store, and not a half-dozen other places around here where he could get soda pop. His brain went there without even thinking about it. His eyes began to burn and his throat suddenly felt clogged. "Pizza and beer." He laughed bitterly and put his hands on top of his shaved head. "What's more natural than that?" Unconsciously, his brain was already waiting in line with money in hand.

Caleb moved in for a sneak attack. "Let's pretend we don't have penises." He wrapped his arms around Logan's waist and hugged him hard. Logan dropped his arms, letting them hover for a moment before returning the embrace.

"Do me a favor and don't freak out," Caleb said. "I can't deal with that shit."

Logan laughed. Caleb was damn good at it. It made Logan wonder why he was so determined to deny himself any comfort when he fell apart. Reluctantly, he pulled away and walked stiffly toward the door.

Caleb followed him, slipping money into his hand. "Call me if you need help… finding the place."

WHEN Logan returned with the famous pie in hand, he found the door unlocked again and he noticed a baseball game on the TV with the sound turned low. Caleb sat on the leather couch. It looked like it was taking every ounce of his will not to pounce like a starving jackal. Logan set the pizza box on the coffee table. Seeing Caleb's barely contained glee, he decided Klass had to be wrong in denying him something that made him so happy. Disgusted by his own sappiness, he flopped onto the couch.

Opening the box, Logan said, "Eat before you drool all over the carpet."

Caleb took a deep satisfied breath before snagging a slice.

Logan started in on his own piece. The crust was crispy, the cheese thick, and the pepperoni spicy enough to make the roof of his mouth tingle. He preferred deep dish, but it had been forever since he'd had pizza anywhere close to this good. The floorshow wasn't bad either.

Caleb really could charge $9.99 a minute just to listen to him eat the pizza, let alone watch him. Logan had to adjust himself as Caleb's tongue went hunting for a stray dollop of sauce on his bottom lip. He hadn't realized someone could purr and chew at the same time, but Caleb was pulling it off. He needed a distraction before he was tempted to find out whether the tangy sauce tasted better on Caleb's tongue. Tilting his head toward the TV, Logan asked, "Did you ever play in high school?"

Caleb dropped the piece of pizza in his hand back into the box. "I wanted to, but… uh… I needed to get home right after school and help my mom with the housework and stuff."

Logan was wishing he hadn't asked when Caleb's expression brightened again. He retrieved the slice of pizza and said, "The track coach, Mr. Connors, used to let me run on the track in the morning even though I wasn't on the team. It was always the best part of my day. After about ten minutes, I would hit my stride and everything else would disappear and it would just be me and the sound of my feet pounding on the asphalt." He hunched forward and focused on eating the slice in his hand. "Did you play any sports?"

"I played football, but I was more interested in the after-game party."

Caleb accepted this answer without comment. "I doubt I would've been very good if I'd had the chance to play baseball. I'm a better spectator."

Logan faithfully watched the Chicago Bears, but he'd never had much interest in baseball, not seeing the appeal. Too much slow-moving strategy and not enough violence. Caleb's eyes kept returning to the game, watching with rapt attention and Logan found himself wanting to know more. "What is it about baseball you like?"

Caleb tilted his head as if thinking over the question. "Each pitch has the potential to change the course of a game, series, or season. Perfection is rare and errors can cause everything to spiral out of control."

"That's a good thing?"

Caleb smiled. "There's always another eight innings to get it right."

Logan was living proof that second chances happened. He hoped that Caleb would get one too. Seeing Caleb lick sauce from his thumb, Logan couldn't help asking, "Did you know in high school which team you batted for?" He took a sip of water from his bottle for his suddenly dry throat.

"Considering the first time I ever got myself off I was thinking about the first baseman, Mark Grace—"

Logan sputtered and choked, sneezing as the water went up his nose. Caleb thumped him on the back and offered him a napkin. Just when he thought he was going to live, Caleb said, "You wouldn't believe the batboy fantasies I had." He smiled sheepishly, seemingly oblivious to the effect his words were having.

Leaning forward, Logan tried to regulate his breathing, but the image of Caleb in a tight baseball uniform, bending over to retrieve a bat wouldn't leave his head or his cock. Phrases and images from the game filtered through his head: hitting the sweet spot, working the rosin bag over the bat, going deep in the hole, doubleheader.... Baseball was a filthy, dirty sport. Thankfully, Caleb assumed he was still choking. He rubbed Logan's back and cooed until he recovered.

Logan kept eating after he'd already had enough, because watching Caleb devour the pizza with orgasmic delight fascinated him more than the game. He was reluctant to leave and Caleb didn't seem inclined to shove him out the door. He felt comfortable here in a way he didn't feel anywhere else. He knew he was venturing into dangerous territory, but he couldn't seem to stop himself. *I'm not planning on putting the moves on him*, he told himself sternly. *Even though I'm apparently his type*. It was just nice to have someone to talk to and hang out a bit. Most of the guys at the warehouse were either married or only interested in going to bars. *God, I'm fucking pathetic*. The last thought gave him pause. He couldn't help feeling like he was taking advantage of Caleb's generosity. Hell, he hadn't even paid for the pizza.

Caleb leaned back on the couch, his hands on his stomach. Looking deliciously limp and sated, he said, "God, that was so good."

"But not enough to make us even."

"What do you mean?"

"I want you to let me help you get your own pizza next time."

Caleb stiffened. "I don't need your help."

Logan snorted. He was way too familiar with those five little words. His mind gave him a replay of the faces of people who'd tried to help him only to be shot down. He'd taken an almost visceral pleasure in seeing the resignation in their eyes as they turned away from him. All but Michael, but thinking about his former best friend hurt too fucking much. "I had to lose everything before I figured out I needed help."

He'd sacrificed his future, his friendships, and his freedom for what? To become as much of a bastard as his old man? How could he ever have thought oblivion was worth such a price? More than anything, he wished he could correct those mistakes, but he didn't deserve their forgiveness. He couldn't change the past, but he could maybe help Caleb in the here and now. Caleb had created his own personal prison, and Logan was determined to help him break out.

Caleb was quiet for several minutes before he spoke. "W-what w-would we d-do?"

A plan forming in his head, Logan said, "We'd take it one step at a time."

CHAPTER
THREE

Rubbing sleep from his eyes, Caleb plopped on the leather couch. The last time he had left his apartment the police were called. While attempting to check the mail for an ailing Mrs. Simon, he had a panic attack in the stairwell. He had only managed two floors before losing it. *What had been the trigger? Voices?* A woman walking up the stairs complaining about an unfair parking ticket. Hardly a terror-inspiring situation. But logic had very little to do with fear.

The woman had called the police when she saw him huddled against the wall with his arms covering his head. His memory of the event was fuzzy after that point. He remembered the police attempting to talk to him, but not what they said or his responses. He also remembered the burning humiliation of being carried like a child by Marco back to his apartment. Mrs. Simon must have been the one to call Marco. Or had she called Uncle Harrison and he had sent Marco in his stead? Caleb wouldn't be surprised.

Today, Logan expected Caleb to risk falling apart again. *There's no way I can do it.* Caleb would have to call Logan and cancel the trip out. Logan would understand. It wasn't like he cared either way. He was just being kind to his boss's freak nephew. A knock on the door squashed Caleb's hope of canceling over the phone instead of in person. *Maybe I could pretend to be asleep?*

The next knock was hard enough to make the door shake and chain rattle. Caleb rose and walked over to the door. The police would be showing up *again* if Logan kept at it. *What if they arrested him for disturbing the peace?* Moving quickly, Caleb unlocked and opened the door.

Logan entered, looking annoyingly chipper and gorgeous for three o'clock in the morning, dressed in cargo shorts and a fitted black T-shirt. Logan's dark gaze dipped, then rose again, making Caleb wonder for the hundredth time if Logan was gay. He seemed more comfortable talking about Caleb's gayness than any other straight man Caleb had encountered, but he had never trusted his so-called instincts. Even if he did, he would never have the guts to act on them.

"I'm sorry I made you get up early, but I don't think today is a good day to try going to the roof. I didn't sleep well last night and being too tired can trigger an attack."

Logan leaned against the doorframe. "Are you saying it would be better if I just showed up unannounced one morning so you wouldn't stay up late worrying?"

Caleb's breath caught audibly in his throat. "N-no, I'd have to k-know ahead of t-time."

"In that case, we might as well try today since you'll worry either way." Logan handed him an insulated cup. "I got you this since you don't drink coffee."

Seeing the determination in Logan's eyes, Caleb sighed and accepted the cup. *At least Logan won't have any trouble hauling my ass back into the apartment.* After popping the tab, he took a deep drink. "It's good. Thanks." He was proud of himself for not spitting it out on the floor.

"Really? It smells awful, but the shopkeeper said the tea was relaxing."

Caleb took another sip to hide his grin. It wasn't so bad if you didn't mind sucking on tree bark. "We should get going. I don't want to make you late for the early shift at work."

"You're going to need shoes."

Caleb looked at his socks, a sudden surge of panic flooding through his system. *Do I have shoes?* He couldn't remember. He had given away a lot of stuff in the past couple of years. "Shoes... shoes, shoes."

"You don't have shoes? No wonder you don't leave the apartment. I'd get ten different diseases before I reached the ground floor if I walked around barefoot at my apartment complex."

Caleb scowled. "I have shoes. There, next to—" He spun around and headed for the bedroom. Stepping over to the treadmill, he grabbed a worn pair of Adidas from the floor. He threw them on and drained the last of the awful tea.

When Caleb returned, Logan was tossing his own cup in the trash. It was time to go. His keys thankfully hung on a hook by the door. He grabbed them as they exited the apartment, dropping the keys twice before he managed to secure the door.

Logan stood behind him at the foot of the stairs with his hands resting on Caleb's shoulders. Caleb took a deep breath, which was a mistake. The witch's brew in his stomach threatened to take flight. He should never have agreed to let Logan help him with his agoraphobia. He blamed the pizza. And hormones.

Logan leaned in close, his coffee scented breath warm against Caleb's cheek. "Tell me about your first time with a guy."

Caleb was pretty sure he blacked out for a second or two as the sound of Logan's gravelly voice traveled from his head to his toes. Logan squeezed his shoulders, giving them a slight push. As Caleb started to climb, his mouth decided to act without his permission. "I was running on the track and a guy started jogging behind me. He didn't try to talk to me or anything, so I just kept running."

"Hmm, giving him a great view of your ass."

Caleb was glad Logan couldn't see him right now. They could roast marshmallows off his face. *That answered the whole straight or gay question. Right?* He cleared his throat. "I finished my last lap and headed for the locker room. I wasn't expecting him to follow me."

A few more steps and they had reached the landing. They walked a short way down the hall to a metal door. A cheap-looking padlock on the door barred access to the roof. Continuing the story, he said, "I was shocked when he showed up while I was in the showers."

"Did you drop the soap?"

Scowling, Caleb crossed his arms over his chest. "Now what? You need a key to access the roof."

Logan looked at the padlock for a moment before he said, "Close your eyes." He held up his hand when Caleb started to speak. "Better for you not to know."

Caleb reluctantly complied. He heard the sound of metal crinkling. After only a few moments, he heard the swish of the door opening. As he opened his eyes, he spied Logan stuffing something into his pocket that looked like part of a can of Coke. Lowering his voice, he asked, "What if someone calls the police?" He didn't want to be responsible for Logan violating his parole.

"We won't be up here long enough for it to matter." He stepped through the door, holding it open for Caleb to follow.

As Caleb moved through the entryway, the smell of early morning air invaded his nostrils. The muggy air coated his throat, smelling faintly of fuel and garbage. Standing under the alcove over the door, he looked out at the city he had not set eyes on directly in nearly three years. The city lights and the moon shining above cast enough of a glow to see the pebbled surface of the roof. According to Mrs. Simon, there was talk about putting in a rooftop garden. He hoped they did, for her sake. The much-taller surrounding buildings made the roof look small and bleak. It needed a bit of color. Looking at the space, Caleb waited for the surge of panic to rise, stealing his breath and his composure. Nothing happened. By now, he should be drowning in fear, but instead he felt calmer inside than he had in years.

Logan wrapped his arms around Caleb from behind and said, "So, you're in the showers soaping that lean body of yours and the water's pouring over you. Then what happens?"

Caleb sighed, letting his head rest against Logan's firm chest. He assumed Logan was only touching him and prompting the sex talk to distract him, but damned if it didn't feel good. "He walked up to me still fully dressed and asked if I was a fag."

Logan's body tensed, and his voice hardened. "This story better have a happy ending."

The protectiveness in Logan's voice sent a shiver racing down Caleb's spine. "He lunged at me, pressing me against the wall and kissing me breathless."

Logan turned them and pushed forward until Caleb's back pressed against the door. Hunching a little, he asked, "Like this?"

"It wasn't long before we both got our happy endings," Caleb said, looking down and cursing his blushing cheeks. Somehow, they had managed to end up much closer, their chests touching as Logan rested his hand on Caleb's hip. Logan's musky scent mixed with freshly cleaned skin enveloped Caleb, giving him the ridiculous urge to bury his nose against Logan's broad chest. Logan put one finger under Caleb's chin and tilted his head back to look into his eyes, watching him with a strangely intent expression. Caleb was amazed to see so much heat in his dark eyes.

Caleb licked his lips. "Doesn't your shift start soon?"

"Let's go over to the edge for a minute first." Logan pulled back, taking hold of Caleb's hand. They worked their way over the uneven surface to the cement railing that bordered the rooftop. The sputtering of a car engine turning over drew Caleb's eyes to the street below. Even at this hour, the streets weren't deserted. Looking around, he realized they were directly in view of dozens of apartment buildings. Anyone could pull back the curtain and see him. Putting a hand to his chest, he said, "The air's too humid. I can't breathe."

Logan moved behind him again, placing his arms around Caleb's waist. "Close your eyes and stop breathing like a crank caller."

Caleb tried to comply, his fingers digging into the gritty cement railing. He hated this feeling so much. Shame and guilt flowed through him as he realized Logan's hands on him were the only thing keeping him from bolting toward the door. His legs trembled from the forced inaction. *Breathe*, he commanded his errant lungs. *Breathe.*

Logan's hold on him tightened. "I knew I was a switch hitter by the time I was in junior high, but I never did it with a guy until my senior year of high school. By then, I wanted it so bad, I could barely stand it."

Caleb's brain short-circuited at the thought of Logan bubbling over with pent-up sexual desires. It was almost too much to contemplate. Taking a deep breath, he reminded himself that it didn't mean anything. Logan used the sex talk to distract him. Oh, God did it work. It was so easy to imagine Logan as a lanky teen, not yet filling out his tall frame. His dark hair grown out, framing his almost-black eyes.

"I was at a party, buzzed but not drunk yet, and I went looking for an open bathroom."

Rubbing the corded muscles of Logan's biceps, Caleb wondered if it bothered him to talk about his past drinking. He had zero experience with alcohol. He had always been too afraid of the idea of losing control over himself.

"I walked in on a guy pissing and saddled right next to him, too impatient to wait. I caught him looking at my dick and the guy freaked out, like I was going to hit him or something," he said, sounding indignant even after all these years. "After we got through the 'No way, I'm not gay—whoa, nice dick, bud!' shit, we jacked each other off, coming on a pink fluffy towel."

Caleb snorted. "I bet it even had a lacy hem."

"The whole room smelled like dried flowers and perfume. I'm lucky I didn't end up a cross-dresser."

"Now there's an image I didn't need."

Logan cuffed the back of his head. "With that hair of yours, you'll have straight boys pinching your ass, thinking you're a chick."

"I'm not built like a chick," Caleb grumbled, running a hand through his blond hair. "I tried cutting it myself once, but Marco said I looked like an escaped mental patient."

After a pause, Logan said, "It's weird wanting to kick somebody's ass without ever meeting them."

Caleb blinked, realizing he hadn't painted a pretty picture of Marco. His head was all twisted up about the man. It was ridiculous to resent Marco for moving to Florida when Caleb had been the one to encourage him to apply to the management position. He had even convinced his uncle to write a glowing letter of recommendation. Marco deserved the position, and Caleb had been happy for him when he got the promotion. Mostly. Marco spent his last two weeks on the job clucking like a momma hen, while Caleb refused to talk about it. Thanks to caller ID, there were three unheard messages on his voice mail. Caleb sighed. "He's a stubborn—albeit gorgeous—ass, but he's a good person. I was lucky to have him as long as I did and to call him my friend."

Logan grunted and headed for the door.

Caleb grabbed Logan's hand before he could escape. "Thank you." At Logan's questioning look, he clarified, "Three years is a long time not to see the smog-covered stars."

Squeezing Caleb's fingers, Logan said, "You'll be sucking up exhaust fumes and dodging taxis in no time."

When Logan said it, Caleb could almost make himself believe it.

CALEB opened his closet and frowned at the contents. Stacks of neatly folded but worn-looking T-shirts and sweats lined the wooden shelves. The only hanging clothes were a faded green hoodie and a Cubs pullover. Months ago, he had badgered Marco into accepting his nicer clothes for his two teenage sons, who at fourteen and fifteen were already nearly six feet tall. It felt good to have the reminders of his old life gone and be able to help Marco's family. He had kept the comfortable clothes he had lived in during college and tossed his ragged collection of ill-fitting jeans. He had thought about replacing some of the items since he had put on a bit of weight and muscle. He even went online to buy them, and much to his amusement, he found that new jeans looked more distressed than the ones he had tossed. He had gotten as far as the checkout before closing the browser. Why bother replacing them? He didn't have anybody to impress. Except today of course. When Logan's parole officer was supposed to stop by for a visit. Caleb sighed, closing the closet door. It was too late to do anything about his lack of wardrobe.

Through the peephole, Caleb spied a man with a salt and pepper beard and square-rimmed glasses. Giving himself a mental reminder not to act like a freak, Caleb took a deep breath. He wiped his clammy hands against his sweatpants before unlocking the door and opening it.

Caleb shook hands with Logan's parole officer as they exchanged greetings. Stepping back, he said, "P-please come in Mr. Dabb."

Dabb wore khaki shorts and a polo shirt, which shouldn't have been surprising considering the heat, but it was. *I can see the man's toes*, Caleb thought absurdly. Dragging his eyes from the man's sandals, he asked, "Would you like some water or lemonade?"

The lines around Dabb's eyes and sprinkling of gray in his dark hair and beard put him likely in his mid-forties. He had the kind of face that got better with age; his body was compact and fit looking. His blue-gray eyes seemed to be taking in the details of the room when he spoke. "Lemonade would be great."

Caleb gestured for Dabb to have a seat on the couch while he headed for the kitchen. He pulled out a pitcher of lemonade from the fridge and filled two glasses. He then added frozen lemonade cubes from the freezer. He had frozen a raspberry in the middle of each ice cube, which was seriously overdoing it, but he couldn't seem to help himself. He had spent an embarrassing amount of time this morning deciding which raspberries to select.

"I appreciate you taking the time to see me, Mr. Klass," Dabb said as he settled onto the couch with a weary sigh. He wiped a bead of sweat from his forehead.

"You can call me Caleb and I'm happy to help Logan however I can." He brought the glasses into the main room, handing Dabb the lemonade before sitting on the couch as well.

Dabb took a small sip from the glass. "Oh, wow. The real kind." He took a deeper drink. "God, that's good." He put the glass on a coaster on the coffee table and opened his briefcase. "Let's take care of the preliminaries." He took out a file folder and a pad of paper. "I'd like your permission to ask you a few questions. If you're not comfortable answering at any time, just let me know."

"O-okay."

Dabb clicked open a pen, his hand poised over the pad of paper. "Are you on disability?"

Caleb took a deep drink from his glass to give himself more time, the lemonade tart and sweet on his tongue. His mother had been forced to go on disability, and he swore he wouldn't follow in her footsteps. "No, I have my own internet-based business. I offer services such as website creation, copywriting and editing of web pages, and interactive features such as surveys, basic flash animations, and customer ordering systems."

"You don't need to meet with clients?"

Caleb paused, wondering how much Logan and his uncle had told the man. He knew his aversion to having strangers in his home bordered on social phobia. He didn't know why he cared what Dabb thought of him, but he did. "It's mostly handled through e-mail or on the phone. Whatever can't be sent to me electronically is sent to my PO box. I generally deal with small businesses that want a site that will get noticed without a lot of cost or difficulty maintaining. I also have a number of steady customers that have me maintain their sites on a weekly or monthly basis."

"It sounds like a lot of work."

Caleb smiled weakly. "More like a lot of little work. I charge by the hour and negotiate with the client on an estimated time to complete the job. The Internet boom isn't what it used to be, but more and more businesses are creating sites so customers can easily find information about them or to advertise promotions."

Dabb clicked the pen several times. "Will Logan be required to pick up alcohol for you?"

"No, I don't drink alcohol. And the grocery store knows not to add anything to the order without hearing from me directly." He had learned his lesson the hard way. His uncle had been furious when he found out the first man he hired had been slipping in booze and charging it to Caleb's account. Caleb had been more dismayed at the thought of having to invite a new stranger into his apartment. Screwed up priorities? Yep.

"That's good. Logan's continued success with AA is a condition of his parole." Dabb scribbled some more in his notebook before continuing. "I've expressed concerns with... your uncle about the appropriateness of Logan helping you in this capacity."

Caleb heard the same reproach in Dabb's voice toward his uncle that he had heard in Logan's. He felt the ridiculous urge to stamp his feet and declare he wasn't a child in need of protection. The irony didn't make him any less annoyed.

Dabb must have seen some of that in Caleb's face, because he raised a bushy eyebrow. "There are qualified individuals who could help you with your situation." His voice softened, sounding less formal. "If money's an issue, there are programs designed to help."

"I don't want a nurse." The gravel in his voice startled even him.
He cleared his throat. "I know there are people better trained to deal
with panic attacks and Logan is more likely to be shocked or even
horrified by it." He paused, needing to take a deep breath. Talking
about this with Dabb made him feel as if his ribs were being
compressed by a python. He shifted in his seat and told himself he was
getting enough air. "I absolutely hate the idea of it happening in front
of him." He wasn't sure he could face Logan after he had seen how
pathetic the panic made him. "Every time I'm able to open that door
and let him in, it's a tiny victory." He wasn't comfortable talking to
Dabb about Logan helping him leave the apartment. He hadn't even
mentioned it to his uncle, who'd been trying to get him to see a
therapist for years. It was too new and too fragile.

Dabb sat silently for a dozen heartbeats, looking at Caleb with
those hawk eyes of his as if peeling away at the skin to get to the tasty
meat. When he spoke, his voice was devoid of emotion, listing off the
details without needing to look at the file in his hands. "A girl sat next
to Logan at the bar and started flirting with him. He was too wasted to
pay her much mind until her boyfriend showed up." He paused, his
eyes asking if it was okay to continue. Caleb nodded his assent, not
trusting himself to speak.

Dabb didn't look convinced, but he continued anyway. "The guy
took a swing at Logan and Logan tossed him over a five-foot bar and
into the glass shelves holding the liquor bottles." He opened his
briefcase and took out an eight-by-ten color photo, plopping it on the
couch between them.

Caleb looked at the photo, unable to touch it, feeling his chest
tighten. The picture showed a close-up of a man's partially shaved
head. A long gash held together with more than two dozen stitches ran
from the middle of his forehead to the back of his ear. The skin was
puckered and angry looking.

"Logan wasn't done yet." Dabb pulled out another photo,
showing the smashed shelves and the floor covered in blood, glass, and
liquor. "He climbed on the bar to go after the boyfriend. Three guys
tried to stop him." He pulled out a stack of five-by-seven photographs.
He laid out the photos like a card dealer, listing off the injuries
sustained to the men who tried to prevent Logan from hurting the man

further. "Fractured wrist, broken nose, dislocated shoulder, and numerous bruises and cuts." Logan had been enraged and unstoppable.

Caleb gathered the photos and handed them back to Dabb. "You're showing me these because you think he'll start drinking again and do something to hurt me?"

"I know this doesn't feel real that the guy who's been delivering your mail is capable of doing something like this. But he is. He did."

Caleb felt like someone had poured sand down his throat. He took a deep drink from his glass before continuing. "I know how weird it is that checking the mail is more terrifying than having an ex-con bring it to me." It was the truth. He wasn't afraid of Logan, even if he should be for more reasons than Logan's record. He looked at his drink. The glass was cold and slick against his hands; the contents rippled ever so slightly.

"I'm not judging you. I want Logan to succeed." Dabb pulled off his glasses and began polishing them with the bottom of his shirt. "I also want to limit the damage if he fails."

Caleb swallowed hard, the lemonade feeling like acid churning in his stomach. "What do you want me to do?"

"I think I should force him to find another part-time job. I think you'd both be better off. I'll help him find another one."

Caleb put his glass on the coffee table, afraid it would shatter in his tightening grip. "If you think that's best for *Logan*," he said, stressing the name, because he didn't want Dabb's pity or his protection. "Then I'll go along with whatever you decide."

"You still want him working for you after seeing those?" Dabb gestured toward the closed file folder. "I won't hold it against him or you if you want to hire someone else."

Dabb was right. It didn't feel real. He couldn't imagine the man he had gotten to know over the past few weeks capable of such a brutal attack. *Could the booze really change him so much? What if he starts drinking again?* He reined in that line of thinking. It wasn't fair to Logan. "I refuse to be afraid Logan might slip back into bad habits. He's earned the right for a second chance."

Dabb looked Caleb in the eyes for the next few moments, and then he sighed. "Let's give it a couple of weeks. I'll look into some prospects for another job in the meanwhile." He handed Caleb a business card. "Call me if you have any problems."

Caleb accepted the card numbly, wondering if he would ever get his own second chance. Not to get his old life back, but a new one. Where he would select his own produce. Eat a hotdog bigger than his head at the ballpark. Go to a movie with a friend. They had seemed like impossible goals only a few weeks ago, but a flicker of hope burned in his belly.

"Caleb." Dabb said it like it hadn't been the first time. "Come lock the door after me."

Caleb shook off the thoughts and rose. Dabb stood in the threshold with a pained look on his face. "Take care of yourself," he said, making it sound like an order instead of a request.

Something in Dabb's intense gaze made Caleb's stomach clench. *Uncle Harrison looked at my mother that way.* He didn't want to be seen as fragile, breakable.

Caleb smiled stiffly. "I will. Thank you." Only after he had secured the door, did he hear Dabb walking away, his feet pounding on the steps.

Flopping on the leather couch, Caleb covered his face with his arms. His mother would be devastated to know how far he had sunk since her death. When she got upset, her heart would race and she would get dizzy, even faint if she got flustered enough. Caleb tried very hard never to be the cause. When the panic attacks first appeared, he did everything he could to keep her from finding out about them. The campus doctors subjected him to a barrage of tests to see if he had a heart condition like his mother. The tests all said the same thing. His heart was fine. His head was screwed up. He managed to hide it from her until six months into his first job after graduating. He had been pushing hard to meet a deadline for a client, living on caffeine and too little sleep. His meltdown occurred in the middle of a family dinner. His uncle used to say she would worry herself into an early grave if she wasn't careful. That was exactly what she did. And her son had helped put her there.

LOGAN leaned against the front of the apartment building, trying to give Caleb time to get his shit together. On Friday, they'd only made it a block before Caleb needed to turn back. He'd probably spent the weekend berating himself, in spite of Logan's attempt to reassure him that he'd made it further than he'd been in three years. Logan knew without a doubt that the only reason Caleb was standing here was that he wanted to help Logan and saw this as the only way to do it. *I'm helping him too*, he told his bristling pride. Squatting, he pressed his shoulder against Caleb. As Caleb tried to stop gasping like a dying goldfish on the exhaust-thickened air, Logan eyed the flow of people shuffling on the sidewalk. The late-morning traffic wasn't too bad, and the weather had cooled to a balmy 70 degrees. Most of the business commuters were already tucked away in their cubicles, and the teens that seemed to wander the streets endlessly in the summer were still snoring in their beds. Those that remained were an eclectic collection: power-walkers, nannies and their charges, wide-eyed tourists, people trying to walk and text on cell phones and doing a piss poor job of it, real and wannabe homeboys, and the invisible vagrants with their pushcarts and layers of baggy clothing.

He leaned close to Caleb's ear to speak over the murmur of voices and the sounds of traffic. "Do you think that guy," he said, tilting his head toward a middle-aged man with a hideous Hawaiian shirt, "knows the chick he's hitting on has a dick?"

That got Caleb's attention. He stopped hyperventilating long enough to sneak a peek. The tranny had platinum-blond hair down to her pert ass and she was playing with the guy's copious chest hair with her blood-red nails. She caught them gawking, and her eyes locked with Logan's for a moment before trailing to Caleb. A wicked smile crossed her lips, and Logan had the irrational urge to haul Caleb upstairs and hide him away. *Great, I can add possessive to my list of admirable traits.* He pushed off the wall, dragging Caleb with him. It was only two blocks to Meng's Market, but it seemed to take forever.

"People are staring at me," Caleb said, his voice barely audible over his ragged breathing.

Logan wished he could put his arm around his shoulders, but he didn't want to draw any more attention to them. They were turning heads all right. Men and women were swiveling their heads to check out Caleb's ass, encased in a pair of gray sweats that looked glued on. His long-sleeved white T-shirt was so thin Logan could just make out Caleb's tight nipples. Caleb's luscious lips were parted slightly and his breathing heavy, like any second he was gonna throw his head back and come. *Yeah, they're staring. Wondering how I can afford such a hot rentboy.*

"Who says they're looking at you? Remember back to when you first met me."

Caleb remained quiet for a few steps. "Does it bother you?"

Up ahead, Logan spotted a mother and her young son. She pulled the boy in close and inched over until she was as far away as she could get on the sidewalk. Her wary eyes never left Logan until she'd passed by them.

"No big deal." When Logan glanced away, he caught Caleb giving him a look that seemed to say so much: *bullshit* and *I'm sorry* and *they're idiots.*

Caleb squeezed his elbow. "I guess I should be happy my freakiness is curable." He bumped Logan's arm. "You're stuck being a giant."

"Smartass." Logan flicked the back of Caleb's ear.

Caleb gave him a toothy grin, not looking the least bit chagrined. He then stopped. "We're here."

Logan stepped through the sliding door, trusting Caleb to follow. Caleb licked his lips, his eyes darting around the store as if counting the potential number of witnesses if he fell apart. His eyes lit when he spotted Min and Mr. Meng approaching. With a squeal of delight, Min wrapped her arms around Caleb, hugging him close. Logan felt that ridiculous urge again, wanting to peel Min off Caleb. Caleb didn't look any happier about Min touching him. Logan tried not to be happy about that.

Oblivious to or maybe in spite of Caleb's discomfort, Min took hold of Caleb's hand, snatched a box from below the counter, and dragged him toward the back of the store. Logan leaned against the counter, enjoying the view of Caleb's retreating backside. Just as they reached the dairy case, Min looked over her shoulder and giggled in a way that could only mean trouble. A yank on his sleeve had Logan glancing down at the storeowner.

"You dating Mister Klass?"

Amused, Logan peered at the old guy. "Not yet."

Meng nodded thoughtfully before walking away. A few minutes later, he returned, carrying a large plastic bag. Holding out the bag with both hands, he offered it to Logan with his head bowed. Confused, Logan accepted the frozen bag of... something. Through the frosty plastic, he saw what looked like an earthworm on steroids with tentacles glued to its face.

"Comjang O," Meng said, gesturing toward the bag. "Make you big."

"Uh... thanks?" Logan had no idea what the proper response was to being given a creature straight out of a Stephen King novel or possibly *Dune*.

Apparently satisfied by the response, Meng smiled and headed back to the counter.

A few minutes later, Caleb appeared at his side, carrying a now filled box of groceries. Examining the bag, he said, "It's even uglier when alive."

"Uglier? What the hell is it?"

"It's called a hagfish and alive it's covered in this slimy mucus it uses to ward off predators."

"Why would he give me this?"

"I guess he thought you needed it," Caleb said with an air of absolute innocence that didn't fool Logan for a second. After a beat he added, "It's a Korean aphrodisiac."

Logan groaned. "To make me big."

After letting Logan take the box, Caleb held up the bag and peered at the contents. "It looks to be about a foot long. That would certainly be big." He smirked. "I'll go grab some spices to go with it." He ran off before Logan could stop him.

As they left the store, Caleb said, "You should be honored. They don't sell hagfish here. Mr. Meng must've given you one from his private stock."

"Honored the guy thinks I need Korean Viagra?"

Caleb's grin faltered, and Logan turned to see what had caught his eye. Karen Foster strutted toward them. Caleb's face said he was familiar with the redhead. He wasn't running away, but he looked like he'd be okay with the sidewalk opening up underneath him. Logan wondered if Foster had tried to sink her claws into Caleb. The thought bothered him.

Foster leaned in too close, and Logan got a whiff of her cheap perfume. Did she bathe in the shit?

"I was hoping to run into you." Foster's eyes widened when she caught sight of Caleb standing next to him.

"Hey, Karen," Caleb said, taking the box from Logan as if suddenly feeling the need for a barrier between himself and the diminutive woman.

"Caleb, it's great to see you," Foster said, with enough false cheer to make Logan's teeth hurt. She looked back at Logan, answering his unasked question. "Caleb worked at the warehouse part-time on the Night Sort when he was going to college."

Logan had worked that shift a few times when they were short package handlers. He couldn't imagine working from 11:00 p.m. to 3:00 a.m. and then putting in a full day's worth of classes. He remembered from his orientation that employees could earn money toward college tuition. Caleb had to have been dedicated to work those hours and still have time to study. It was no wonder the pressure eventually reached critical levels.

"I don't think I've seen you since"—she lowered her voice—"your breakdown at the warehouse." She put a hand to her chest. "That was so heartbreaking. I'd never seen a grown man cry before."

Caleb's shoulders twitched, hunching further over the box of groceries as if it could shield him from the backhanded barbs Foster was flinging at him.

"I'd heard you stopped going out entirely. And here you are risking having all these people see you fall apart." Foster laughed, a harsh grating sound. "I don't think I could do that."

Trying to keep his tone even, Logan said, "We need to get the groceries back."

Relief flashed across Caleb's face, and he ducked his head too late to hide it.

Foster stuck out her bottom lip. "I was hoping we could talk, Logan. I'm sure Caleb can find his way home on his own. Right?"

"Yeah, I'll take a c-cab h-home," Caleb said, moving over to the street.

Logan grabbed Caleb's elbow and whispered, "What the hell are you doing?"

"I'll be fine."

"I'm worried about me, dumbass. She'll figure out I'm a fag and disembowel me with her five-inch nails."

Caleb shook his head. "If you pick me over her, she'll be mad. You don't want her mad at you, Logan."

Caleb had a point. Pissing off Foster all but guaranteed she'd complain to Dabb. But leaving Caleb to make his way home alone wasn't an option. "I'll make nice and give her what she wants," Logan said, grabbing the box of groceries from him. "But we go back together." Before Caleb could protest, Logan stepped back over to Foster. "I'm working right now. How about we meet later or maybe tomorrow after shift?"

Foster raised her sculpted eyebrows. "Afraid Caleb will go tattling to his uncle if you don't walk him home?"

Logan didn't respond, letting her think what she wanted. "Being nice" was a hell of a lot easier if he kept his mouth shut.

When he didn't rise to the bait, she continued with an aggrieved huff. "It shouldn't take you more than ten minutes to get Caleb home and come back," she said, making Logan wonder how the hell she knew that. With a flip of her too-red hair she continued, "I'll get us a booth at Buck's across the street."

"Fine. I'll see you soon," Logan said, making his way back to Caleb.

Caleb had his arms wrapped around himself so tightly it reminded Logan uncomfortably of a straightjacket. Surprisingly, the fear in his eyes seemed to be directed at Foster and not the swarms of people shoving past him. Logan hailed a cab, holding the door open for Caleb to climb inside. Scooting over the seat, he placed the box of groceries near the door so he could be closer to Caleb.

After giving the cabbie the address, Logan turned toward Caleb. He wanted to pepper the man with questions about Foster. What was her problem with Caleb? Why did she know so much about her boss's nephew? But Caleb looked like he needed a distraction, not an interrogation. The whites of his green eyes showed all around, and his breathing sounded painful.

Leaning over close to Caleb's ear, Logan said, "If you don't stop breathing like a porn star, I'm going to be forced to molest you." He put his hand on Caleb's knee and gave it a squeeze.

Caleb made a sound between a hiccup and a laugh. "Your hand on my leg isn't going to slow my racing heart."

"Hmm. Then I'll just have to move it somewhere else." Logan trailed a finger up the length of Caleb's thigh, sliding over the too-thin cotton pants. "Is this better?"

The blare of a car horn startled them both. Far too soon, they arrived at Caleb's building. Logan jumped out of the cab before Caleb could protest. He heard Caleb ask the driver to wait.

Frowning, Logan said, "I have time to walk back."

"This way she'll be more sober when you get there."

Logan couldn't argue with that logic.

The four flights flew by with Caleb's ass in the tight sweats as a motivator. When Caleb unlocked his door, Logan dropped the box and turned Caleb around, pinning him against the scarred wood.

Caleb gasped, no doubt feeling how much Logan had enjoyed the view. Instead of pulling away, he shifted his stance, allowing Logan to press their bodies closer. Logan could feel the thumping of Caleb's heart and it sent a thrill racing through him to know it was caused by desire and not fear.

"You did good today." Logan kissed Caleb's forehead. "How about I come back after I'm done talking with Foster?" The mention of his supervisor caused a worry line to form between Caleb's brows, so Logan kissed there too. "Don't worry about her. I can handle her."

Caleb didn't argue, but he didn't look particularly reassured. Placing his hands on Logan's chest, Caleb slid down slowly, brushing against clenching muscles until Logan needed to step back to make room. Caleb grabbed the box and smiled up at Logan from his knees. Logan had thought he was hard before. For a moment, he feared he'd swoon like a Hollywood starlet.

Caleb took advantage of his distraction to stand and open the door. Over his shoulder he said, "You can help me prepare the hagfish when you get back."

The walk back down the stairs was a lot less fun.

THE bar Foster chose looked like the kind of dive Logan used to love. Still loved, if he was feeling the need to be honest. Dark wood furniture, dim enough lights to hide the grime, the heady combination of spilled liquor and old smoke that lingered years after the smoking ban went into effect. Not many customers occupied the bar, but it wasn't surprising for ten o'clock in the morning. He resisted the urge to look around surreptitiously, half-convinced Dabb would pop up and call him a parole violator. Even though he had no plans to get smashed, his parole agreement was clear: "no visiting bars or lounges where intoxicants are sold." He'd agreed to Foster's choice of location without thinking about it, too concerned about getting Caleb safely home. Hopefully, he could get this meeting with Foster over quickly.

Seeing Logan, the bartender asked, "What can I get for you?"

"Rum and Coke," Logan said, reflexively. He swore under his breath. "I mean just a Coke. Uh... with no booze."

"Coming right up."

Logan spotted Foster at the back of the bar. Registering the predatory look on her face, he picked up his Coke and joined her at a small, wooden table.

Petting his hand, Foster said, "I'm so glad you could come," as if she hadn't coerced him into it.

"What's up, Karen?"

She seemed absurdly pleased he'd relented and called her by her first name. Or maybe the mood was due to the empty glass in front of her. Margarita, going by the salt rim. Breakfast of champions. She signaled the bartender. "Give me another with extra cherries." She looked at Logan, silently asking, and he shook his head.

"Since I know you worked construction," she said, slurring her words slightly, "I was hoping you could give me some advice on my kitchen redo."

It took all his concentration not to roll his eyes at the transparent pretext. He'd much rather be eating that mutant worm than listening to Foster prattle about her home remodel woes while she sucked back a margarita like a Hoover vacuum. He'd worked enough residential remodels to know indecisive homeowner syndrome when he heard it. There was nothing worse than a vague client who got pissed off when the contractor didn't read their mind. They'd demand changes and then bitch and moan when it added cost and time to complete the job. From the sound of things, Foster was looking for an excuse to skip out on the bill.

Foster cut off mid rant. Either she was more perceptive than he gave her credit for or his neutral expression needed work. "I saw your PO heading for Klass's office as I was leaving today." She licked salt off her upper lip. "Is he tryin' for PO of the year or somethin'?"

"What do you mean?"

"I talked to him last Monday right before my shift ended and today he's back."

Logan remembered seeing her at Meng's. *You went running for a bottle of tequila after talking to Dabb.* He doubted it was a coincidence.

"When my good for nothin' boyfriend was on parole, his PO showed up like three times in a year."

Dabb struck Logan as the type of man who took his job very seriously. But there was no way he had time to visit all his parolees' work places twice in two weeks. *So why is he paying me so much attention?* "Dabb visited Caleb this week, so maybe Klass is last on the list."

Caleb had said that the meeting had gone okay, but he'd been vague on the details. Maybe Dabb was trying to convince Klass to find someone else to look out for Caleb. His throat suddenly dry, Logan took a sip of the watered-down Coke.

She sucked her teeth. "I should've realized Klass had roped you into doing Marco's old job." She gave him a grin that was supposed to be seductive but looked more like she needed a bran muffin. "He always selects hot guys to dangle in front of his nephew."

That Klass picked him based on his looks still chafed his ass. *I'll bet old Harry didn't count on me wanting Caleb back.* As much as he'd like to see the look on Klass's face, he didn't relish being unemployed. No way would his boss want him anywhere near his nephew if he knew. Was that what worried Caleb? That Foster would out him to Klass?

"Caleb is a good guy. What do you have against him?"

She shook her head slowly. "Poor Marco ran all the way to Florida to get away." An ugly, sour look crossed her face. "But that was better than lettin' the boss's pervert nephew paw at him anymore," she said, with no small amount of disgust.

Logan hadn't realized how angry he was until he saw her disgust morph into panic. He closed his eyes and took a deep breath, trying to get a handle on the emotion slamming through his system. By the time he'd opened his eyes, she was offering excuses and scurrying out of the bar, and his rage was dissipating with each step she took. *Huh, maybe those anger management classes are working.* He hadn't bashed in her lying face with his watered-downed glass of soda pop, so that had to count for something.

CHAPTER
FOUR

CALEB set the box on the counter and started putting away the groceries. Seeing a small brown bag buried at the bottom of the box, he felt his cheeks flush even though there was no one to see it. He had added a tube of lube to his order, since he was nearly out. He had contemplated ordering it online instead before dismissing the idea. Even with planned purchases, he sometimes wasn't able to answer the door. *God help me if the lube was delivered to Mrs. Simon when I didn't answer the door.* He would never survive that kind of humiliation. She would take one look at his face and *know* he had something dirty in the package. He opened the paper bag and dumped the contents on the counter. It took his brain a few seconds to process what he was staring at. Condoms. Min had stuck a box of condoms in with the lubricant. He had assured Min that he wasn't dating Logan when they were in the store. Just two guys helping each other out and maybe getting to be friends. Apparently, she wanted him to be prepared just in case. The fresh flush of embarrassment made him remember the first time he had gotten condoms. It was the morning of prom....

A knock on his bedroom door had woken him. Rubbing sleep from his eyes he asked, "What do you need, Mom?" He was surprised when Uncle Harrison opened the door. Yanking back the covers, he asked, "Has something happened—"

"Your mom is fine," his uncle said, closing the door behind him. "I didn't mean to wake you, but I need to go into work today and I wanted to see you before the dance." His uncle brought the desk chair over and sat in front of the bed. He was red-faced and jittery, looking

at the walls as if he'd never seen the shrine to Kerry Wood, Gracie, and the Cubs.

Feeling self-conscious in only boxers, Caleb rose and threw on a T-shirt and sweats. It wasn't unusual for his uncle to stop by, but it was obvious something was up. Out of habit, Caleb quickly made the bed and sat cross-legged in the middle, wishing he had another chair.

Finally looking at him, his uncle said, "I know prom is a big deal nowadays."

Caleb took a deep breath and prepared himself for the "I'm sorry" that was sure to follow. His mother had been giving him wide-eyed looks since he'd told her that Melissa had agreed to go to the dance with him. She was probably panicked they would end up killed by a drunk driver. Surely, she knew he'd never risk upsetting her by getting drunk. His uncle must be here to let him down gently. He swallowed a lump in his throat. He really didn't mind for himself, but Melissa would be devastated even though they were only going as friends.

"I should've given you these years ago, but you've always been a quiet kid and never showed much interest in dating." His uncle handed him a plastic grocery bag.

Confused, Caleb opened the bag and found a box of condoms. His jaw dropped and he felt his face flush. Before he could think of a response, his uncle continued. "I'm not saying anything will or should happen tonight, but I wanted you to have them, just in case."

"We're just friends," Caleb stammered.

"Like I said, just in case. I know how embarrassed I was the first time I bought them and you being so shy, I didn't want you to take the risk of not having them." He shook his head. "God knows it would kill your mother if you knocked someone up."

"I'm gay." The words were unplanned and irretrievable once uttered. He held his breath, waiting for his uncle's reaction. He knew his uncle was a fair man and didn't tolerate prejudice at home or at work. But tolerance was a long way from acceptance.

"You can't tell her." Uncle Harrison's voice teetered on the edge of panic. He paused and took a long, slow breath. "What with AIDS and homophobes she just couldn't handle it. She'd be too afraid for

you." He ran a hand through his prematurely white hair. "I've tried to look out for you and your mom since that good-for-nothing boyfriend walked out on you both."

Lips pressed together, Caleb closed his eyes for a moment, willing tears not to fall. "You have," he breathed, hardly managing to form the words.

"I'm proud of you, boy, and knowing you're... gay won't change that. You can talk to me about it whenever you need to." He put his hand on Caleb's knee. "We just need to keep it between us for now. We'll work on easing your mom into the idea when you're older...."

Drawing back from the memory, Caleb felt a pang of regret that his mom died without really knowing him. Looking back, he understood his uncle's fears, but they didn't hold the same weight as when he was sixteen. His mom would have worried, but she also would have wanted him to be happy. Hiding his life from her became a habit he was never able to break. The ring of the telephone brought him back from his thoughts. Seeing Marco's name flash on the caller ID, Caleb sighed before answering the phone.

"Hey, Marco."

"I am glad you answered, *flaquito*."

He really hated that nickname. "I'm not skinny. I've gained four pounds since you left. I barely fit into my clothes anymore."

"This new guy, Logan, has renewed your appetite?" Marco asked, the rich timbre of his voice gliding over the syllables.

For more than just food, but he didn't intend to tell Marco that. Hoping to change the subject he asked, "How are you guys settling in? Do your kids like their new schools?"

"Do not try to change the subject. I know my beautiful wife has e-mailed you all about the move."

Resisting the urge to sigh, Caleb tried another tactic. "Logan and I went to Meng's today and I didn't freak out." Much. His cheeks flushed as he remembered how Logan brought him back from the border of freak-out land while in the cab. He knew better than to mention encountering Karen outside of Meng's. Marco's contempt for his former supervisor was legendary.

"It does my heart good to hear such things. Tell me, *flaquito*. How did this Logan convince you to go out?"

"Um," Caleb said, his face grew hotter as he remembered Logan's method of distraction. The feel of him pressed close and the way "dick" rolled off his tongue while they stared at the alluring tranny had left Caleb reeling.

Marco made an exasperated clucking sound. "My friends at the warehouse tell me this Logan has a rough past."

Caleb had a sinking feeling he knew the direction of this conversation. If Marco didn't approve of Logan, he wouldn't hesitate to call Uncle Harrison, and that would not be good. Knowing his uncle, he didn't even bother looking at Logan's personnel file. He just zeroed in on the hottest guy at the warehouse. Caleb had never been brave enough to ask his uncle *why* he selected such attractive guys. He doubted his uncle wanted him to get laid. He needed to convince Marco that Logan was a good replacement. Never mind the fact that Caleb paid for the delivery service. That didn't mean he actually got a say in who worked for him. He frowned. Maybe Logan was right about the bullying.

Feeling petulant, Caleb said, "I'm not one of your kids. I can take care of myself."

"You are not a child, but you are innocent. You are also my friend."

Caleb's throat tightened. He had convinced himself he wouldn't hear from Marco after he moved to Florida. It was nice to know he still cared enough to check in. Even if, as usual, he showed it in the most annoying way possible. "I don't care about his past. I only know what I feel when I'm around him." He silently willed Marco to understand. It had been so long since he had felt any motivation to leave the comfort of his apartment. The prospect of going out still terrified him, but each day, home felt more like a prison than a sanctuary.

Marco was quiet so long Caleb thought the line might have gotten disconnected. No such luck.

"Does he feel the same way?"

"He's gay, but I doubt...." Caleb sighed. "It doesn't matter. If I start going out, I can shake my ass at the nearest dance club until Mr. Right stumbles along."

"That is not a comforting thought, *flaquito*."

Caleb snorted. "You're telling me. I can't dance worth shit."

Marco sighed dramatically. "You try a man's patience, my friend. I see I will need to be more direct."

"What does that mean?"

The dial tone was the only response.

THE next day, a stocky Latino man called out to Logan from the truck bed next to his spot on the line. "Marco say...." The man paused as if trying to remember the correct words.

"Hablo español," Logan said, making the transition to Spanish easily. It had been essential when working in construction. "You are Hernandez, no?"

"Yes," he said, looking relieved he didn't have to fight to find the right words. He set a package on the conveyor belt and reached into his pocket, pulling out a scrap of paper. He handed the paper to Logan. "Marco asked me to give you his phone number and to ask you to call him today before your shift is over. He was most insistent he speak with you."

Curious, Logan headed for the break room, punching in the number as he walked. In spite of Caleb's grumblings, he seemed fond of Marco. Logan wasn't sure the guy deserved it, but he couldn't help wondering about him. He entered the sad excuse for a break room, noticing it was empty. In spite of several no-smoking signs, the room reeked of stale cigarette smoke. He made his way over to the only seating, four plastic chairs around a cheap laminated table, and hit the Send button on the phone.

A man with a thick Spanish accent answered the call after only two rings. Without preamble he said, "I was hoping you would call."

"I take it you're Marco."

"Yes, and you are the drunk who ended up in prison for beating a man. I wonder then why Mr. Klass decided to hire you to watch over his nephew."

In the background, Logan could hear the happy melodies of a kids' television show. The muted high-pitched chatter and occasional giggle signaled the likely viewers of the program were watching with rapt attention.

"That life's behind me." Logan sat on a chair, wondering at the purpose of this call.

"That is good to hear. I myself left many friends behind in Chicago and I count Caleb among them."

The unspoken threat in Marco's voice was unmistakable and Logan's opinion of the man shot up several points. He wanted Logan to know 1,200 miles wouldn't stop him from protecting Caleb.

"I am also told Karen Foster has taken an interest in you. This concerns me greatly."

Logan muttered, "You and me both, pal."

"That *woman*"—Marco said the word as if he'd rather use another if there weren't little ears within hearing range—"has caused problems for Caleb in the past."

"What's her problem?" Logan couldn't imagine what Caleb could have done to piss her off. He had tried to get the details out of Caleb without success. Was she just a homophobic bully or was there more to it?

"A couple of months ago, Klass moved her to the early morning shift and she was very angry about it."

Logan snorted. "I'm not surprised. Getting to work by 4:00 a.m. is bound to cut into her social calendar."

"She is rumored to be very much the party girl, but she must be a daylight drunk since her old shift was the Night Sort."

Huh. The same shift Caleb worked during college. That might have explained how she knew him, but not why she preferred the evening shift. *Maybe she has kids and prefers working at night while they sleep?* She didn't strike Logan as the maternal type, but he was hardly one to judge.

"What does that have to do with Caleb?"

"A few days after the schedule was announced, someone shoved a nasty note under Caleb's door. I only know about it because his neighbor saw the look on Caleb's face when he retrieved it. Caleb would not let me see it, and I suspect there were more."

His anger returned in full force. Foster couldn't lash out at Klass directly without risking her job, so she attacked Caleb instead. It was the act of a petty vindictive bitch, but the reasoning didn't make any sense. What could she possibly gain from harassing Caleb? It had been years since he had worked at the warehouse.

"Then, a couple of weeks later, I came to the apartment and there were police and a fire truck in front of the building. In the lobby I saw Caleb holding a fat orange cat and helping his elderly neighbor down the stairs through a cloud of smoke. When he saw me, he handed me the cat and took off, racing back up before I could stop him."

Logan swallowed hard. He could imagine the lobby too vividly. The blaring alarm, a swarm of pissed off and scared residents expelled from their apartments, emergency personnel trying to tame the chaos, and the threat of fire billowing down the staircase. It was a recipe for a panic attack if there ever was one.

"Someone had set off a smoke bomb on Caleb's floor. Caleb inhaled a lot of smoke, but refused to let the paramedics check him out."

Logan unclenched his jaw with a pop. "You think Foster was responsible?"

"I have no proof she—or one of her boyfriends—was responsible, but the next day, Klass came in looking haggard and I saw the look on that *puta*'s face."

A chorus of *bad word, bad word* rang in the background. Marco grumbled something and then Logan heard delighted squeals and the smacking sound of messy kisses. "Daddy is sorry for saying a bad word." Marco cleared his throat, and Logan swore he could hear the man regrouping his dignity.

The happy domestic sounds helped Logan pull back on his growing temper. Getting angry wouldn't change what happened. He was grateful to Marco for telling him about it and for caring enough about Caleb to follow up on him. "Do you want me to put in a good word with Mommy?"

Marco sighed. "I will be forgiven… eventually," he muttered. "My wife is very fond of Caleb and always includes him in her prayers. I would not have this job if not for him and I am now able to save for my children's futures."

"Why not go to Klass and tell him what you suspect about Foster?"

"*Mijo*," Marco admonished.

Logan winced and said, "Right, stupid question," giving himself a mental smack for suggesting Marco accuse his white supervisor without a shred of evidence.

He harrumphed. "Besides, I would never have convinced Caleb. He refused to talk about it. I think he would rather her go unpunished than risk accusing her wrongly. Without proof, I could do nothing."

Logan was convinced Foster's actions outside of Meng's had been deliberate. She'd wanted to upset Caleb and possibly send him into a panic attack. She also seemed to be going out of her way to weasel herself into Logan's life. He wasn't vain enough to think it was his bod making her try so hard. There had to be another reason.

Marco's voice drew him back from his musing. "Perhaps," he said, drawing out the word until it purred. "You will have better luck persuading Caleb than I."

"You talk to Caleb lately?"

"Of course, I would be a poor friend if I did not call to see how my replacement was faring."

Marco paused. If he was waiting for Logan to ask what Caleb had said about him, he'd be waiting indefinitely. He didn't intend to rise to the bait, in spite of how much he might want to. "If any of your *friends* hear anything about Foster, let me know."

"Yes, yes, of course. Now you must tell me why I could hear my Caleb blushing through the phone line when I asked about you."

"Sorry, I gotta run."

"Bah, you are no fun."

Grinning, Logan ended the call.

CALEB smiled when he heard a knock at the door. Logan usually came by on Mondays and Fridays, but he had started showing up on Wednesdays too. He claimed it was because Thursday was hell day, with a double shift at the warehouse followed by an anger management class and an AA meeting. He came by just in case he was too tired to come on Friday. So far, Logan hadn't missed a Friday.

Logan took two steps into the apartment before stopping and inhaling deeply. He swayed on his feet, and Caleb's stomach fluttered at the sight of him. The navy-blue tank top covering his chest looked like it barely contained his thick, rippling muscles. The cut-off shorts put his long and slightly hairy legs on display.

"Cookies?" Logan licked his lips. "God, you bake too?" He followed Caleb and sat on an island stool, facing toward the kitchen. "How's everything going?"

"Good. I'm channeling another ex-con—good ol' Martha Stewart—after talking to Mrs. Simon in the hallway." Caleb pulled a cookie sheet out of the cabinet and placed it onto the island. "She's visiting her grandkids this weekend." Unrolling a sheet of parchment paper, he continued. "But she can't bake, and I said I'd help her out," he said, laying the paper over the cookie sheet.

Logan smirked. "She afraid of losing her grandma card? I'd think her kid would know she can't bake."

Caleb chuckled. He turned and opened the fridge, pulling out a covered bowl of cookie dough. "Her son has no idea she can't bake. Her deceased husband, a burly butcher named Herb, secretly did all the cooking and baking and let her have the credit."

Logan's brow rose. "Why would he do that?"

Caleb opened a drawer and pulled out a teaspoon. "He loved to cook, but his mother thought it was women's work." He snorted. "Mrs. Simon's convinced old Herb married her just because she nearly set the kitchen on fire trying to cook him a roast chicken." He took the plastic wrapping off the top of the bowl and handed Logan the teaspoon.

Logan's forehead wrinkled. "What's this for?"

Caleb quirked an eyebrow. "Scoop out spoonfuls and place them on the cookie sheet. Be sure to leave a couple of inches of space between the balls."

Logan shook his head and took a step back from the counter, still holding the teaspoon. "No way. I screw them up and she'll feed me to her cat."

Caleb gave an exaggerated sigh. "Then I guess I'll just have to give her the batch I've got in the oven and freeze this dough for another time." He fought to keep the smile off his lips as Logan inhaled, closing his eyes.

"I expect you to rescue me from the jaws of that monster," Logan grumbled, stepping back toward the counter. He detoured to the sink and washed his hands.

Caleb grinned. "I promise." Hearing the beep of the timer, he said, "Get to work so we can get eating." Turning back toward the stove, he put on an oven mitt and opened the oven door, taking out a sheet of cookies. He heard Logan's murmur of appreciation when the smell of freshly baked goodness invaded the kitchen. Carefully, he slid the parchment paper off the cookie sheet and onto the cooling rack. When he turned back, he watched Logan measure out a spoonful of dough with painful precision. Logan frowned when the dough failed to slide off the spoon and onto the parchment.

Caleb bit his bottom lip to keep from smiling. "You can use your finger to slide it off." He opened a drawer and pulled out another teaspoon. He then scooped out a ball of dough and deposited it onto the sheet. He repeated the action a few more times while Logan watched him intently. Leaving Logan to the rest, he wiped his fingers on a hand towel. "I'll make a burly baker out of you yet."

Logan scowled, but he dug out another ball just as carefully and deposited it on the cookie sheet. There was a small, satisfied smile on his face. "Ain't wearing no frilly apron."

Turning toward the cabinet, Caleb opened it and got out a plate and two glasses. "That's too bad. I think frilly aprons are hot." He laughed when the hand towel hit the back of his head. Using a spatula, he slid half a dozen cookies onto the plate. They were warm enough to be a bit gooey, just the way he liked them. He then filled the glasses with milk from the fridge. By the time he was done, Logan had finished preparing the cookies. "Thanks," Caleb said, lifting the tray and putting it into the oven. After resetting the timer, he slid a plate of warm cookies and a glass of milk in front of Logan. "Eat, before you get drool on my counter."

Logan bit into the soft cookie, his eyes closing in apparent ecstasy as he groaned. Caleb watched his long lashes flutter with pleasure. He was still staring, thanking God for the counter between them, when Logan turned a sizzling, speculative look on him. "Perfect," Logan said thickly.

Caleb felt himself blush, absurdly pleased by the compliment. Lowering his eyes, he took a bite of the cookie in his hand. It really was good—the chewy texture, the richness of the white and dark chocolate, and the saltiness of the cashews.

Selecting another cookie, Logan shoved the whole piece in his mouth and chewed it noisily, making muffled sex noises. "God, what I woulda given for food like this in prison."

"I fully acknowledge the irony, but I can't imagine being in prison."

"You make sure to keep it that way." He pointed a crumb-covered finger at Caleb. "A guy as pretty as you wouldn't survive prison."

Caleb nearly choked on a piece of cookie and he felt his cheeks flushing again. "You think I'm...."

"Pretty?" Logan grinned and grabbed another cookie. "That depends. Are you freaking out? 'Cause if you are, then I'm only saying you're hotter than a bunch of crusty cons."

Caleb laughed, but then he froze when Logan leaned forward. He held his breath as he felt Logan's finger brushing against his lip. Logan then stuck his finger in his mouth, sucking it off. His dark eyes never wavered.

Caleb licked his lips, tasting chocolate and Logan all blended together. Logan leaned forward, his eyes searching for something and his lips parted. He reached a hand out and ran his thumb along the underside of Caleb's jaw, curling the rest of his fingers around his nape. He pulled Caleb toward him for a long, open-mouthed kiss. Caleb tasted the chocolate heated by the warmth of Logan's mouth. Logan slid his tongue along the seam of Caleb's lips, coaxing his mouth open and running his tongue lightly along the rim of his lower lip. The buzz of the timer startled them, causing them both to pull away. Caleb looked back, realizing he had mistakenly set the timer to five minutes instead of fifteen.

"Oh, crap, is that the time?" Logan said, rising to his feet. "I'm meeting with my parole officer today. I need to get going."

Caleb heard the regret in his voice. Turning toward the cabinet, he pulled out a small Tupperware container, put the remaining cookies into it, and sealed it. Handing the container to Logan, he said, "For the road."

Logan's grin made Caleb's toes tingle.

After securing the door, Caleb cleaned the kitchen, rinsing off the baking pans and scrubbing the counter. It didn't stop his thoughts from going back to the kiss. He couldn't remember feeling like that before. He wanted to devour Logan, to run his tongue over every inch of his chiseled body. Surprisingly he had seen the same heat in Logan's eyes and felt the urgency in his touch. Logan could have his pick of gorgeous guys. *Why would he settle for me?* The buzzer brought him from his musing. He pulled the cookies out of the oven and transferred them to the cooling rack. Glancing down at his shirt, he noticed a blob of cookie dough sticking to the front. *What a sexy beast I am.* He left the cookies to cool and headed for the bedroom. The package from Old Navy sat on the bed where he had left it. Impulsively, he had bought a new set of clothes online after Dabb had left, wanting to have at least one decent outfit.

When he had answered the door for the delivery man, Mrs. Simon had spotted him and put in her cookie request. Caleb had eagerly agreed, wanting an excuse to bake something special for Logan. Yanking on the tab, he opened the package and dumped the contents on the bed. He ripped off the plastic covering from a striped button-up shirt in muted earth tones, a white T-shirt, and a faded pair of jeans. He undressed and pulled on the new clothes.

After walking into the bathroom, he stepped into the shower stall to see more of himself in the mirror over the sink. "Huh." It was strange to see himself in the kind of clothes he used to wear. A low-level sense of unease settled in his mind. The collar on the T-shirt felt tight, even though he knew it was at least a size bigger than he normally wore. The jeans hugged his buttocks and thighs in a way that was somehow different than his usual sweatpants. Even as the thoughts occurred, he recognized how irrational they were, but the feelings persisted. *Maybe I just need to get used to them.*

He left the bedroom and went back to the kitchen. He got another Tupperware container from the cabinet and set it on the counter. After testing the cookies to see if they had cooled, he began placing them into the container, putting a layer of parchment paper between each level. Task completed, he headed into the living room. Before opening the door, he took a deep breath.

He knocked on Mrs. Simon's door, clutching the container to his chest. Keeping his eyes focused on the marred wood, he waited a lifetime for her to open it.

"Hello, dear. Why don't you come in a minute, so I can thank you properly."

He shook his head. "No need. I was happy to help and I'm sure you've got plenty to do before your trip."

She took the container from Caleb. "Yes," she said, looking at her feet. "I do, but you've done enough for me already, so I'll let you go."

Caleb cocked his head to the side, less anxious to bolt. "Is there something you need help with?"

She sighed. "I need to get Tiny to Daniel's apartment on the fifth floor." She patted Caleb's hand. "But don't you worry, dear. I'll manage." Her lips thinned, likely imagining carrying thirty pounds of cat up the steep staircase.

Caleb frowned. "Why can't the guy come get Tiny himself?"

"Daniel is… nervous about taking care of a pet. Maybe my son can help me when he comes to pick me up." She frowned. "Of course, Tiny can't stand my William, so I'll probably need to put Tiny in a pillowcase, so he doesn't tear him to shreds." She sighed again. "He's gotten too fat for the cat carrier."

The performance was Oscar-worthy, and even though Caleb knew he was being played, he found himself offering to haul the cat upstairs anyway. She was stubborn enough to try doing it herself, and he would never forgive himself if she got hurt. She barely managed the stairs under normal circumstances. Shuddering, he imagined her trying to walk up them with the squirming monster in her arms. He also knew she wasn't exaggerating about Tiny's utter contempt for her son. Caleb gave the man credit. He drove forty miles twice a month to bring his mother a heavy bag of cat litter even though Caleb had offered to add it to his own grocery order. Tiny showed his appreciation by attempting to maul William to death the moment he set foot in the apartment. Caleb had handed over the last of his first-aid supplies the last time. How Tiny had managed to open the closed bedroom door was a mystery he didn't want to contemplate. Tiny had always been a purring pile of mush when he came to visit.

Mrs. Simon narrowed her eyes and then, much to his horror, looked him over from head to toe. "Did you buy new clothes?" Not waiting for a reply, she continued. "It's nice to see you in something other than those ratty old sweats." The knowing look she gave him made him want to run screaming from the room. She moved into the living room to retrieve a canvas bag with a disposable litter box poking out of the top of it. "I put everything he'll need in here."

Caleb took the bag from her. The orange cat watched him as if deciding whether it was worth the effort to bolt from the room. It was hard to blame the big guy. His options were a pillowcase or a man prone to panic attacks. He would probably much prefer a big bowl of kibble and an uncovered toilet to get him through the weekend. Trying not to give out terrified vibes, Caleb reached out to rub behind the cat's ear, his hand trembling slightly. "It's okay, boy. I'll get you there safe and sound."

Mrs. Simon was staring at Tiny or possibly his traitorous hand when she spoke. "Daniel's in apartment 501. He's a teacher at CSU and seems like a nice young man." She squeezed Caleb's arm. "I could call him and ask him to come get Tiny."

If you can't handle it was her unspoken message. She was giving him an out, and he was grateful for it, but refused to back down. If he wanted a life beyond the walls of his apartment, he couldn't rely on Logan whispering dirty things in his ear to coax him out. "I'll be fine." He lifted Tiny into his arms, kissing the top of his furry head. Pulling the canvas bag over his shoulder, he headed for the door. He looked back and said, "Have fun visiting your family."

Caleb took a deep breath before heading up the stairs, snuggling the cat close to his chest. The tabby purred and nuzzled his neck as if in encouragement as they made their way to the fifth floor. Juggling Tiny into one arm, Caleb knocked on the door of apartment 501. After only a moment, the door opened to reveal a guy with a friendly smile and a set of delicious dimples. His bright blue eyes widened when he spotted Tiny.

"My God, he's massive." Opening the door further, he asked, "Do you mind coming in for a minute while I check out the bag?" He smiled sheepishly. "I've never taken care of a pet before."

"Sure," Caleb said.

They exchanged introductions as he followed Daniel inside. The apartment had the same layout as his place, but it somehow managed to come across as bright and cheery whereas Caleb knew his place appeared dim and gloomy. He noted a casual and comfortable-looking green couch and matching chair that faced a modest flat-screen TV. He handed over the bag to Daniel, still cuddling Tiny. The big cat peeked around the room before burying his head against Caleb's chest. Wanting to avoid looking out the sheer curtains, he turned toward Daniel, who was setting the bag on the island counter. "Mrs. Simon mentioned you're a professor at my alma mater."

Daniel nodded. His carefully styled mass of dark curls made Caleb conscious of his own mop of hair. *Maybe Logan would buzz it off for me.* Daniel unpacked what looked like half a dozen cans of cat food. *No wonder Tiny's huge.*

"I teach Marketing at CSU." Daniel pulled the disposable litter box from the bag. "Any idea where I should set this up?"

"Mrs. Simon keeps hers in the laundry room."

After returning from the laundry, Daniel said, "Mrs. S. said you have your own business. You design web pages, right?"

"Yeah," Caleb said, wondering what else she had said about him.

"I'm always looking for guest speakers, especially alumni. Would you be interested?" His expression faltered, and his cheeks flushed. "We could do it via webcam."

Caleb swallowed hard and used his free hand to yank on the collar of his T-shirt. "I'm pretty busy right now. I'll have to let you know."

"Sure." He looked like he was struggling for something to say. Caleb wondered if he could get away with pretending he had left the stove on. *Would that make me look like more of a basket case?* He wasn't sure he cared as long as it got him out of here.

Before he could voice his excuse, Daniel asked, "Have you watched Tiny before?"

"No," Caleb said, more emphatically than he meant to. Daniel blinked rapidly.

Caleb lifted his hand in apology. "I'm too worried he'll get sick and I'll need to—"

"Oh, God!" Daniel said, loud enough to make Caleb jump. "I can't believe I let Mrs. Simon convince me to take care of him." He pointed a finger at Tiny. "I'll kill him!"

Caleb swore under his breath when Tiny's claws pierced his shirt. Smart cat. He took a couple of steps toward the door. *If he admits to drowning a kitten, we're out of here.* Tiny howled as if he had heard the words.

"I lied," Daniel said, like he was admitting to murdering a busload of nuns. "I got a Panda Moor goldfish this past Christmas. He was this big fat guy with bulging eyes and a black-and-white pattern." He ran a hand through his hair. "And I killed him in less than two weeks."

"Um," Caleb said, fumbling for the words that might calm the guy. And wow, wasn't that ironic? "How do you know he wasn't sick when you got him?" he asked, sincerely hoping his nostrils didn't flare like that when he was freaking out.

"I put the tank by the window so he could see outside." He collapsed on an island stool, covering his face with his hands. "On top of the radiator cover."

Caleb mentally winced as the hagfish soup he had made for Logan on Monday came to mind. He wouldn't be eating fish again anytime soon. "You'll be fine," he soothed, patting Daniel's shoulder awkwardly. "Oh, but keep the door chained."

"Why?"

Caleb started to explain that Tiny was the Houdini of cats and then thought better of it. "Bring the bag and let's sit down." He walked over to the couch and sank into the soft cushions.

Daniel hesitated a few moments before sitting on the opposite end of the couch. Prying Tiny from his chest, Caleb placed the cat on the cushion between them. "You're only watching him for forty-eight hours and he'll be asleep for most of it." Tiny looked back at him as if to say *what did I ever do to you?* He tried to pet his head reassuringly. "Give him a can of food in the morning and one in the evening. Keep a bowl of fresh water out for him and you'll have no problems."

Daniel didn't look convinced. He regarded the cat as if he expected him to burst into flames any minute. Tiny yowled pathetically.

"Reach into the bag and grab the kitty crack."

"Huh?"

"Grab the little brown sack and give it to him."

Daniel reached into the bag and pulled out the catnip. He tossed the sack toward the cat. Tiny went crazy, pinning the sack with his massive paws and rubbing his face all over with it.

Caleb grinned. "Congratulations." He rubbed a finger behind Tiny's ears. "You'll be his new best friend."

Daniel watched in apparent fascination as Tiny batted the sack back and forth. "Thank you, for helping me and for not making me feel like an idiot."

"Not a problem," Caleb said with a smile. "I aced Panic 101."

LOGAN handed the cup to the bored-looking cop on piss collection duty. Drugs had never been his scene. He'd watched his old man shoot every dollar he could get his hands on up his arm. Activating the sensor on the sink, he washed his hands. They had given him a breathalyzer test earlier. Who would be stupid enough to show up drunk to the parole office? Enough guys to warrant the need, apparently. He knew Dabb carried one around in his briefcase. He'd made Logan use it outside the grocery where Logan got Caleb's food. Logan hadn't had a drink since detox in prison. After shaking off his hands, he wiped them against his jeans as he exited the bathroom.

This was his first time going to Dabb's office. He met with his PO once a week, but mostly at places near Logan's work or at his shit apartment. Today marked his one-month anniversary of being free, relatively speaking. The preteen curfew of eight o'clock would continue for another eleven months, but he'd get to scale back on his in-person check-ins if everything went okay today. He walked down the hallway, following the signs to the office area. He found the correct room, noticing Dabb sitting at his desk. *What the hell?* His PO was wiping his computer screen with a plushy M&M doll bigger than his hand.

Seeming to sense Logan's presence, Dabb turned and invited him in by waving the doll at him. Logan hesitated, looking at the bright red M&M doll and then back at his PO.

"It's a screen cleaner," Dabb growled, like that made it any less weird.

Logan suddenly found his nose itchy as he stifled a laugh. He didn't remember there being a clause in his parole agreement about mocking his PO, but it didn't seem worth the risk. He entered the office that was the size of a walk-in closet, and took a seat in the chair across from the desk. In spite of his resolve, he couldn't keep from gawking. There were at least a dozen boxes of bulk M&M packages and an M&M mouse pad with a matching mouse in the shape of the blue character. Magnets covered a pair of battered-looking filing cabinets. Plushy dolls of every shape and size, coffee cups, and even something that looked like a candy dispenser were spread over nearly every available surface. The scowling visage of his PO amongst the sea of brightly covered items was too much.

"I like M&M's," Dabb said.

"Clearly."

Dabb's gray eyes narrowed. "My girls are young, but they still like to pick out presents themselves." He pulled out a framed photo of two curly-headed girls from his desk drawer, likely elementary-school age. Someone—hopefully the kids and not Dabb—had glued M&M's all around the frame. It was disgustingly adorable.

"They're real cute."

Dabb looked at the photo with a sappy smile on his face before he tucked it back into the desk drawer. Logan started to wonder why he didn't keep it out when the reality of his PO's job hit him. *He likely deals with some sick fucks.* It was a sobering thought, but he was glad that Dabb wasn't afraid to show him the picture.

"Okay, we need to fill out a monthly report of your activities. I am hoping you brought the information we talked about. It asks for info on your residence, employment, police encounters, alcohol treatment, and payment of supervision fees." Dabb handed Logan a sheet of paper on a clipboard. "And here's a pen," he said matter-of-factly, as if daring Logan to comment on the M&M-shaped cap.

Logan bit his lower lip to keep from smiling and started on the form. The contact information was easy to enter, but he hesitated when he got to the employment section. "What should I put for hours?" His regular shift was 4:00 a.m. to 8:00 a.m., but he took on additional shifts whenever he got the chance.

"Put the time for your regular hours and I'll put in a note about you texting me when you get an extra shift that has you out past curfew. The HR department agreed to fax me the timecards weekly. Did you remember to bring a pay stub?"

"Yeah." He actually had two. Caleb had printed him one on company letterhead and provided a signed time card. Logan had been impressed by how professional it looked. He frowned. The form Dabb gave him only had space for one job. "Where should I put Caleb's info?"

A look that made Logan's gut clench passed over Dabb's features. *Why would mentioning Caleb create a flash of irritation in Dabb's eyes?* He looked away from Logan and said, "Fill out the rest of the form for now."

Logan concentrated on the report, trying not to panic. He filled in the information about the AA meetings and the anger management classes he'd attended and verified he had paid the supervision fees to the court. After signing his name and dating the form, he handed the clipboard back to Dabb.

His PO pulled out a notebook and flipped to several pages in. "According to Mr. Klass, you're responsible for retrieving Caleb's mail from the PO box, taking back any mailers, removing any refuse or recyclable material, and visually inspecting the apartment for hazards or potential problems." He flipped to the next page. "He also requires you to spend ten minutes talking with his nephew and occasionally picking up Caleb's grocery order."

Logan shifted in his seat. "That's right."

Dabb put down the notebook and folded his hands across the desk. "Then you want to tell me why that took you sixty-three minutes on this past Monday?" His voice was calm, without a hint of anger, but his gray eyes bored into Logan. It was hard to pull off badass while surrounded by colorful plushy dolls, but Dabb made it look easy. "I want to know what other *services*," he said, managing to make the word sound filthy, "he's paying you to perform."

"You think I'm…." Logan laughed. The image of Klass in pimp gear flashed in his head, and he laughed harder. "Sorry," he said, wiping his eyes.

Dabb looked both relieved and annoyed. "I've known Har—uh, Mr. Klass a long time and he definitely got squirrelly when I asked him why he selected you for the job. I needed to be sure he wasn't putting pressure on you."

"To fuck an incredibly hot guy?"

Without missing a beat, Dabb said, "To prostitute yourself to avoid losing both jobs and put your probation in jeopardy."

"Klass ain't pressuring me to do nothing!" Logan made a conscious effort to lower his voice. "You've met Caleb. Do you honestly believe he'd coerce a guy into having sex with him?"

Dabb shook his head. "He'd only have to switch on the webcam and guys would be begging to come over and rock his world, but that doesn't mean something isn't going on. You need to talk to me, Logan," he said, pulling off his glasses. "I can't help you if I don't know what's going on."

Logan scrubbed a hand over his face, not wanting to think about anybody else rocking Caleb's world. "Klass wants Caleb to leave the apartment. He just has an ass-backward way of doing it. He hires guys he thinks Caleb will be attracted to and has them ask embarrassing questions. It's like he's trying to shame Caleb into leaving." It wasn't until he said the words that he realized how angry the idea made him.

Dabb leaned back in his chair looking smug. "Then I take it Klass doesn't know you're gay."

With a jolt, Logan realized he'd been played. No way did Dabb think Klass hired pros for his nephew. He'd just wanted to provoke Logan into talking. Manipulative bastard. "I don't deny it, but I don't get asked often."

Dabb snorted. "I wasn't looking forward to it myself. And you still haven't answered my question."

"Mostly, Caleb cooks and we talk a bit. As far as I can see, Caleb don't have many friends and I'm being overpaid. It's only right I spend time with him and make sure he's doing okay."

"So you're doing it because you feel obligated? Or maybe sorry for him?"

"It's not like I have many friends either." When he had come up for parole, he'd deliberately asked to move into a neighborhood on the other side of town from his old place, needing to break away from the people who'd watched him slide into a bottle and not climb out. He couldn't stand the thought of facing Michael again and seeing the hurt in his eyes. "He don't drink booze and he's a good guy."

"So, you're getting to be friends with him?"

Logan started to say yes, but then stopped.

Dabb made a frustrated noise. "This," he said, pointing back and forth between them, "doesn't work if you're not honest with me."

"I want us to be friends, but I wouldn't mind if we were... uh... more than friends." It was the first time he'd admitted even to himself what he really wanted. He'd wanted to fuck Caleb from the moment they'd met, but the urge to get closer to him had grown as he'd gotten to know him better. He'd had enough meaningless fucks in his life and too many he couldn't even remember. He wanted more than that from Caleb. He wasn't sure if he should act on it, but there was no use denying it.

Dabb massaged his forehead. "You know, this isn't the first time in twenty years I've played Dr. Phil to a parolee's love life, but it has to be the strangest."

"Don't get a lot of gay romances, do ya?"

"Plenty, but they don't usually sound like the tagline to a porno." His voice took on the tone of a TV announcer. "The delivery guy can't wait to deliver his package to the housebound hottie."

Logan barked a short laugh. Then felt his cheeks flushing when he remembered his first fantasy about Caleb had been along those same lines. *Housebound and Horny.* Pulling back from his thoughts, he saw Dabb smirking at him. *Two girls in the photo, but no wife.* It could be nothing, but something told Logan the glint in Dabb's eyes meant they batted on the same side. He knew better than to ask his PO, but that didn't mean he wasn't tempted to.

Dabb cleared his throat. "Having successfully completed your first month on probation, you won't need to come back here for another three months, provided you continue to attend the AA meetings and successfully complete the anger management class. And avoid getting your ass arrested. We'll scale back the phone check-ins to once every three weeks. But that doesn't mean I won't randomly show up at your work or your apartment." He picked up a minibag of M&M's and tossed it to Logan. "Stay out of trouble and call me if problems arise."

"Will do," Logan said, rising to his feet. After a moment's hesitation, he said, "Thanks."

WHEN the phone rang, Caleb glanced at the clock, noticing the late hour before answering it. It was Logan on the line. Remembering yesterday's scheduled meeting, Caleb put the book he had been reading on the nightstand. "Did everything go all right with your parole officer?"

Logan's deep sigh did nothing to alleviate Caleb's unease. After an eternity, Logan said, "I woulda rather stayed with you, but it went okay."

"I'm glad," Caleb said, feeling his face heat up. "That it went okay." He recalled his conversation with his neighbor when he had returned from Daniel's apartment. "Mrs. Simon says 'time's up', but she refused to tell me for what."

"She said that when you took her the grandma cookies?"

"Yeah, after she had me deliver Tiny to a guy on the fifth floor that's going to watch him," Caleb said, feeling ridiculously proud of himself for holding it together long enough to deliver the cat. Hell, he managed better than Daniel.

"Is that right?"

Caleb thought Logan's voice sounded strange, more serious. *Maybe he's tired and not looking to hear about my pathetic success.* "I should let you sleep. I know how long your day was."

"Not until you tell me about the guy you met."

Caleb shrugged and then realized Logan couldn't see him. "Seemed nice enough"—*for a fish killer*—"and Mrs. Simon sings his praises."

"Gay or straight?"

Caleb blinked several times. "How would I know? I talked to him for less than ten minutes."

"Knew about you that first day."

"Really?" *Am I that obvious*? He chewed on his bottom lip, consoling himself with the knowledge Logan was the most gorgeous guy he had seen in the flesh. *Who wouldn't drool over him?*

"I'd bet money I don't have that that biddy is scheming to hook you up with the guy. No straight man's gonna volunteer to cat-sit an old lady's pet."

Caleb laughed. "You've gotta be kidding."

"Was he pretty?"

A picture of Daniel when he had first opened the door popped into Caleb's mind. "Um…." He heard a low grumbling sound. Pulling back the receiver, he looked at the phone before putting it back against his ear. "Did you just growl?"

"I don't wanna talk about Mr. Fifth Floor anymore."

Caleb grinned. Was Logan actually jealous? "You know, you're starting to slack on the job. You forgot to ask me about my sex life yesterday." In a flash, he remembered the moment in the kitchen. The heat he saw in Logan's eyes and the warmth of his mouth. He dragged his attention back to what Logan was saying.

"You little shit. I just got out of the shower and you're gonna send me right back in there."

It took a moment for Caleb's brain to process the words. "Are you saying…." He covered his face with his hand. "You're going to…."

Logan chuckled. "Get off thinking about you? Oh yeah, but it's up to you whether you listen."

"I don't think I can do it," Caleb blurted out.

"Get off?"

"Talk about, uh, stuff. I've never done it on the phone."

"But you have done it with a guy, right?" Logan asked quietly.

"Huh? Oh, yeah." Four years ago. But Logan didn't need to know that.

"We can just talk. We don't have to do nothing, baby."

Caleb blew out a slow breath. Logan giving him permission to back down eased his growing anxiety. It made it easier to go forward. "So," he started, feeling ridiculous. "What are you wearing?" He smiled when Logan gave a throaty chuckle in response.

Caleb heard what sounded like the bedsprings squeak as Logan said, "Too hot to get dressed." He sighed as he settled into place. "Are you wearing those tight sweatpants?"

"They're not that tight."

He made a sound of appreciation. "Tight enough for me to know you don't wear nothing underneath."

Caleb was sure his face would burst into flames any second. Hearing rustling, he closed his eyes and visualized Logan leaning back on the bed, dark eyes hooded, towel wrapped loosely around his hips as water dripped down the length of his hard chest. *Yum.*

Logan's voice in his ear sounded low and rough. "Take off your shirt, but leave those sweatpants on. I want to hear you come all over them."

Caleb couldn't believe they were about to do this. The thought sent shivers of anticipation and trepidation riding down his spine. "Hold on, let me get something." After taking off his T-shirt, he reached into the nightstand and took out a bottle of lube. Placing the bottle next to the phone, he snapped the cap.

"Oh, fuck," Logan said, "was that lube?"

"Yep," Caleb said, as he squirted a dab into the palm of his hand, "and I have you to thank for helping me get it." Logan's strangled curse was particularly satisfying. Caleb wished he were brave enough to mention the condoms Min had snuck into the bag.

Closing his eyes, Caleb snaked his hand into his sweatpants. He pressed his lips together as his fingers curled around his hardening erection. He let his fingers twist and glide along his length, relishing the feel of warm skin and wet friction. *What would it feel like to have Logan's strong hands on me?* His breathing grew shallow as he began to squeeze his cock lightly, then harder, moving his hand up and down the velvet-smooth flesh pulsing against his fingers. The cloth restricted his movement, forcing him to go more slowly than he wanted. He hesitated, unsure what to do next. Licking his lips, he said, "Tell me what you like."

"Are you asking me to talk dirty to you?" Logan asked, his voice one part amusement and two parts growl.

Caleb's heartbeat sped, breath hitching in his chest. "Please."

"Do you want to hear about how I want to shove my cock into you?" Logan asked, his voice velvet-edged and strong. "How I want to ride you until you can't walk? How I wish it was my hand on you, making you come?"

"Oh, God," Caleb said, gripping the receiver so tight his fingers ached.

Logan's groans of "So good, so good" made Caleb's balls tighten in response and he quickened his pace. The sound of slapping flesh became louder and more erratic. Caleb panted into the mouthpiece and pumped harder, ignoring the stickiness clinging to his pants. Full and hot, his balls tightened against his body, ready to burst as he stroked himself again and again. Within seconds, Caleb released a guttural groan, coming in his hand, seed soaking his sweats.

Moments later, Logan cried out, Caleb's name on his lips. Neither of them spoke for a few minutes.

"Good night," murmured Logan. "I'll see you tomorrow."

"Night," Caleb said, before ending the call. His sweatpants were damp and sticking to his leg, but he couldn't bring himself to care about the mess. He quickly wiped his hand and groin with his T-shirt and turned off the light. He fell asleep easily.

CHAPTER
FIVE

ON FRIDAY, Caleb woke when the morning sun found the gap in the curtains and attacked his eyeballs with a sharp ray of sunlight. Squinting, he peered at the bedside clock and groaned when he realized it was well past eight. Logan would be here in less than half an hour. Caleb felt a wave of sympathy for Logan. He had already been at work for hours, and Caleb was still lazing around in bed. He dragged himself from the warmth of the covers and cringed when he saw the state he was in. He would be lucky to get the pants off without giving himself a bikini wax. He needed a shower desperately.

Caleb entered the bathroom, turned on the shower, and adjusted the spray until it was scorching hot, the way he liked it. Considering the late morning hour, he needed to move quickly before the hot water ran out. He peeled himself out of the pants, wincing when he lost hairs in the process. *That's what you get for not cleaning up after phone sex*, he thought as he stepped into the shower stall. He felt his cheeks flush and not from the billowing steam and near scalding water. He couldn't believe he'd had phone sex. With Logan. Who would be arriving in a matter of minutes. *God, what if he regrets it? What if we sit there in awkward silence?*

Caleb leaned his forehead against the wall, his vision clouding and his legs and arms tingling and distant. A crush of emotions and thoughts rushed through him and he felt the fear build in his chest. Time drifted and shifted, leaving him feeling dizzy. Until the hot water decided it had had enough.

"Fuck!" Caleb leapt backwards away from the icy spray. One foot landed on a soapy tile. He skidded, lost his balance. His arms windmilled, and he snatched at the shower curtain. The blue-checkered fabric ripped under his weight, the curtain hooks popping off the rod as he tumbled forward. He fell halfway out of the shower, his upper body crashing against the edge of the toilet and his head cracking against the cabinet. Letting out a short, harsh gasp of pain, he rotated his body away from the toilet, cradling his arm against his chest. The pulsing pain shooting up his arm and elbow battled with the throbbing ache in his head.

His vision blurred and he thought about getting to the phone to call Logan. Rapidly, thoughts flooded through his mind in a blinding whirl. *What if the door jams and I'm stuck in here forever? What if my arm's broken and I end up crippled? Or it turns gangrene and they want to cut it off?* His stomach churned and his head spun. He was going to be sick. With his good arm, he pulled himself to his knees and flipped open the lid of the toilet. The universe blinked out of existence. He was there for two minutes, or maybe it was ten, wracked with cramps and spasms. *God, would they ever end?* The thought made him retch again, while every muscle and bone in his arm cried out in protest.

The terror immobilized him. So he went still, lying on the torn curtain while the cold spray splashed out of the shower onto his legs and back. A familiar sound rang in the distance. It was an important sound, but he couldn't latch on to it. The universe blanked out again.

LOGAN stepped back from the door, hands on his hips. No answer. He took out his cell phone and dialed Caleb's number. His unease increased as Caleb's phone repeatedly rang before going to voice mail. He hit the End button on the phone. After a moment's hesitation, he pulled up Klass's number and hit Send. His boss sounded harried when he answered the phone.

"I'm at Caleb's place, but he's not answering."

Klass's voice seemed temporarily muted as though he were switching the phone from one ear to another. "When did you last see him?"

Logan rubbed the back of his neck. "Saw him on Wednesday and talked to him on the phone yesterday."

Logan heard a murmured woman's voice. Klass agreed with what she said before continuing. "You say you called him?" He paused. "Why exactly?"

"Just checking in 'cause I couldn't stick around too long on Wednesday like I usually do."

"That's very kind of you, Mr. Sellers."

"Weren't no big deal. He's a good guy."

"I'm glad you think so," Klass said, sounding downcast. "Did he mention anything unusual happening when you talked with him yesterday?"

Oh fuck. He was glad Klass couldn't see his face. "Uh... he mentioned visiting Mrs. Simon at her place and carrying her cat to a neighbor on the fifth floor." *And then we had phone sex.*

"Ah, that explains it," Klass said, sounding like he'd solved a mystery. "When he pushes himself to break his patterns, it can be upsetting to him. He tends to retreat, needing time to recover. It's best if we give him that time."

Logan privately thought letting Caleb slide backwards after he made progress seemed like the wrong approach, but what did he know? He wondered if Klass knew about the trips out they'd taken. Caleb had made it all the way to Meng's without freaking out, but maybe it was different going up the stairs with only a fat cat for company. "So you want me to just leave?"

"Yes, let's give him the weekend. If he doesn't answer the door on Monday, you can use my spare key."

Logan wanted to argue, but maybe Klass was right. The idea of meeting Dabb in his own apartment made Caleb shake and stutter. Dealing with the old bird's attempt at matchmaking was bound to be stressful. *Yeah, right. Blame the old lady and not the fact that you went from one kiss to phone sex.* Caleb was probably hiding in his place, too embarrassed to answer the door. The request had been impulsive and more than a little possessive. The idea of Caleb meeting some hot guy had bothered him more than he wanted to admit. He'd wanted to stake his claim on Caleb in a way his curfew didn't allow. The result had been too fucking hot for him to regret it, but he could acknowledge, if only to himself, the reason behind it. He'd have to wait and see if Caleb regretted it.

LOGAN opened the door to his apartment and made his way inside. He stood in the middle of the room for a full minute before turning around and heading back out. He'd go crazy if he stayed here. He needed a distraction, something to keep his mind off Caleb. It wasn't until he started AA he realized so much of his life revolved around booze. Watching football at a local pub, playing pool, and even slaughtering his buddies at poker were all just excuses to get plastered. *So what the hell do I do now?* He could go for a run around the lake if he wanted to experience a heat stroke. Not for the first time, he wished he could afford a gym membership. *Passive thinking*, scolded the voice in his head that sounded suspiciously like Stacy. It was a valid point regardless. Caleb could probably help him find someone online interested in selling a set of used free weights. *Assuming he ever speaks to me again.* Logan felt a pang of unease at having to wait until Monday to see him. He took out his cell phone and pulled up Caleb's name from the contacts. He hesitated, finger poised over the Talk button. Sighing, he hit the End button and shoved the phone back into his pocket.

Exiting the apartment building, Logan heard a man's voice call out. A twitchy-looking guy with greasy hair and a backpack that looked like it weighed more than he did emerged from the narrow gap between buildings. Moving to block Logan's path, Twitchy opened his mouth to speak.

Logan stopped abruptly, holding his hand out to keep the guy at a distance. It wasn't often that even the panhandlers approached him on the street. His size was usually enough of a deterrent. "Not interested," he said, moving around the man.

Twitchy sidestepped and blocked Logan's path again. "Got me a li'l somethin', right here, you wan' it?" He held up a small bottle of what looked like scotch. "Only a fin and totally legit," he said, showing off his broken yellow teeth in a manic smile.

Logan snorted. Minibottles of booze were illegal to sell in Chicago. Twitchy had to have bought them in the 'burbs or online, assuming he'd actually paid for them instead of swiping them off the back of a truck. "You ain't got nothing I want," he told the man, wondering why his feet hadn't gotten with the program. That the guy had stationed himself between a halfway apartment complex and the shelter down the street showed he knew how to spot an opportunity.

Looking at the bottle Twitchy was waving back and forth, Logan remembered the message he'd scribbled on the packet of oatmeal for Caleb: "in case of emergencies." Wouldn't it be better to have a small amount of booze on hand if shit became too much instead of risking going to a bar or binge buying at the liquor store? He would only need to get through the weekend and then he could toss it. *Just 'cause I buy it don't mean I have to drink it.* Logan fished out a ten from his wallet, handing it to Twitchy. He accepted the scotch, checking to make sure the seal was still in place. And then shoved it into the front pocket of his cargo shorts, not bothering to try to get change from the guy.

Logan started walking without any clear idea of a destination. He plowed through block after block without paying much attention until his calves began to ache. He stopped, realizing he was only a couple of blocks from his old apartment. He must've walked for miles while the fog swirled around in his brain.

"Logan?"

Logan zeroed in on a familiar man blocking the flow of traffic on the sidewalk, his gut clutching at the sight. The last time he'd seen Michael was from the prisoner's side of a cubicle. They'd talked through a heavy window of glass. Or Logan had talked. Michael had just sat there looking devastated. His blond, curly hair sticking out in puffs like he'd run a sweaty palm through it over and over again. He didn't even protest when Logan told him not to come back, ending a more than decade-long friendship.

"Michael," Logan said, shaking the other man's hand. "Good to see ya." He was surprised to find that it was true. Michael was a part of the past Logan didn't like remembering. They'd been the closest of friends since junior high and stayed close after graduation. Cutting all ties with Michael had felt like severing a limb.

"Can I buy you a cup of coffee or lunch if you have the time?" Michael asked, oblivious to the annoyed pedestrians moving around him.

Logan thought about saying no, but the hopeful look in Michael's bright blue eyes stopped him. It wasn't Michael's fault Logan had let himself be sucked down so deep he couldn't climb out. Michael had done more than he should have to try to drag Logan out and gotten a fractured wrist for his efforts. "Sure."

They headed down Milwaukee Avenue to the Pancake House. Logan had spent many a Sunday morning nursing a hangover in the diner. He wondered if Michael was thinking the same thing as he frowned at the small, red-brick building. Stepping around him, Logan opened the door.

The place smelled like it always did, of hot coffee and sizzling bacon. It wasn't as packed on a weekday, but they still opted to sit at the counter. Their waitress greeted them brightly. Logan wouldn't be surprised to learn she'd been working there since the forties. She gave them menus and went to fetch them coffee. After a few minutes of staring at a menu they'd both memorized years ago, the waitress returned.

"What can I get for you boys?" she asked, setting down their coffees.

Impulsively Logan said, "Belgium waffles."

"Do you want strawberries and whip cream on them, hon?"

"Uh… yeah."

Michael raised an eyebrow, but didn't comment. He ordered the meal they'd usually gotten when they came here, the fiesta skillet. It had enough chorizo and jalapeños to burn any remaining alcohol from your body. It was also tasty as hell, but Logan couldn't stomach anything that brought back so many memories, good and bad.

The waitress drawled out their order in diner-slang to the fry cooks, leaving them to sit in silence once again. Logan wished he had a list of instructions to navigate this conversation. Michael stared at his coffee cup like he expected the dark brew to surge up and swallow him.

"Your family doing okay?" Logan asked.

"Yeah, my folks retired to Florida and Lisa's living with me."

Logan wasn't surprised. Michael had acted more like a parent to his baby sister than their parents. *God, she must be in high school.* No wonder her older brother looked so ragged even in his designer suit. She'd be a heartbreaker for sure. "Her living with you working out?"

Michael grinned, bright and eager like the boy he'd been a lifetime ago. "She's decided she's a lesbian."

Logan barked a laugh. "Meaning no teenage boys will be groping her."

Michael's smile faded, and he sighed as if the weight of their combined baggage had reappeared. They didn't speak again until the waitress delivered their orders. Logan looked at the mass of waffles smeared with strawberries and cream, wondering why he'd ordered it. He picked up his fork and started eating.

Michael swallowed a mouthful of the hash and then asked, "Do you remember all those times we took my sister ice-skating?"

Logan smiled, remembering the perky blonde who was ten years younger than they were. At the first snowflake, she'd start begging to go to the ice rink. She'd been so cute in her poufy pigtails and bright pink skates. "She always insisted on going around by herself."

While Logan darted around on the ice, Michael hovered close but not too close behind his sister, waiting for the eventual moment when she fell. She was as awkward as a seal on land, spending more time on her ass than not, but it didn't stop her from trying.

Eyes on his skillet, Michael said, "When you were arrested, a part of me was relieved."

No more waiting for the inevitable fall, Logan thought. He understood the feeling. He had gotten his first taste of it not long after he'd graduated high school. When he walked into his father's bedroom and found he had OD'd during the night, he'd felt relief rather than grief. You could only go so long expecting someone to die before it numbed you. His mom had been smart enough to take off when Logan was in junior high. Occasionally, he wondered how his life would have turned out if he'd agreed to go with her.

Michael cleared his throat. "That day I went to see you in prison. Was I one of your AA steps?"

Logan nodded, forcing himself to take another bite of the too sweet waffles. He chewed and then said, "Step nine, make amends to people I've harmed." The bottle in his pocket felt like it had doubled in size, pressing into his thigh. *It's preventative*, he reminded himself. Pushing his plate away, he leaned his elbows on the counter and rubbed his face with his hands.

"Is the food all right, sweetie?" the waitress asked.

"Yeah," Logan said. When she stared at the plate disapprovingly, he resumed eating.

Michael wasn't doing any better with his own meal, moving the hash and eggs around the skillet without eating much of it. After a swallow that looked painful he said, "I convinced myself the reason you wouldn't let me sit in the courtroom or visit you in prison was because you were angry with me. I didn't know what to think after I got an apology and a get lost permanently."

"You tried to help me, but I wouldn't let you. I don't have nobody but myself to blame."

"Then why cut me out of your life?"

Logan couldn't bring himself to say the words they both knew. Michael was better off without him. Logan was sober now, but there were no guarantees he'd stay that way. Michael didn't know how to walk away from someone he loved, even when he should. Logan pushed his plate away again. No wonder Caleb was hiding in his apartment. He was smart enough to back off before he got sucked into Logan's world.

"I know how that thick skull of yours works," Michael said, pointing a finger at him. "You're listing off all the bad things in our friendship and totally ignoring the good. If you don't want me in your life, I won't try to force you, but don't you for one second think I'm better off without you."

Logan shook his head. "How can you say that? You know damn well your wife divorced you because you were spending too much time dealing with my shit." He lowered his voice when he spotted their waitress looking like she was contemplating an intervention. "And that night in the bar wasn't the first time I'd hurt you when I was too shitfaced to care."

Michael rolled his eyes. "Her tennis coach had more to do with it than you."

Logan hadn't heard about the tennis coach, but he wasn't surprised. Melissa had been a slut in high school. No reason to think marriage would reform her. But he'd bet *she* had been the one to initiate the divorce and not Michael.

Michael pulled out his wallet and smacked a few bills on the counter. "I was your best friend, Logan, not some battered boyfriend." He stood up from the stool. "And you hit like a girl when you're drunk."

Logan followed him out of the café. Michael leaned against the brick building, fishing a pack of cigarettes from his pocket. Logan kept the *I thought you quit* to himself as Michael leaned forward to light the smoke.

Michael blew out a puff of smoke. "I made it worse." When Logan opened his mouth to object, Michael slashed a hand through the air. "I can see it now, but back then I was in such denial. I thought there's no way you'd follow in your old man's footsteps. You just needed to get your shit together and everything would be okay."

Logan gave a choked, desperate laugh. He'd managed to top his old man. In spite of the drug addiction, his dad never served time. "You shouldn't have had to deal with my shit in the first place."

"You want to spend the rest of your life hiding from people you *might* hurt, I can't stop you." Michael said the words as if the truth of them burned hotter than the smoke. With eyes too bright, he asked, "Would you just tell me if you're doing okay?"

Logan wondered why he was bothering as he told Michael about his job and the conditions of the parole. People in AA talked about relapse like it was inevitable, and Logan couldn't argue with them. He hadn't had a drink in over a year and he still craved it every damn day.

Even without taking a single drink, Caleb understood that loss of control in a way Michael never would. He knew what it felt like to become a passenger in his body when fear got behind the wheel. If Logan let Michael back into his life, his friend would eventually end up a busted speed bump.

Michael's forehead wrinkled. "The shipping warehouse by the docks?"

"That's the one."

Michael's jaw dropped, nearly causing the cigarette to fall to the ground. He swore under his breath as the ash struck his blue silk tie.

A thought occurring, Logan asked, "Do you have a professional interest in the company?" Michael was a forensic accountant at a security company. He referred to it as the cool branch of accounting because they specialized in fraud investigations. He had always been a jock with geeky tendencies. It was one of the things Logan liked best about him. He had been just as comfortable wearing a pocket protector as he was a football uniform.

Michael rolled the cigarette between his fingers and his thumb. "A couple of months ago, the Loss Prevention division within your company identified the Night Sort as the source for an increase of lost packages. They were unable to determine the person or persons behind the employee thefts. They hired my firm to evaluate their prevention plan and offer recommendations. We were also going to conduct our own investigation, but the manager, Harrison Klass, decided not to go forward with the investigation."

Logan's mind whirled, replaying what he'd learned in the past few weeks. The sudden shift change for Foster made sense if Klass suspected her of stealing. It would force her to adapt, making her more vulnerable to exposure. Was she trying to recruit? Was that the reason she was so eager to jump into his bed? If Klass was anything like Caleb, he'd wait to be sure she was guilty rather than risk firing her unjustly. *Unless Klass is in on it and wants to cover it up.* Logan's gut rolled at the idea. What if Caleb wasn't making enough at his business and Klass needed money to support him? He couldn't see Caleb allowing his uncle to help pay his expenses, but fear was a hell of a motivator.

Reluctantly, Logan asked, "Why do you think Klass called off the investigation?"

Michael shrugged. "He might not have wanted to incur the expense, hoping to handle it internally." His eyes widened. "You think he might be dirty?"

Logan decided to ignore the question for the moment. "How do the employees pull it off? Every inch of the warehouse is videotaped and you can't bring nothing on the floor."

"There are a number of methods. Someone swaps the label on a package, getting it sent to another address. Or a more elaborate method is to create a dummy company. The dummy company sends empty packages that look like they've been tampered with and then claims insurance on them after they're delivered. Sometimes the packages are just sliced open and resealed. There's no way to know without a full investigation."

He couldn't see Klass stealing from the company, but he could imagine his boss looking the other way to protect Caleb. It put their encounter with Foster outside of Meng's in an all-new light. "Klass's nephew, Caleb, is a friend of mine. A couple of months ago, someone set off a smoke bomb on his apartment floor."

Proving just how smart he was, Michael said, "You think it was a message to Klass to back off?"

Logan nodded. "Caleb's an agoraphobic and was housebound at the time. He didn't know there wasn't a fire when he barricaded himself in his apartment and refused to leave."

Michael's lips parted; a look of complete and utter shock evident as he stared at Logan.

"I think my supervisor, Karen Foster, might be behind the smoke bomb and she used to work the Night Sort before Klass moved her to another shift. Could you... look into her background... uh... unofficially?"

Michael's expression changed, and he gave Logan a long, assessing look. "Is this Caleb a friend... or a friend-friend?"

Logan felt his cheeks heat. "We're not dating." Which was the truth. Phone sex hardly counted as a date.

"Did you fall in love with another gorgeous straight guy?" Michael asked, exhaling a stream of smoke.

"Fuck you," Logan said, without heat.

Michael wagged his finger at Logan. "There are limits to my friendship and seeing your hairy ass is one of them. But looking up info on your supervisor won't be a problem."

I've missed you, Logan thought, feeling his chest tighten. "You won't get in trouble or nothing if you investigate Foster?"

Michael bumped their shoulders together. "I'll be fine." He pulled out his wallet and fished out a business card. Handing it to Logan, he said, "Give me a call in a few days and I'll have the information for you." He took a last drag of his cigarette, then dropped it, and ground it under the heel of his shiny dress shoe. "Take care of yourself, Logan."

"Thanks, man," Logan said, watching Michael walk away.

CHAPTER
SIX

FOSTER had been prattling at him for close to ten minutes. Logan only needed to work three hours today before he could head over to Caleb's, but the shift seemed endless. The redhead's attempt at flirting wasn't making it go by any faster. He couldn't help wondering what game she was playing. On the surface, a guy with a record seemed like the right person to approach if she really did need new recruits. If Logan thought about ratting her out, she could get him fired or make a complaint to Dabb. The best thing to do was to avoid pissing her off, but he lacked patience today.

He'd tried calling Caleb several times over the weekend, getting a busy signal every time. He remembered their first meeting when Caleb said he sometimes had trouble with the phone when upset. Considering their last phone call, it wasn't surprising he'd disabled the phone. That didn't mean Logan wasn't going to give him shit about it. What if there was an emergency? Caleb could screen his calls instead of taking the phone off the hook.

"You haven't heard a word I've said," Foster said, dragging Logan back to the conversation.

Hoping to avoid antagonizing her, Logan said, "Sorry, I've got a lot on my mind and I've got work to do before I head out."

"Right," she said, her face twisted in an ugly smirk. "Today's the day you play nursemaid to the boss's nephew. Do you get a thrill out of sponge-bathing the little freak?"

Logan gritted his teeth. "He ain't no freak."

"Temper, temper," she said, running a finger down his chest. "You'll be nice to me, if you know what's good for you."

"Fuck off, sweetheart," Logan said, moving past her and pulling out his cell phone. His gut churned when once again he got a busy signal. *Why the fuck isn't he answering?* He hit the End button on the phone and headed for the exit.

Two steps out of the warehouse, the phone rang and Logan nearly dropped it. He looked at the display before answering. "Michael," he said, his voice sounding frazzled to his own ears.

"Are you okay?"

Hell, no. "I need to check on Caleb. He's not answering the phone."

"Sorry to call like this. I found out some info on your supervisor I thought you should know. Do you want to call me back later?"

Whatever Michael had discovered, it had to be big. He'd found the info fast. "Go ahead and tell me what you found out." *It'll keep me from going crazy on the ride over.*

"The file wasn't officially closed. I'm guessing the investigators hoped Klass would change his mind about going forward with an investigation."

A cab pulled to the curb in front of Logan and stopped. He climbed in the backseat and barked the address to the cabbie. Leaning back against the squeaky vinyl upholstery, he asked, "What were you able to find out?"

"In forensic accounting, there are red flags that we look for when trying to ferret out employee theft and fraud. Karen Foster hits every one. Company dissatisfaction, which you mentioned when they changed her shift. I also learned her live-in boyfriend was fired at the same time when he refused a transfer to another facility. One of the security improvements my firm suggested was a policy forbidding dating or relationships between supervisors and hourly employees."

She has plenty of other boyfriends to fill the gap.

"A credit check showed she is in deep financial trouble."

"Then why's she paying to have her kitchen redone if she's so tight on cash?" In a flash, the answer came to Logan. "She keeps making the contractor redo shit because she can't pay for it when the job's done."

"I'm guessing she's short on cash because of a misdemeanor charge she got six months ago. She was arrested for public drunkenness at the riverboat casino. Booze and bets are two big red flags."

Logan had been around her enough to see signs of his former self in her, as much as he hated to admit it. Craving tequila at nine in the morning was a hell of a tip off. Adding gambling to the mix would only make her sink that much faster. "So what do I do next?"

"Stay the hell away from her or better yet, start looking for a new job. Eventually, greed will get the better of her and you don't want to be anywhere near her when it does."

"Why not go to Klass and get him to call the police?"

"Most of our investigations into employee theft don't end in criminal charges even when we've got solid evidence."

"Why the hell not?"

"Because it's about business and not justice. Companies believe it is better to keep it quiet—avoiding media attention—than to prosecute."

"Let me get this straight. They catch the employee stealing and all they do is fire the guy? That's just asking for someone else to try it."

"I tend to agree, but the alternative isn't much better. It's harder to convict than fire, and civil suits are expensive and the company rarely ends up recouping losses."

Finally understanding, Logan said, "And even if you caught the guy with a box of iPods, you couldn't prove all the other shit he likely stole before then."

"Exactly, and that's when there's proof. Everything I've found out about Foster is circumstantial. It shows she has the profile of a typical employee that steals, but it doesn't prove anything."

Logan rubbed his aching forehead. "I can't just quit, Michael. A steady job is a condition of my parole and my PO was the one who got me this job. There aren't many options with a felony conviction for assault on my record."

"If you need—"

"Don't. Just don't, man. I don't want your money."

There was a long pause and then Michael said, "How about my friendship, Logan? Do you want that?"

Logan knew the answer he should say, but he couldn't get the word "no" past his lips. Instead, he found himself saying, "They have Al-Anon meetings at the center where I go. Would you be willing to try going to one?"

"Isn't that for family members of alcoholics?"

"Friends, too. But you're more family to me than my old man ever was."

His voice sounding a bit strangled, Michael said, "Just let me know where and when."

Grateful, Logan ended the call with a promise to call back with the information. When he reached Caleb's building, he found himself heading up the stairs, three at a time. Once at the door, he knocked, louder than usual. When he tried again and got no response, he pulled out Klass's spare key. He hesitated a moment before putting the key in the slot and unlocking it. He tried to open the door, but the security chain was actually in place this time.

"Hey, Caleb. It's Logan. Get off your ass and unchain the door." He listened, trying to hear any sign of movement from within the apartment, but heard nothing. "Open the door or you'll be paying a locksmith to fix it." When he got no response, he turned to the side, butting his shoulder against the door. He grabbed the doorknob and shoved against it with all his weight. The metal snapped under the strain, sending wooden splinters flying. He quickly scanned the main room and kitchen. Finding no sign of Caleb, he headed for the bedroom.

He'd never been in Caleb's bedroom before. To the right, he spotted a doorway that presumably led to the master bathroom. A treadmill sat on the left side of the room and a king-sized bed in the middle. Logan spotted a motionless lump buried under a mound of dark blankets. His heart made an appearance in his throat, and he forgot how to breathe. He rushed over to the side of the bed, but hesitated for a moment before touching what he thought was Caleb's shoulder. After an incredibly long three seconds, Logan heard Caleb groan in his sleep, his body rocking back and forth slightly. Logan dropped to his knees and rested his forehead against the comforter, trying to calm his racing heart. Looking down, he realized the damp towel he knelt on was clicking. He pushed back the towel, revealing the phone off the hook. "Caleb," he said, peeling back the blanket from Caleb's head.

Caleb was lying on his side with his arms crossed like a mummy, looking every bit as pale as the walking undead. Logan noticed how pronounced the bags were under Caleb's eyes and how sallow his skin appeared. Logan blinked and then squinted in the dim light, pulling the blanket back further to get a better look. *Duct tape? Why would he have tape wrapped around his wrist and hand?* "Aw, hell." Caleb's fingers had swollen to twice their normal size and the skin looked red and angry.

Logan flinched when Caleb's eyes snapped open, pupils blown wide. For the span of two ragged breaths, no one moved. Then adrenaline kicked in. One minute Caleb was buried under the covers and in the next, he was across the room, scrambling on his hands and knees with no regard to his likely broken wrist. Logan imagined he could hear the bones grinding as Caleb moved toward the other side of the room. *Jesus.* He needed to stop him before he caused permanent damage.

"Let me help you," Logan said, kind of loud, and Caleb jerked back, scrunching himself into the corner, his head bowed on his knees, cradling his injured arm to his chest at an awkward angle.

When he got no response, Logan tried again, willing his voice to sound calm. "Everything's going to be okay." He held out his arms the way one would when pacifying a frightened horse. He moved sideways, not approaching Caleb yet, to position himself in front of the bedroom door. Caleb might be frantic enough to make a break for it. "You need to go to the doctor and get that wrist fixed," Logan said, moving closer and ignoring Caleb's flinch from either his words or his sudden nearness.

"Please don't make me," Caleb whispered, lifting his head to look at Logan.

Logan swallowed hard. The pain and misery in Caleb's eyes was difficult to witness. "You gotta let me help you."

Caleb's whole body seemed to wither as his shoulders slumped even further and his chin dropped to his chest. His voice sounded like a ragged plea. "Let me stay here. My wrist is fine." Logan could hear the tears in Caleb's voice even though his cheeks were dry. Caleb kept repeating the word *fine* over and over again as if he could wish it so.

Logan wanted a drink so badly, but the booze would never make it past the lump in his throat. Part of him wanted to agree, to let Caleb stay home just to stop his voice from sounding so goddamn broken. But Caleb needed help and hiding under the covers wouldn't magically reset bone. Logan pulled out his cell phone and texted a message to Klass: *Need help. C hurt.* He hoped the old man was wearing his cell phone. He didn't want to risk talking to Klass on the phone in front of Caleb, and he couldn't bring himself to leave the room. Caleb had spent far too much time alone and in pain. *My fault.* Guilt threatened to rise up and take hold of Logan, but he pushed it down. Caleb needed him now.

His cell phone beeped, and Logan fumbled to turn off the sound as Caleb started hyperventilating. Logan read the one word message: *ambulance?* He looked at Caleb trembling against the wall as he gulped in huge breaths. He texted *Y* and hit the Send button. He was so focused on the button, he nearly missed Caleb's escape attempt. Caleb darted to the side pushing off the wall in an effort to get around Logan. Logan grabbed him around the middle, and lifted him in the air before settling the frightened man in his lap. He made shushing noises against the back of Caleb's neck as Caleb whimpered and struggled against the hold, trying to pry Logan's hands from his waist. The pungent smell of sweat and the faint odor of vomit made Logan's nose itch, but he didn't dare loosen his grip. "I'm so sorry, Caleb. I shouldn't have waited. I shoulda made Klass hand over the key on Friday."

Caleb sobbed into his hand, refusing to look at Logan. The sight of his tears tugged strings Logan didn't know he had. "You're okay," Logan said into the side of Caleb's throat, kissing his warm skin.

A few minutes later, Logan heard loud knocking and the sound of voices from the main room. *The paramedics move fast in this neighborhood.* He could hear Klass's voice, likely explaining about the panic attacks.

Logan felt faintly embarrassed when the paramedics and Klass stopped in the doorway, eyes wide as they took in the sight of Caleb cradled in his lap. His glare compelled the guys to get moving. He slid Caleb to the ground, but stayed close by. The paramedics traded info back and forth that meant nothing to Logan as they assessed Caleb's condition. Heart rate one-fifty. Blood pressure one-forty over ninety. Sweating but not diaphoretic. "We're here to help you, sir," said the paramedic on blood pressure duty. "I need you to tell me what happened, Caleb."

The other paramedic turned to Logan. "Can you get us some more light?"

Logan leaped to his feet, glad to have something to do. He took two steps toward the window before Caleb made a low keening sound. Turning, Logan saw the paramedics scramble to keep Caleb from moving.

"You're hurting him," Logan said, and it came out in a snarl that surprised even him. Caleb twitched violently and the paramedic holding his arms looked warily over his shoulder. Logan sighed and made an effort to lower his voice again. "His wrist looks broken." Something caught his eye and he angled his head to see into the bathroom. "The shower curtain's been torn off the rod."

The paramedic's expression changed, looking chagrined and then crossing over into concerned. "If he fell, there's a possibility he hit his head as well. He could be suffering from a head injury in addition to the anxiety." He shared a look with his partner, and Logan's gut rolled. "Sir, when you fell in the shower, did you hit your head?" the paramedic asked as his partner rose and walked to the bathroom. "Did you lose consciousness?" He moved his hand slowly over Caleb's scalp.

Caleb froze, and his eyes grew distant. "It hurt and then time got all slippery like the soap."

The partner came back into the room, looking grim. "There's some blood and vomit on the floor." Looking behind Logan, the man said, "We need to prep him for transport."

Logan had forgotten Klass was in the room until he spoke. "Are you sure that's necessary?"

Logan valiantly resisted the urge to strangle the man.

Seemingly unfazed by Klass's question, the paramedic said, "He has obvious physical signs of trauma in addition to the psychological. He needs to see a doctor and we're more likely to get him to the hospital quickly and safely than you can. But he needs to consent before we can take him, unless you're his medical proxy."

Caleb vigorously shook his head. "No hospital." He struggled into a sitting position. "They'll chop, chop, chop. Not going." His faced went even paler, and he swallowed hard.

While Klass stood there waffling, Logan kneeled in front of Caleb. "You need to go to the hospital." When Caleb turned away, Logan grabbed his face, forcing their eyes to meet. "I won't let nobody hurt you. Do you hear me?"

"Promise?" Caleb asked, sounding like a child desperate to learn that monsters weren't real.

Logan brushed a hand across Caleb's stubbled jaw. "I'll squash their tiny heads with my size twelves." He kissed Caleb's forehead. "I promise." Klass's clearing his throat caused Logan to pull back and stand. Logan stared straight at the wall, not wanting to see the expression on his boss's face. *I'll be lucky if I still have a job after all this.* He knew he should be more upset about the prospect of unemployment. His focus was entirely on the man struggling to his feet. The paramedics moved to either side of Caleb, walking him into the main room and lowering him onto the stretcher.

Logan walked in front of the paramedics, wanting to be in place if Caleb reacted badly while they negotiated the stairs. The last thing Caleb needed was to take another tumble.

As they loaded Caleb into the ambulance, Logan asked, "Which hospital are you taking him to?"

"Mr. Sellers," Klass said, putting his hand on Logan's arm. "Thank you for your help, but I can handle it from here." When Logan opened his mouth to protest, he said, "I'll speak with you tomorrow at *work.*"

Logan gritted his teeth. "I promised him."

The paramedic put a hand on Logan's shoulder. "He's going to be okay, but we need to get moving."

Not wanting to delay treatment, Logan stepped back.

Hand clutching the ambulance door, Klass asked, "Did we lock the door?"

Logan shook his head. "I had to bust the chain to get in, but I can fix it no problem."

"That won't be necessary. I will arrange to have the door repaired and the locks upgraded. Could you lock the door in the meanwhile?"

"Yeah." Logan ground the word out between his teeth.

"Thank you, Mr. Sellers," Klass said, scrambling into the back of the ambulance.

Logan watched them secure the door and pull off, hating how helpless it made him feel. He reentered the apartment complex, adrenaline draining away with each step he took. The trip back to the fourth floor felt like he was walking up the wrong way on an escalator. He wanted to stop resisting the flow and let it take him out of the building, away from the crushing weight on his chest. He found himself standing in front of Caleb's bathroom. Forcing himself to step inside, the sharp smell of sickness and fear hit him. The blue-checkered curtain hung by only one plastic ring and covered the floor like a painter's tarp. A smear of blood stained the pine cabinet below the sink. *The fall was bad, but it coulda been worse*, Logan thought, fingers tracing the corner of the granite countertop. *He coulda been bleeding out while I walked away like a fucking coward.* His knees buckled at the thought, dumping him on the floor. He felt a sharp jab of pain on his ass, and he reached into the back pocket of his cargo pants. He'd retrieved the bottle of booze from under the bed this morning with the intention of tossing it out. *Liar. Just don't want Dabb to find it.* Looking at it now, he noticed the plastic seal was frayed from the times he'd fingered it this weekend, but it remained unbroken. Logan closed his eyes and dropped his chin to his chest. He couldn't afford to fall apart now.

His fingers felt fat and clumsy as he took out his cell phone and pulled up the number. He heard murmuring voices and phones ringing in the background when Michael answered.

Tapping the bottle against his bottom lip, Logan said, "I need you to remind me of what it was like."

"What do you mean?" The sound broke a little as if Michael were on the move. "Is everything okay with Caleb?"

Logan smacked the back of his head against the wall. "Tell me what it was like to have a drunk for a best friend."

"What's going on?" Michael asked, his voice echoing.

Logan guessed where Michael was headed. The ambient noise of traffic and howling wind in the background confirmed that he had escaped to the roof for a nic fix. Michael swore under his breath, and Logan pictured him with his hand cupped around the lighter as the wind conspired to steal his flame.

"I've been carrying a minibottle of booze around in my pocket for the past three days. I bought it off a panhandler before I ran into you."

Michael made a noise of disgust. "You shook my hand after touching something a homeless guy touched."

Logan snorted. "Way to focus on the important part, OCD man."

Michael cleared his throat. "Right, did you drink it?"

"I haven't had a drop of liquor since detox and I need to remember why."

For a dozen heartbeats, Michael didn't speak. When the words finally came, his voice didn't break. It shattered. "You were a cruel drunk," he said, his breath hitching. "You seemed to get off on rooting out people's insecurities. You'd pick at their scabs until they bled."

Logan couldn't remember when a few drinks became a bottle and then two bottles every night. He couldn't point to one single moment or event as the cause. From his first drink at fourteen, alcohol began soaking into his skin, the moisture rotting him on the inside. Every few years he'd use a chisel to hack away all the wet, unsound wood without trying to find the source of the moisture. The rot always came back, stronger than before.

"That night in the bar was the first time I was afraid *of* you instead of *for* you. You grabbed my wrist and honest to God snarled at me. It was like there was nothing human left in you. You were going to kill that man and anyone who got in the way."

Logan threw the bottle into the cabinet and slammed it shut. He didn't trust himself to pour the contents into the sink instead of down his suddenly dry throat. Leaning his forehead against the door, he asked, "Why would you want anything to do with me after going through all that?"

"Because you stopped," Michael said quietly.

Logan sat up. "Stopped drinking?"

"The girlfriend of the man crawled over broken glass to get in your way and to put her hand on your arm. And I remember thinking that if you hit her, then you really had become your old man and there'd be no saving you." Michael took a long indrawn breath before expelling it. "But you didn't hurt her. She begged you to stop and you did."

Logan remembered almost nothing about that night, but he was sure of one thing. "I didn't give a shit about that girl. I was thinking they didn't serve shots in lockup. I don't want that drink any less now than I did then."

"You've changed, Logan. You may not be able to see it, but you have. You might have wanted that drink today, but you picked up the phone instead. Shouldn't that count for something?"

"You sure you don't want me to lose your number?"

"I want you to get off your ass and go wash your hands before you get hepatitis."

Logan's mouth curled unwillingly into a smile. "The AA meeting I go to meets on Tuesdays and Thursdays at 6:00 pm. They have an Al-Anon meeting that goes on at the same time down the hall. You up for it?"

"Yeah."

Ending the call, Logan realized what Michael must have felt. The feeling of wanting to help someone and being powerless to do it. Looking around the bathroom, he decided there something he could do.

In the kitchen, Logan rooted around until he found a trash bag, paper towels, and cleaner. Detaching the torn curtain from the pole, he folded it up roughly before shoving it into the trash bag. After scrubbing the mess on the cabinet and floor, he tossed the paper towels away. He doubted his efforts were up to Caleb's standards, since he was a bigger neat freak than Michael, but at least Caleb wouldn't have to come home from the hospital and clean up his own blood and vomit.

WHEN he entered the warehouse, Logan headed straight for Klass's office. He'd spent last night in anxious misery. None of the local hospitals would tell him if Caleb was even a patient, let alone how he was doing. His attempts to call Klass and Caleb had gone unanswered. Dabb stopped by just long enough to tuck Logan into bed and tell him to be nicer to his supervisor in the future. Since he was a cryptic bastard, Logan couldn't tell if his PO believed whatever Foster told him or not. Eventually, he collapsed into a troubled sleep.

Before Logan could get through the doorway, Klass said, "I want to thank you for your help with Caleb, Mr. Sellers." He sat behind the desk with his hands pressed flat against the wood like he was using it to hold himself upright.

Logan counted to five in his head before he spoke. "Is he doing okay?"

Klass looked like he was debating what to say. "The doctors diagnosed him with a broken wrist, a mild concussion, and dehydration. He's been treated and is resting at home."

Home. It wasn't a home; it was a prison. And Klass might not be Caleb's warden, but he wasn't making it any easier for Caleb to escape.

Klass pinched the bridge of his nose, like he was getting a headache. He sat like that for a few long moments before he dropped his hand and spoke. "Caleb will no longer need your services and he has asked me to pay you four weeks' severance pay. Also, a full-time position will be available next month when Hank Nelson retires, and in light of your efforts on behalf of my nephew, I would like to offer you the position."

Logan swallowed hard. It was obvious Klass wanted him away from Caleb, and Logan wanted to tell him where to shove his pathetic excuse for a bribe. The smart thing to do would be to just thank the little weasel and walk away. He couldn't afford to lose his job. Instead he asked, "Are you planning on hiring another ex-con for him?"

Klass pursed his lips. "Not that it's any of your concern, but Caleb has decided to switch to a courier service and do his shopping at an online grocery."

Solitary confinement. Logan stared at his boss long and hard, and for a moment, something raw and naked touched Klass's eyes before it disappeared. Stepping right in front of the desk, Logan said, "You think you're helping him. You're not."

Klass's shoulders stiffened and his eyes narrowed. "And you think a couple of weeks being his errand boy makes you qualified to know what's best for my nephew?"

Logan knew the signs all too well. Klass wasn't angry; he was afraid. So terrified of failing his dead sister he'd rather do nothing than the wrong thing. He wanted to help Caleb, but was doing the opposite. "I know nobody ever got over being afraid of the dark by never turning off the lights." He turned and walked out before Klass could respond.

Rather than finishing his shift, Logan decided to leave work. Exiting the warehouse, he knew he needed to call his sponsor, Stacy. He didn't trust himself to keep it together, and he couldn't help Caleb if he was passed-out drunk.

LOGAN looked up at the sound of the bell as his sponsor entered the cafe. Stacy was wearing a tailored black suit, white shirt open at the neck, revealing enough cleavage to turn heads as she joined him.

After they exchanged greetings, she said, "You sounded frazzled on the phone. What's going on?"

Just as Logan was about to reply, the waitress appeared with a coffeepot in one hand and menus in the other. "Today's soup is chicken noodle and our lunch special is a toasted Reuben with fries." She dropped the menus in front of them. "Coffee?" She held up the pot, and when they both nodded, she filled their crockery mugs and deposited a handful of creamers on the table. "Be back in a jiff." She spun away to answer the sharp ping of the pick-up bell from the kitchen.

Logan delayed the conversation by swirling cream and sugar into his mug and sipping the hot coffee. "I screwed up and I don't know how to make it right."

"Tell me what happened." She reached across the table and covered his clenched fist with her hand. "Does it involve the guy you told me about? Caleb?"

Logan nodded. He then told her an abbreviated version of what happened to Caleb and his conversation with Klass.

"Are you ready to order, folks?"

Stacy shot Logan an apologetic glance and turned to the menu. "I'd like a bowl of today's soup and a side salad."

The woman jotted down Stacy's order and glanced at Logan.

"Just the coffee."

Another quick notation, a gathering of menus, and their waitress disappeared.

Stacy took a deep sip of coffee. "I take it Caleb is refusing to speak to you."

"Yeah, he doesn't answer when I call." He shrugged his shoulders. "I'm guessing he's pissed at me for breaking in and calling his uncle."

"It's possible, but I doubt it. If he's refusing to talk to you, it's not because you got him the medical treatment he needed."

"Then why?"

"From what you've told me there are a lot of similarities between addiction and anxiety disorders. They both have the potential to control a person's life and there's a lot of shame in allowing it to happen." She took a sip of her coffee. "Shame makes it worse. Making you more likely to sink further."

Logan rolled his shoulders, tilted his head from side to side to pop his neck and to ease his tension, trying to force himself to relax. He was too familiar with that vicious cycle. "I shouldn't be bothering you with this and dragging you away from your job."

"Don't do that," she said, loud enough to turn heads. She sighed and continued more quietly. "I told you I went three years on the program before I relapsed, but not what happened. One lousy fight with my then girlfriend and all that work was gone. My sponsor was a crotchety old lady named Gertrude. She came by my place and found me worshiping the porcelain god, reeking of booze and vomit. She looked at me and said, 'I think it's time you sponsored someone.'" Stacy grinned as if lost in the memory. "That crazy bat was right. Helping you helps me. I haven't had a relapse since I started being a sponsor three years ago."

"I don't know how to help him, Stacy. And I need to find a way."

"It sounds like your friend is sinking hard, but you can't save him. You can try to be his friend if he lets you, but the only way off that boat is for him to take that first step. It's not easy to talk about personal struggles, but I believe it's necessary to move beyond them."

Logan rubbed the back of his neck, realizing they weren't just talking about Caleb anymore. "I haven't missed a single AA meeting and I've completed more homework in the past month than my senior year of high school."

The waitress returned, bringing a wilted pile of lettuce and one solitary slice of tomato. Stacy thanked her and proceeded to drown the salad with sharp jabs to a bottle of low-fat Italian dressing. "You attend, but you're not an active participant. That's not unusual when you first join a new group, but eventually you need to start sharing."

"I'm not required to speak or share with the group. I just gotta show up."

"Bullshit," she said, smacking the bottle of dressing against the table hard enough to make the dishes rattle. "There are some people who can never say a word at meetings and still see improvements in their lives just by going and listening. You're not one of them."

Stacy's eyes dared him to contradict her. He hadn't told her about buying the scotch, but she didn't need the details to spot the pattern. Before AA, she'd spent years carving the design into her own skin with every lie, every evasion, every excuse.

"I haven't gone back to drinking," Logan said, half-expecting a neon "YET" to appear above his head. He knew he could tell her about the booze and she'd offer him support and understanding. But he wanted the focus on Caleb and not himself.

"If alcohol was our only problem, then the detox centers would be turning out winners all the time."

Logan winced. "He needs me to keep my shit together and I want to be there for him. I can't remember the last time I felt that. It's enough to keep me sober for now."

"What happens after you help him? What are you hoping for with this, Logan?"

Logan delayed answering for a moment, drinking his lukewarm coffee before reaching up to scratch his forehead. Stacy's soup had appeared at some point, but the murky contents remained untouched. He leaned forward, resting his hands on the table. "I care about what happens to him and hate the idea of him being locked away in that apartment of his." *A prisoner of his fears*. It sounded like the tagline to a cheesy Lifetime TV movie, but it was true. His instincts told him he didn't know what Caleb was really afraid of, and he needed to understand in order to help the man.

"Is that all you want? For him to get the help he needs?" Stacy pushed a stray hair behind her ear. "For both your sakes, you need to be honest with yourself about what you want."

Logan sighed. "He smiles at me and it's all I can do not to tear his clothes off, but it's more than that. I think we could have something more."

"Well, if he won't answer the phone, you could always send him a letter, but—" She looked at her sculpted nails. "You need to consider whether being in a relationship with Caleb, given the struggles he's going through, is the best decision for you, considering you're still in the early stages of recovering."

Logan slumped in his chair. He wanted Caleb. Plain and simple. For the first time in his life, he had a reason to get his shit together beyond keeping his ass out of prison. At the very least, he knew he couldn't walk away without knowing Caleb would be okay. But Stacy was right. He needed to think about whether he could handle getting everything he wanted.

LOGAN eyed his boss as he drifted through the warehouse, looking distracted and exhausted. He hadn't spoken to Klass since Klass had pried him away from his nephew. He couldn't help wondering how much influence Klass had on Caleb's decision. Shopping online for groceries wasn't the same as having Min hand-select items for him. Hell, Meng's would probably be willing to deliver the groceries for a lot less money than Caleb had been paying to have Logan deliver them.

He'd spent the last week doing what Stacy told him to do, thinking about what he wanted. He hadn't had much choice. Michael refused to give him any more details about what he'd found out about Foster, claiming he couldn't talk about an ongoing investigation, which was Michael code for "I'm going to protect you whether you like it or not." Logan would have argued with him if he hadn't been so damn grateful for the help. Swallowing his pride was a hell of a lot easier when it meant potentially protecting Caleb from that bitch.

Logan entered Klass's office without knocking. "I get why you wouldn't be thrilled with someone with my background… uh… dating your nephew, but I don't want more from Caleb than he's willing to give. I'd be lucky to have him as a friend."

Klass seemed almost as though he had been waiting for Logan. "I won't pretend to be thrilled about my nephew… dating someone with a violent and criminal past. But he trusts you and he doesn't trust easily."

"Then why make me break my promise to help him get to the hospital?"

"The doctors had him so doped up he could barely remember his own name let alone notice you weren't there."

"That's not the point and you know it." Logan took a breath, trying to calm down. Pissing off his boss wouldn't get him any closer to Caleb. He needed a new approach if he wanted to get Klass on his side. "Did Caleb tell you that we've been going out?"

Klass's jaw dropped. "Out of the apartment?"

Logan nodded. "He made it all the way to Meng's Market without panicking."

"He never said anything," Klass said, his body sagging like a blown tire on the freeway.

Logan wasn't surprised. "You have me ask him those questions about how he's doing, but you don't ever ask me what he said. How come you don't want to know the answers?"

His eyes focused on the far wall, Klass said, "Caleb thinks he killed his mother. It's the reason he stopped going out."

Logan frowned, confused by the change in topic. "I thought she had a bad heart."

"She did. I invited them over to celebrate her fiftieth birthday. I knew Caleb was pushing to make a deadline at work, but I expected him to rearrange his life to accommodate her, like he always had. Sarah had suggested we wait until the weekend, but I didn't listen...."

Klass began to speak as if he were the only person in the room, his description so vivid Logan felt as if he were actually there.

Harrison had joined Sarah on the couch, handing her a mug of peppermint tea. She had unclasped her hands and accepted the beverage.

"Thank you, Harry," she said, falling back on the childhood nickname he had always despised. Her eyes drifted to the mantel clock that had been their grandfather's pride and joy. "Did Caleb call and say he'd be late?"

The urge to lie crept in as it always did when faced with her growing unease, but he suppressed it. She would see right through the attempt and become all the more fearful because of it. "I'm sure he's just stuck in traffic."

Her eyes widened, and he noticed new lines on her face, making her look closer to his own sixty years than fifty. "What if he was in an accident?"

The door buzzer saved Harrison from answering. He leaped from the couch and made his way down the hallway and opened the door far enough to berate his nephew. "Your mother has spent the last twenty minutes convinced you were dead in a fiery crash."

"I'm sorry. The meeting ran late and I still needed to go home and get the cake."

"Harry, is it Caleb?"

"Yes, Mom." He moved past Harrison and made his way into the living room to greet his mother.

"Looking back on that night, I can remember how thin Caleb looked, how ragged. I can see the dark circles under his eyes that looked like bruises and the fine sheen of sweat across his brow. I can remember all those things, but I can't remember acknowledging them back then. He was crumbling before me. Why wasn't I able to see it?"

Caleb stumbled to his feet, knocking the dining room chair to the floor. "I'm sorry, I have to...." He swayed, and Harrison rose and gripped his forearm. Leaning in close to his nephew's ear he whispered, "Get a hold of yourself, boy, before you send your mother into a panic."

Panic. Caleb moved as if his body had been waiting for the word to be voiced. He tripped over the chair, tumbling to the ground. In the next moment, he was across the room with his back pressed against the wall and his hand clutching his chest.

"Oh, God. His heart, Harry." Sarah rose from her seat and made to go to Caleb.

"Shhh, his heart is fine." Harrison wrapped his arms around her shoulders and ushered her into the living room. "The doctors said it's just a case of nerves," he said, encouraging her to sit on the couch.

When he tried to stand, she grabbed the front of his shirt. Her voice sounded high and thin, on the verge of hysteria. "The doctors can be wrong."

She was a walking testament to how wrong they could be. The doctors had said it would be a miracle if she lived to her first birthday. It was why he insisted on celebrating every birthday for the miracle it was. He pried her fingers from his shirt and squeezed them gently. "They're not wrong about this. He's just having a bit of trouble adjusting to the new job. I'll help him find a new one."

"Harry, I don't feel so good," she said, pressing a hand to her chest. She slumped forward, and Harrison barely caught her before she hit the hardwood floor. He gathered her small body in his arms and laid her on the couch. "Sarah, Sarah, open your eyes." He lightly tapped her cheek and then moved to take her pulse. Fast. Much too

fast. "*Caleb, you've driven your mother into a heart attack. Now get in here and help me with her!*"

Sarah touched his face. "Don't say that, Harry."

Harrison shook his head. "You're right. I'm sorry."

"Tell... him."

Caleb ran into the living room clutching a cordless phone. When he spoke, it sounded like he had been gargling glass. "Ambulance is on the way." He turned his attention to his uncle. "Did you give her the medication?"

Harrison stared at him. "No, I...." He couldn't even say the words. How could he forget?

Caleb left and returned with the bottle of pills and a glass of water.

"Are you okay, honey?" Sarah asked.

Caleb nodded. "Now I need you to take your pills."

"Love you," she murmured before closing her eyes. They would never open again.

"I blamed Caleb for his mother's death because I didn't want to deal with my own guilt."

Logan looked at his feet, not sure how to respond to Klass's story. A part of him wanted to rail at his boss for riding Caleb so hard only to turn around and blame him for his mother's heart attack when he crashed. It wasn't right, and he didn't intend to pretend it was, in spite of how broken Klass looked. Focusing on the present, he asked, "Did you tell Caleb not to return my calls?"

Klass shook his head. "My sister was plagued by fears, but never for herself. Caleb is the same way. More than anything, he's afraid of becoming a burden to those he loves and of them being hurt because he can't control his fears. If he's refusing to talk to you, that's likely the reason." Klass's jaw twitched as if holding the raw emotion in place. "I tried to do what was right, but now I know I've failed them both. I found a behavioral therapist who makes house calls, but I haven't been able to convince Caleb to see him. Tell me what to do and I'll do it."

"Tell me about the courier service you hired for Caleb."

CHAPTER
SEVEN

LOGAN felt conspicuous hovering outside of Caleb's apartment building like a creepy stalker. His thoughts drifted back to his boss as he waited. The past week had obviously strained Klass. Frankly, Logan thought the man *should* feel guilty for his part in this mess. But he was glad Klass cared enough about Caleb to go along with the plan, seemingly desperate to find a way to reach his nephew.

Logan had debated just following the courier up and shoving his way into the apartment when Caleb opened the door. It was what he wanted to do, but Stacy's words kept ringing in his head. He couldn't force Caleb to see him; it needed to be his choice. He didn't know what he would do if Caleb chose to ignore him.

When the courier approached, Logan stepped in front of him. "I need to add something to that envelope."

The balding little man frowned at Logan before moving around him. "I'm afraid I can't help you. Tampering with the mail is a federal offense."

The guy let out a squeak when Logan grabbed his arm. "Hold on a minute." Logan saw the guy reach into his pocket. Probably to take hold of his phone or a can of dog mace. He sighed, releasing the man's arm. "I need to add a note to the mailer before you deliver it. The guy who set up the service called into your office, but you had already left. You can call him and he'll tell you.

"You mean Mr. Klass? My instructions do say to call him if I have problems making the delivery." The man sounded thrilled to have a possible solution that didn't involve being squished by an angry giant.

Logan made a "get on with it" gesture. The courier pulled out his phone to make a call. He stepped back so Logan couldn't see what number he dialed. He wouldn't be surprised if it was to the police instead of Klass, but it was a risk he was willing to take. *Dabb will rip me a new one if I get arrested.*

The man spoke too quietly for Logan to hear on the busy street before closing the phone. He handed over the package without a word. Logan unraveled the string holding the envelope closed and slipped in the note he'd written.

CALEB took the package from a twitchy courier and secured the door. Even though typing made his wrist ache, he was happy for the distraction work brought him. He had been miserable since he had gotten back from the hospital. And itchy. He had been digging through his desk in search of an envelope opener to find some relief from the constant urge to scratch under the cast when the mail came. He had spent all last week taking sponge baths in the kitchen, not being able to deal with stepping into the tight confines of the shower stall. His uncle had been the one to replace the curtain, fluttering around the bathroom looking as uncomfortable as Caleb felt.

This morning, Caleb had had enough, not able to stand the smell of himself anymore. Navigating the shower with the cast wrapped in a garbage bag hadn't been pleasant. He had nearly lost it when he had had to use duct tape to keep the bag closed. In spite of his efforts to keep it dry, the cast had the musty smell of wet plaster, but he felt marginally clean. Emptying the contents of the package on his kitchen counter, he found a postcard of Wrigley Field on top of the contract he had been expecting. Confused, he flipped it over and noticed that someone had written on the back of it.

When he read the words "Don't freak out," he had to close his eyes. He took a quick breath, fighting the sick surge of panic spreading outward from his stomach. He had been both dreading and hoping to hear from Logan with equal fervor. He had turned off the phone, not able to deal with the uncertainty of Logan's reaction. *I sobbed in his lap like a child.* He didn't want Logan to see him as broken and pathetic.

I don't have to read it, his reptilian brain reasoned. He could just toss the card away and forget all about it. But God help him, he didn't want to forget Logan. He opened his eyes and read the next instruction: "Don't assume I don't know what you're going through." He felt his nerves flutter and his stomach began to twist and turn, shooting slivers of ice through his arms and legs. He hated the feeling so much. He took another steadying breath and read the last instruction: "Open the door." He walked over to the door and leaned his forehead against the wood. *Maybe we can just be friends.* Logan was a good guy, so it shouldn't surprise Caleb that he had followed up on the accident. He wasn't the type of man to walk away without knowing Caleb was okay. It was one of the reasons Caleb felt so drawn to him. Sighing, he unlocked the door and opened it.

Logan was across the hall, leaning against Mrs. Simon's door. The sight shattered any illusions Caleb had of being around Logan and not wanting him. He was dressed in jeans, and wearing a coffee-colored T-shirt, which showed off the muscles of his chest and stomach. It was hard to tear his eyes away from him. Caleb cleared his throat and said, "Do you want to come inside?"

"Are you okay with—," Logan said, but he ended up flat on his back before he could finish.

Mrs. Simon leaned over him and said, "What on earth are you doing down there, sonny?"

"Ow," Logan said, rubbing the back of his head. "Somebody cut down my beanstalk."

Caleb exchanged a few quick words with Mrs. Simon, reassuring her that he was recovering as he extended his unbroken arm to Logan. Logan accepted the hand up, not letting go until they sat on the leather couch in Caleb's apartment. Logan had gone to a lot of trouble to see Caleb, but he seemed at a loss for something to say now that he was here. Caleb saved them from the awkward silence by saying, "I've missed you, but I think you're better off walking right back out." He looked away. "You deserve better than what I can give you."

When Logan didn't respond right away, Caleb looked back and sucked in a breath. Logan stared at him with an intense gaze filled with too many emotions for him to interpret. Every muscle in Caleb's body tensed, making his wrist twinge unpleasantly.

"That's some self-esteem you got there, if you think I'm such a freaking prize."

"You are." He smiled wanly. "I felt almost normal around you and not a candidate for a jacket with extra-long sleeves."

Logan put an arm around Caleb's shoulders and relaxed back against the couch. Caleb shivered, and worked hard to remind himself not to be afraid. He trusted Logan, but having Logan witness his panic attack had shaken him. Logan tightened his arm around Caleb's shoulder, and Caleb felt his dark eyes watching him, warming the side of his face. He had felt a connection to Logan from the moment they had met, but they were not only united by their screwed-upness; they got along well together, and they were easy with one another in a way that Caleb hadn't experienced with anyone else. He could admit to himself how much he wanted Logan, but that didn't mean he should act on those feelings.

"You need to understand that I might never get better. I might never leave this apartment again." Caleb's wrist twitched under the cast, as if to remind him he would have to figure out a way to take off the cast in six weeks. *I could order a hack saw.* He closed his eyes tight at the images suddenly racing through his mind.

He heard the deep tone of Logan's voice over the roar of his own blood in his ears. "I'm not going to give you no ultimatums because I know how useless they are. The state forced me to attend rehab sessions, but they couldn't make me accept their help. Only I could do that." He brushed a strand of hair off Caleb's forehead. "But I won't apologize for getting you the help you needed."

Caleb grabbed Logan's hand. "I needed help and I'm glad you were there to give it to me." He rubbed his thumb across Logan's knuckles. "I was just too afraid at the time to see it."

"Your uncle says he knows a behavioral therapist that's willing to come to your apartment. I want you to agree to see her. And I want us to keep trying to go out like we did before."

Caleb paused, waiting for more demands. "That's it? I just have to try to get help?" He shook his head. "That's not fair to you."

"What do you mean?"

Caleb stood and started pacing in front of the couch. "Meaning if it doesn't work you'll settle for conjugal visits instead of the normal couple things like going out or having me at your place sometimes."

Rising to his feet, Logan said, "You honestly think you're not good enough for an ex-drunk ex-con package handler?"

Caleb felt his face tighten. "You're more than that, but there's no way it can work."

Logan studied him for a moment before moving forward. Caleb felt his heart rate climb with each step Logan took toward him. He retreated until he ran out of space, his back touching the wall. Raising his hands, he tried to stop Logan's approach right there, at an arm's length.

With a firm but gentle touch, Logan moved Caleb's arms to his sides—being especially careful of the cast—and put his own hands against the wall on either side of Caleb's head. Caleb's breathing was coming fast and shallow. Logan moved closer until he stood within inches, crowding his personal space. "One, I wouldn't let you walk in my neighborhood with an armed guard in tow."

His eyes locked on Logan because looking away was impossible. Caleb wanted him so much his chest ached, making a panic attack seem like heartburn in comparison. But what he wanted didn't matter, because he couldn't let himself be that selfish.

Caleb held his breath. For a moment, he expected Logan to kiss him, but Logan turned his head to the side, and then it was cheek rubbing against cheek, the burning rasp of stubble moving back and forth. Logan froze in place with his mouth next to Caleb's ear; his body so close Caleb could feel the heat radiating from him from head to toes. His voice sounded strained when he finally spoke again. "Two, I'm better off not going out to places I used to get shitfaced every night."

Logan pushed forward until they were plastered together; so near Caleb could feel Logan's belt buckle against his stomach. "Three, we can find new places to go, because you *will* leave this apartment again."

Caleb let Logan's words sink in, hearing his sincerity. He wanted to believe Logan was right. He had had some success, but the farthest he had managed alone was the fifth floor.

"Let me help you, baby," Logan said in a guttural whisper.

"Will you talk to me if you're struggling to stay sober?"

In an instant, Logan's body felt like granite, hard and unyielding. Confused by the reaction, Caleb explained, "I want you to be able to talk to me. I don't want you to stay silent just because you think I can't handle it."

The stiffness melted away as Logan let out a deep sigh. "We'll help each other."

Stronger together. This time Logan let him push him back far enough for Caleb to tilt his head and draw up on his toes for a kiss. The first touch was short, light, and dry. Logan didn't react at all, just stayed impossibly still. Caleb rested his forehead against his chest and breathed him in, savoring his spicy scent before releasing the breath again with a contented sigh.

Logan made a strangled sound, and then there were hands cupping Caleb's face, and lips descending on his, wet and warm and open. Logan's tongue plunged into Caleb's mouth, claiming, demanding, and Caleb gave back as good as he got. Logan tasted both sweet and bitter, and Caleb realized what it meant to crave, what addiction felt like.

Drawing back, Logan said, "We'll take it slow."

"You mean take the going out stuff slow, not the sex, right?" Caleb asked, his voice cracking like a teenager's.

"I was thinking thirty seconds until the sex stuff. That work for you?"

"No," Caleb said, grabbing the back of Logan's neck and pulling his head down. "Can't wait that long." He pressed his mouth against Logan's, softening his lips after a moment and tickling Logan's lips with his tongue. Logan opened his mouth as if to retort and Caleb pressed the advantage, slipping his tongue between Logan's lips as he stroked the spiky hairs at the back of his neck.

After the kiss ended, Logan buried his face against Caleb's throat, nibbling at the curve of his neck. He smoothed his hands down Caleb's sides, over his hips, and settled on his ass.

Logan lifted Caleb until he had virtually no choice but to wrap his legs around Logan and hold on.

He barely prevented his cast from smacking Logan in the back of the head. "We need to talk about your habit of hauling me around like a rag doll."

"Later, munchkin." Logan swallowed Caleb's squawk of protest.

Logan carried Caleb into the bedroom and lowered him to the bed slowly as if he weighed no more than the packages he spent hours hauling around. "Now you're just showing off," Caleb griped, before tilting his face for another kiss.

Logan stood upright and toed off his shoes. "I need the workout. Your cooking's making me fat," he said, lifting his shirt and revealing rippling abs and not an ounce of excess on his sculpted chest.

Absolute perfection. The thought threw Caleb out of the mood, his self-consciousness rearing its ugly head. *What if he's disappointed in me? What if*—With a force of will, Caleb halted the thought. He closed his eyes tightly and pressed his fingers against them so hard that he saw swirling shapes dance on the back of his eyelids. He begged, "Not now, not now," as if he could bargain with the growing monster of fear lurking in his belly. He inhaled deeply, trying to even out his breathing without hyperventilating. He had only been on Xanax for a week, and he knew the anti-anxiety meds were helping, but not quickly enough to save him from this humiliation.

"Hey," Logan said, sitting on the bed and putting his arm around Caleb's shoulder. "Open your eyes."

Logan's deep-timbred voice stabbed through him like a physical blow, and he couldn't help the sharp intake of breath. He desperately wanted to see Logan's reaction and was terrified at the same time. Would he be horrified and disgusted? Or would his dark eyes be filled with pity? Caleb wasn't sure which would be more horrible.

A gentle brush of fingers on the side of his face broke his indecision and forced him to open his eyes. He tried to swallow the emotion forcing its way up his throat and was surprised it didn't simply burn straight through his esophagus. Caleb buried his head against Logan's chest, feeling the crisp hair brush against his forehead with each breath. "I'm such a freak."

"You really are," Logan said, kissing the top of Caleb's head.

Caleb pinched a pert nipple in retaliation and grinned when Logan squealed like a pig. He felt the adrenaline slipping away, and his breathing returned to normal. Logan didn't ask if he was all right. Didn't make him explain the swirling feelings battling in his head: lust and fear and affection all tangled together. Tilting Caleb's head back, Logan just looked at him, letting every ounce of his caring and desire shine through. Caleb was breathless again but for a much better reason. Fingers curled in his hair, holding him in place as Logan consumed him with his mouth. Their tongues tangled together in wet heat.

Logan broke off the passionate kiss to begin lavishing Caleb's neck with his tongue and biting lightly. "Shirt off," he ordered, pulling it up at the collar and making Caleb feel like a kid getting help being undressed when he gently eased the sleeve over the cast.

Caleb lay back on the bed and resisted the urge to squirm under Logan's intense gaze. Logan lightly fingered the fading purple and yellow bruises on his chest, a frown on his face, as if disappointed they didn't disappear when he touched them. He kissed a nasty contusion on his pectoral, and Caleb had the dual urge to roll his eyes and gush at the sweetness. He felt warm and gooey like a fresh chocolate-chip cookie and ridiculously cherished.

Caleb traced a hand over Logan's bristled head, feeling the dents and grooves. Pushing up with his elbows, he kissed Logan's forehead and asked, "How many beanstalks have you tumbled off of?"

Logan snorted in response and began to move, using his tongue and fingers to torment Caleb. Caleb groaned when he started working his nipples, softly nibbling, fingers running down his sides. Logan drifted lower, kissing, licking, his breath heating Caleb's skin as he moved downward. Then, Caleb nearly knocked himself silly when he raised his arms to clench the bars of the headboard and smacked his cast against his forehead. *Ow.* Thankfully, Logan was too busy spreading Caleb's thighs and settling between them to notice him being such a klutz.

When Logan mouthed Caleb's crotch through his sweatpants, Caleb made an embarrassing whimper and he swore he could feel Logan's smug smile against his dick. *The bastard.* Then Logan really got going; he lavished the cloth with his tongue, applying heat and wetness and pressure. But not nearly enough.

"We'll need a lint roller for your tongue if you keep that up."

"You're the one who gave me a sweatpants fetish."

"I'm not in the least bit sorry," Caleb countered, and they both laughed. Logan slid his hands under Caleb's ass and massaged the globes, kneading the muscle with his large hands. One finger slid between his cheeks, and Caleb groaned when the knuckle pushed against his rim. Logan finally moved to pull the sweatpants off and to slide back up the bed. Pushing himself up awkwardly, Caleb reached for Logan's jeans, popping the button and unzipping the fly. He palmed Logan's package and they shared another kiss.

Logan rolled sideways and took off the jeans with more grace than Caleb could ever hope to accomplish with two working arms. He then turned Caleb on his side, reaching forward to put a pillow under Caleb's cast. Logan spooned behind him, chest hard against Caleb's back as they shared a pillow. He bent his head to nibble Caleb's ear and whispered, "Tell me what you want."

Caleb licked his lips. He'd only had sex with a guy a handful of times during college. The panic attacks made the idea of starting a new relationship seem impossible. Until Logan. "Min snuck a box of condoms in with the lube." He felt Logan's grin against the side of his neck. After getting the required items from the nightstand, Logan got back into position. Caleb shivered as calloused hands brushed over his hips. Logan rocked forward, pushing his wet-tipped cock against his ass. Caleb moaned as Logan slipped a finger into his cleft and began circling his perineum in a maddening light touch.

Caleb heard the snap of the lubricant and then Logan pushed a finger inside, stretching his hole. He began to wriggle and to squirm and then gasped as a second finger worked him. Logan's chest hair brushed against Caleb's back, sending a shiver through his whole body. Leaning his head back against Logan, he groaned long and deep as Logan's fingers brushed over his prostate.

Pulling back Logan said, "Tell me if it hurts," a slight tremor in his voice.

Caleb nodded, his voice abandoning him.

Spooning behind him, Logan encouraged Caleb to lift his top leg, bending at the knee to give more room to maneuver. Caleb heard the crinkle of the condom wrapper and then Logan pried open his cheeks, inserting the tip of his cock into Caleb's ass. He breathed deeply at the burn, as his body instinctively clenched around the intruder. It had been a lot longer than he was willing to admit since he had done this.

Logan kissed Caleb's neck. He then backed out, eased gently back and forth, and slowly pressed it in further over and over again until he was all the way inside. Sweat dripped from Caleb's hairline onto his forehead as the pressure of being filled increased.

"God, Caleb." Logan didn't move, but there was something in his voice, something that made Caleb's chest ache. It was desperation and need and maybe something like relief.

Angling his neck backward in a way he would pay for later, he captured Logan's lips in a hard, possessive kiss. Logan slid his tongue across his own, curling and teasing until Caleb couldn't help whimpering. The sound seemed to propel Logan into action. He broke the kiss and pulled back his hips.

Caleb turned back and clutched the pillow in a tight grasp as Logan began pivoting into him, each thrust harder and faster as the bed squeaked in protest. He would have more bruises on his hips from Logan's tight grip, but he didn't give a damn. The idea of Logan leaving his mark on his skin thrilled Caleb. The only other sounds in the room were their heavy breathing, the occasional groan, and the noise made from slapping flesh.

Caleb could feel each groove and notch that ran the length of Logan's cock as it unmercifully plunged in and out of his ass. His muscles were locking together, becoming rigid as his release loomed near. Angling his arm, he tried to take hold of his cock, smacking the hard plaster against his leg and hip. He looked at the cast in frustration, needing more friction.

Seeming to sense his thoughts, Logan said, "Let me." His hot breath sent shivers down Caleb's body. "Before you knock me out and have to get yourself off." Almost too quiet for Caleb to hear, he added, "I'd want to be conscious to see that." He leaned over further, his body nearly covering him. Caleb closed his eyes soaking in the heat from Logan's body and his musky scent.

Logan's strong hands worked Caleb's dick in tandem with his pivoting hips. They moved together higher and higher and Caleb cried out wordlessly. His heart thumped, thumped to the rhythm of the thrusts as if Logan's cock controlled its beat. Harsh breaths disturbed the hairs at the back of his head, sweat dripped down the nape of his neck.

Caleb's balls tightened against his body as Logan alternately drove inside him and stroked his cock again and again. Within seconds, he was coming in Logan's hand. A few strokes later, Logan was right behind him, muffling his moan against the flesh of Caleb's neck.

Later, sprawled on his stomach, Caleb hugged a pillow, burying his face in the soft down. He felt liquid and sated. Turning his head on the pillow, he glanced at Logan, who looked equally boneless, before burying his head in the softness once again.

They slept then. Caleb didn't know how long. When he woke, Logan was still there, pressed against him. Logan's forearm clutched Caleb's stomach, his muscles strangely tense. Wiggling under the tight grip, Caleb turned to face him. He ran a hand over Logan's bristled jaw, looking into his dark eyes. "Are you okay?" A burst of fear drove away his drowsiness. *Was Logan having second thoughts?*

"We should probably talk," Logan, said, not sounding happy about it. "Since I didn't intend to just pounce on ya."

"Are you saying you regret this?"

"Hell no, but we talked about your recovery and not mine."

Suddenly wide-awake, Caleb said, "Oh, God. You didn't…." He couldn't finish the sentence. The fear that had been lurking unacknowledged took hold of him, and his breath seemed to solidify in his throat.

After an eternity, Logan said, "I thought about it, wanted the numbness it would bring."

Caleb closed his eyes against the maelstrom of emotion and memories swamping him. His mother's eyes as she lay dying and the anguish in his uncle's voice when they realized she was gone. He took several deep breaths until he thought he could speak again. "I don't want to be responsible for you relapsing. I'd never be able to forgive myself."

Logan was quiet for several long moments. "It don't work that way. There are always gonna be reasons to drink again." He rolled on top of Caleb and traced a hand over his cheek. "And damn few reasons not to."

Hope. It seemed like a lifetime since he had let himself really feel it. Could they be each other's second chance? Was it worth the risk? Logan had so much more to lose than himself. If fear seized control and caused him to push Logan away, would Logan seek oblivion in a bottle? His earlier words to Dabb circled through his head. *I refuse to be afraid Logan might slip back into bad habits. He's earned the right for a second chance.*

A muscle quivered in Logan's jaw. "But I need to know that you'll walk away if things get bad and I stop trying to stay sober."

Caleb bit his bottom lip to resist offering reassurances that it would never come to that point. Logan needed him to give him one more reason to resist the temptation of oblivion. Without consequences, there was no motivation to change. It was a lesson Caleb had learned the hard way. "You know what my uncle told me today? He gave me the money to start my business expecting me to fail. Once I was bankrupt, he could try again to convince me to accept a voluntary commitment at a treatment center."

Logan sucked in a sharp breath. "He wanted to send you to a fucking loony bin?"

"Treatment center," Caleb said, making air quotes. "I understand why he did it. If the business had failed, I might not have spent the last three years hiding in my apartment."

Logan stared at the cast, his fingers moving gently over the hard plaster. "Tell me about the panic attack."

Caleb sighed. "I jumped in the shower and then I started thinking about how you'd be showing up in a short time. I started to worry that you'd regret it or it would be really awkward. The thoughts are less important than the chain reaction they started. I'd gotten what I wanted and that scared the shit out of me."

Moving down, Logan buried his head against Caleb's stomach. "What happened after?"

Caleb wasn't sure how much to tell Logan. He wanted to be honest, but his memory was a lot fuzzier than he liked to admit, a blur of pain and irrational thoughts. "Post panic is almost worse. I'll endure anything to avoid letting the panic take me again. In the middle of an attack, I feel like I'm dying, but afterward, I would rather die than let the fear grip me again. It makes no sense."

"Jesus, baby," Logan said, sounding hoarse. "Fucking duct tape." He wrapped his arms around Caleb's midriff with bruising force.

Suppressing the squeak that wanted to escape, Caleb cupped the back of Logan's neck, ignoring the hot wetness sliding down his side. It was one of the things he hated most about the fear, the way it could twist his brain into accepting the ridiculous just to avoid another attack. That he actually managed to convince himself the pain in his head and wrist was better than risking another panic attack. Logan pressed his cheek deeper into Caleb's stomach as if he had heard the thoughts. Caleb rubbed the back of Logan's neck, wanting to comfort him but not knowing how.

Logan spoke in a suffocated whisper. "I'm so sorry I walked away."

"There was no way you could have known and my uncle admitted he told you to wait."

"I shoulda busted the door open or gotten the key from Klass instead of waiting all fucking weekend. I convinced myself you'd realized you could do better than me and I didn't want to deal with it."

"It sounds like we both panicked for the same reason," Caleb said, brushing his knuckles against Logan's cheek.

After a few minutes, the desperate quality seemed to leave Logan's embrace. His arms loosened from around Caleb's waist, and he lifted his head to look up at him. His cheeks flushed and he seemed almost embarrassed when he spoke. "Did you take the phone off the hook because of what we... uh... done on the phone?"

It took a moment for his brain to figure out what Logan was asking. When he did, he couldn't contain the bubble of irrational laughter that burst forth. Logan's annoyed glare only made him laugh harder. "Traumatized by phone sex?" Caleb knew he wasn't the most experienced guy, but come on. *Oh, bad thought. Or maybe it was a good one.* His stomach shook like his ass crack was a fault line. Knowing he was just this side of hysterical, he hoped it was the drugs making him cackle like an idiot.

"Quit laughing at me, you little shit," Logan griped, poking him in the stomach.

"Sorry," Caleb said, wiping his eyes. He took as a deep a breath as he could with Logan pouting on his stomach and swallowed his inappropriate mirth. "I wasn't freaked out by what we did," he said, though he couldn't even think about it without blushing crimson. "I was worried it wouldn't mean anything or you wouldn't want to do it again." Logan's grip on him tightened again. "After I fell, my first thought was to call you, because I knew you'd help me. But then I started thinking about the hospital and I lost it." He yanked on a muscular forearm, urging Logan closer for a desperate kiss. "I know the odds are that it will happen again, but it won't be your fault if I fall apart. I'm the only one who can start that chain reaction."

"Ditto, unless you're planning on tying me to a chair and pouring liquor down my throat." Logan sounded self-conscious, and Caleb heard the fear beneath the glib words. Caleb didn't know a damn thing about addiction, but he knew how terrifying it felt to lose control.

Wanting to ease the tension, Caleb said, "If I were going to tie you up, it wouldn't be for *that.*"

Logan growled, low and deep. And then he pounced.

WATCHING Caleb bounce around the living room like a bumper car made Logan want to grab him in a bear hug and refuse to let go. Caleb would end up with dents in his cast if he kept accidentally smacking it against the walls, the bookshelves, and the front door during his restless pacing.

True to his word, Klass had arranged for a therapist to come to Caleb's apartment this afternoon. How he managed that on such short notice—and on a freaking Sunday—was a mystery. Then again, Klass had been waiting for this day for three years. He'd called yesterday while they were passed out on the bed after a pancake-induced orgasm. Logan would never look at syrup the same way again. Ever since then,

Caleb had been on a rampage. The kitchen and living room were so clean Logan's eyes burned from the pungent smell of cleaning solvent. Thankfully, Dabb had agreed to let Logan stay Saturday, but he had already axed the idea of Logan spending another night at Caleb's apartment. Caleb would be alone with his demons tonight.

"Hey," Logan said, grabbing Caleb's arm as he made another circuit of the room. "The place looks great. Let's sit down for a minute." He walked over to the leather couch, dragging Caleb with him.

"I can't sit, Logan."

Logan snorted. "I'm surprised you can *walk* after what we did yesterday with the butter."

"That's... not... I... didn't mean...."

Taking advantage of Caleb's flustered state, Logan dropped onto the couch, pulling Caleb onto his lap.

Caleb sat stiffly sideways over Logan's thighs, his body tight and tense. "I shouldn't have agreed to this. Why can't we just go back to you helping me go out? It was working."

Yeah, until you decided duct tape really could fix anything, broken bones included. Logan put a hand on Caleb's knee. "For the same reason I need to go to AA. You need a person outside of your life to talk to you, and to listen. Somebody who's unbiased and objective. It's important, baby. Trust me."

"I do trust you, but this therapist isn't like the members of your AA group. They know what you're experiencing. This therapist has no idea what a panic attack feels like. She'll just think I'm nuts."

A knock on the door caused Caleb to leap to his feet like his ass was on fire. When he took a step toward his bedroom, Logan scrambled off the couch and put his hand on Caleb's shoulder. "Let's answer the door together."

Logan maneuvered Caleb over to the door, reaching around him to unchain and unlock it. He left Caleb to do the rest.

When Caleb opened the door, he gasped like a man who'd been plunged into icy water.

A flash of long red hair and dark lipstick had Logan's body reacting on instinct. He yanked Caleb behind him.

"I'm Dr. Samantha Ryan. I was told you were expecting me?"

As the adrenaline leaked away, Logan noticed the therapist's resemblance to Karen Foster was superficial at best, just the same build and coloring. But Foster would never be caught dead in a blue-flowered blouse and tan slacks. "I'm sorry about that." Logan opened the door farther and stepped back. "You look a little like someone we know."

Ryan entered the apartment. "Someone you don't like too much, I take it."

Now that she was out of the dim lighting in the hall, Logan saw Ryan was likely in her forties. She had a leather briefcase in hand.

"I'm Logan. Caleb's… uh… he wanted me to be here for this first meeting." Logan closed and secured the door. As he turned around, he half expected Caleb to have disappeared. Instead, he spotted Caleb huddled against the end of the couch with his feet curled under him and his cast pressed against his chest.

"I'm s-sorry my uncle made y-you come here, b-but I c-can't do this t-today."

Ryan approached him with glacial slowness. "This is your home, Caleb. Whether you see me or not is your choice, not your uncle's or anyone else's. If you want me to leave, I will. I just ask that you try to take a few deep breaths for me. I would prefer not to leave you in such an agitated state."

"My choice?" Caleb said, sounding like he didn't believe her.

Ryan nodded. "Therapy is about what *you* want to accomplish, not what your uncle, or Logan, or anyone else wants. You have to want to make a change in your life or it will never happen."

Closing his eyes, Caleb took three ragged breaths before reopening them. "I can end the session at any time?"

"Yes. I'll just ask you to give me three deep breaths and then tell me you're sure you want to stop the session."

Watching the tension ease a little in Caleb's shoulders, Logan understood Ryan's approach. She was giving control back to Caleb. For a man whose will crumbled under the weight of fear, control was very important.

"Okay, I'll g-give it a try."

"I'm glad to hear it." When she looked around the room, Logan snagged the chair from behind the desk and brought it over to her. "Thank you, Logan. Why don't you have a seat on the couch as well?"

Logan looked over at Caleb. "Do you want me to stay? I could go hang out in the bedroom while you guys talk."

Caleb held out his hand. "Stay with me, p-please."

Lacing their fingers together, Logan joined him on the couch.

After taking a seat, Ryan opened her briefcase and took out a yellow notepad and a pen. "Would it be all right if I asked Logan a few questions, Caleb?"

Logan had no interest in talking to the therapist, but Caleb assented readily.

"How long have you and Caleb known each other?"

Logan thought about it for a moment. "About a month and a half?"

"You sound surprised."

"It feels like it should be longer, but my one-month parole review was just a couple weeks back." The moment the words left his mouth Logan regretted them. *Ten seconds into the conversation and I'm admitting to being an ex-con. What the fuck?*

Ryan's gaze drifted to the cast on Caleb's arm, and Logan felt his face heat. "I would never hurt him. That was an accident."

"I'm not here to judge you, Logan," she said, but Logan wasn't sure he believed her. "We call the first session an assessment because I'm trying to understand Caleb's current symptoms and overall functioning. Since it can sometimes be difficult for people to remember details from a panic attack, it's not uncommon to bring a friend or family member to the initial meeting."

Logan wished Caleb would speak up and explain what happened to his wrist, but Caleb remained annoyingly mute. "Just tell him you're not here to commit him to the loony bin or anything, and he should be able to talk to you."

"Is that a concern you have, Caleb?"

"My uncle h-has t-threatened b-before."

"Over my dead body," Logan growled.

Caleb squeezed Logan's hand. "Thank you."

"Okay, let's talk about that. I talked with your uncle about your family medical history and reviewed your medical file. Does your web-design business bring in enough money to pay your bills?"

Caleb cleared his throat. "Yeah, it does. It was hard in the beginning, but I have a s-steady stream of c-customers now, mostly through word of mouth."

"So what I hear you saying is that you have a successful business. I can also see you have a clean and safe home, and good physical health according to your medical file. Does it make sense for a judge to take away your freedom just because you have difficulty leaving your apartment?"

Caleb hesitated a moment before answering. "I guess not."

"Don't let TV programs and the movies fool you. An order of commitment or even a court-ordered psych evaluation isn't something done lightly. In my twenty years of practice, I know of only one case of an agoraphobic being forcibly removed from her home. The woman was in her eighties and was no longer able to take care of herself. Is there any other reason why you might think you'll be committed?"

"During a panic attack, it feels like I'm going crazy. Like I'm losing my mind."

"The feelings you describe are common among agoraphobics. It's my hope that I can help you deal with those symptoms."

"What would you do?"

"I know the emergency room doctors gave you a prescription for Xanax for your anxiety. While the medication can help, I prefer a combination of cognitive behavior therapy and relaxation techniques for a long-term solution. CBT has two components. We work on changing distorted thinking brought on by the anxiety and slowly expose you to fearful situations. I also show you meditation and relaxation techniques to help lower your overall stress levels."

"That sounds like what Logan did when he tried to help me go out that first time. He had me drink this awf… uh, relaxing tea, and then we went to the roof."

Logan sincerely hoped Caleb wouldn't mention what they talked about once they got there. He didn't think he could stand hearing Caleb describe Logan's long-ago illicit sexual experience with a lacy guest towel to his therapist.

"It is my understanding that, until recently, it had been three years since you left your apartment. Is that correct?"

"I went into my neighbor's apartment and the stairwell a few times, but nothing beyond that."

"Okay. I would like to give you some material to read, and then we can hopefully meet again on Wednesday. I'd like to talk more about your experiences with panic attacks. Would that be acceptable? You can have Logan here again if it makes you more comfortable."

Caleb took a deep breath, then exhaled slowly. "I'm willing to meet again."

Smiling, Ryan opened the briefcase again and pulled out a stack of pamphlets. She placed them on the coffee table instead of handing them directly to Caleb. "I honestly believe I can help you take back control of your life, Caleb. As a homework assignment, I'd like you to start thinking about some short-term goals."

"What kind of goals?"

"You could start with a list of places you would like to visit either on your own or with someone. Just give it some thought."

Caleb bit his bottom lip. "I'll… try."

Logan leaned over and whispered, "Like the two of us going on an actual date instead of just a trip to the grocery store."

Caleb ducked his head. "Admit it, you loved that hagfish soup."

Logan grinned. "It was the most disgusting thing I've ever eaten and I loved every bite."

Caleb gave Logan a slight nudge in the ribs. "A date would be a good goal."

CALEB clung to Logan's arm with an iron grip, trying not to think about how much he wanted to be back home in the peace and safety of his apartment. Why had he even agreed to this? What was so great about seeing a movie on the big screen as opposed to seeing it on a flat-screen TV in the comfort of one's living room? It must have been the way Logan had practically salivated when he talked about the big tub of buttery popcorn he planned to devour. The lights of the multiplex seemed too artificially bright for the middle of the day, and the smell of stale popcorn made Caleb feel vaguely nauseous. As Logan paid for the tickets, Caleb shifted restlessly from foot to foot, wishing there was some way he could wiggle out of the coming ordeal.

"So, you wanna go find some good seats first, or get our snacks?" Logan smiled down at him with warmth in his eyes. He was doing a good job of hiding whatever concern he had to be feeling. Caleb appreciated that.

"I-I guess food." Caleb would rather have slunk straight into the theater to hide in the darkness, but it was a sure bet Logan would drag him out again. There was no way they could skip the food step. He looked over at the lines in front of the food counters. It seemed as though a lot of people were milling around over there. "M-maybe we should w-wait until the lines are shorter."

Logan's only answer was to tug on his arm and drag him over to the shortest line. "Uh-uh. The longer we wait, the longer the lines might be. We came early for good seats and short lines, right?" They now stood behind a plump young woman who held a small boy by each hand.

"Margie, can we have soda?" asked one of them hopefully.

"No, honey, your mom only gave us money for popcorn."

"But what if we get thirsty?" the other one asked.

"Don't worry, I've got it covered," Margie whispered. She adjusted the straps of her large shoulder bag, and a clanking sound issued from within. At that moment, she seemed to realize she might have been overheard and glanced nervously over her shoulder at Caleb and Logan.

Caleb tried to give her a reassuring smile, but his lips seemed to have forgotten how. He remembered his own days of sneaking snacks and drinks into movie theaters, back when he was a pre-teen trying to make his allowance stretch.

Logan nudged him with his shoulder to get his attention. "Hey, you wanna get the biggest size and share? Or do you want your own?"

"Sh-sharing is good." Caleb looked down at the floor, fighting a brief wave of dizziness.

"That guy looks like Shrek, only he's not green!" one of the children whispered loudly.

The other one stole a quick look up at Logan before turning back to his brother with a look of contempt. "He does not. And only babies watch *Shrek.*"

"He does so. And *you* watched all the Shrek movies, and you liked 'em too."

"That was a long time ago, Timmy." The boy stuck his tongue out.

"That was last Saturday!" Timmy exclaimed.

Further argument was prevented by the necessity of ordering popcorn and fighting about the size. Timmy made a bid to get Margie to spring for some red licorice, but she shook her head. Caleb figured she had candy in that huge bag of hers as well as drinks.

Logan glanced at Caleb, his expression troubled. "Don't tell me I look like an ogre," he murmured.

This time Caleb's lips remembered how to smile. "Only first thing in the morning. Once you have your coffee, you snap back to your usual gorgeous self."

Logan grinned down at him. "Thanks, I think."

Somehow they negotiated the hallway to their theater, even though Caleb could barely see over the pile of food he had been loaded down with. Logan had gone all out. It was a good thing they'd eaten only a small lunch. He didn't think either of them would be up for eating dinner later if they even got through half this stuff.

Their movie was in cinema number four, unfortunately located at the farthest end of the hallway. Caleb's eyes darted about, noting exits and washrooms. He thought Logan might have been surreptitiously doing the same thing, but it was hard to tell because of the way his eyes were glazing over at the taste of the popcorn he couldn't stop stuffing into his mouth. They passed through the doors and surveyed the rows of banked seats. To Caleb's great relief, their theater was practically empty.

"Where do you wanna sit?" Logan looked around. They had come in on a mezzanine and could go either down or up. "Up at the back?"

"No, here is fine." Caleb indicated the seats closest to where they stood. "Near the door."

"Okay. Pick the one you want."

Caleb handed his bundle of snacks to Logan and started forward on shaky legs. He chose the second seat in from the aisle. If he needed to leave in a hurry, he didn't want to have to climb over a lot of strangers. Nor did he want to be directly on the aisle, so it was better if Logan sat there. Tipping his seat down with one hand, he set his drink in the holder attached to his chair.

The large screen at the front of the theater was showing a commercial for some kind of chewing gum. The high ceilings and empty space around him seemed to stretch out for miles. A powerful urge to turn around and make a break for it swept over him, but he fought it back. Logan was enjoying his popcorn too much and was clearly looking forward to the movie. He had chosen it. It was something to do with comic book superheroes. After a quick glance in Logan's direction, Caleb lowered himself into the seat.

"Here," Logan said, "take the popcorn."

The giant tub came at Caleb, and he had no choice but to lift his hands for it.

"And these napkins," Logan added.

Caleb glanced down as a giant wad of napkins slapped down onto his thigh. A family-size package of candy landed on top of it. Beside him, Logan maneuvered his giant self into a seat obviously designed for mere mortals. This apparently could not be accomplished without a certain amount of huffing and swearing, which brought them a disapproving glare from a bespectacled elderly man who had just entered the cinema.

"I don't think we'll be sitting anywhere near these young hoodlums, my dear," he announced to his female companion and led her away, his back very erect. The woman glanced back at them curiously, as if she had never seen a hoodlum before.

"Good! Get lost, why don'tcha," muttered Logan under his breath, and he settled deeper into his seat. It made alarming creaking sounds under his weight.

"Logan, are you sure that seat can hold you?" Caleb wriggled experimentally in his own seat, but unlike Logan's, it didn't make any noise.

"Yeah, probably. Never had one break on me yet." Logan reached for the popcorn and crammed another handful into his mouth. He winked at Caleb and crunched away happily. "Man, there's nothing like movie theater popcorn," he said after a minute. "Feels like forever."

Caleb handed him a napkin, thinking there probably hadn't been much popcorn in prison. Apart from using surprisingly lyrical descriptions of his love for popcorn, Logan had also played the "I haven't seen a movie since before I went to the pen" card. It had been effective. Caleb was here. He would just have to try to make the best of it. He snuck a quick peek at his watch. If it really was a ninety-minute movie, he just might be home in two hours. He hoped he could get through them without embarrassing himself.

"Sure you don't want some?" Logan shook the tub of popcorn at him.

"Maybe later." Caleb clutched the huge packet of candy and took a couple of deep, calming breaths.

"You sure?" More crunching. "'Cause it's still warm right now. And it's making my fingers all… slippery and buttery."

Caleb's eyes snapped open. Sure enough, Logan was busy licking butter off his fingers in a most provocative way. His eyes shone with mischief, and Caleb felt his cheeks getting warm. He couldn't look away.

"Oops, forgot my thumb," Logan murmured and turned his head to offer Caleb a side view as he slid the whole length of it into his mouth. His lips closed over it tightly, and he moved it in and out several times while watching Caleb sidelong.

"OhmiGod!" exclaimed a soft female voice nearby, and both Logan and Caleb jerked, startled, as they realized that a trio of teenage girls had just come in and stood stock still, staring at them.

"Kelsey, don't just stand there," hissed the tallest of the three. "Let's go sit down." She attempted to nudge her friends forward.

The one called Kelsey seemed reluctant to move. "But, Anna, did you—I mean, that guy, he was…." She glanced back at Logan and Caleb, her eyes very round.

"I think we should sit right here," said the third girl in a decisive tone of voice.

Caleb heard the rustle of her jacket and felt a slight bump against the back of his seat as she entered the row directly behind them.

"Fine with me." That was Kelsey's breathy voice as she hurried after her friend.

"Shove over, you guys," snapped Anna. "I am not sitting behind the Incredible Hulk here. How am I supposed to see the screen?"

"Shh, he can hear you," insisted Kelsey as softly as possible, but she obeyed Anna.

The girls and their purses and backpacks bumped and smacked against the backs of Logan and Caleb's seats as they all shifted over by first one seat, and then another after Anna made the discovery that she didn't want to get stuck behind "Blondie," either. Her friends grumbled and complained but did as she said. Caleb wished they didn't have to sit so close to him. But on the other hand, he couldn't blame them after Logan's little performance. He became aware that Logan was refraining from eating any more popcorn. Maybe he was feeling self-conscious. Caleb gave in to the desire to rib him a little.

"Afraid to get more butter on your fingers?"

Logan grinned back. "I ain't never been afraid to get butter on my fingers, baby."

The whispering behind them abruptly stopped, and Caleb had a sense that three pairs of teenage ears were waiting to hear his response. Suddenly he wanted to laugh.

"Oh?" he said. "Why don't you tell me about some of those other times when you got butter on your fingers?"

There came the sound of a smothered giggle followed by a brief admonitory "Shh!"

"Well, there was this one time," drawled Logan, and the little tilt of his head told Caleb he was playing to the gallery, "when it was really late at night, and I was in a real adventurous mood…."

"And you needed some butter?" Caleb tried to sound encouraging.

"Well, we needed something. And butter was all we had."

"'We?'"

"Uh. Yeah. It's not like I had this butter adventure all by my lonesome."

"I should hope not," said one of the girls in a very low voice. Caleb wasn't sure which girl it was, but judging by the way his seat was shaking, she was getting smacked by the other two.

"So," Caleb said in the most casual tone he could muster. "Who did what, and to whom, with the butter?"

Logan cleared his throat and then said, "Hey, it looks like the trailers are starting. Guess we'd better stop talking."

A collective wail of disappointment went up behind them, but it was almost immediately drowned out by the noise of music and explosions from the speakers. The sudden increase in volume made Caleb flinch, but when Logan winked at him and dipped his fingers back into the popcorn, he relaxed a little.

The movie was okay. Logan had assured him it would feature hot guys with their shirts off, and it did. The male lead was handsome enough, although not quite Caleb's type. The plot was predictable; the special effects exciting. But the most enjoyable part of the movie for Caleb was the snarky commentary being delivered in undertones by the three teenage girls behind him. They had something to say about almost every scene, and Caleb found that between the movie and the girls, he was sufficiently distracted to forget to panic most of the time.

About twenty minutes into the film, his stomach settled down enough that he felt he could try the popcorn. The peanut gallery remarked on that too.

"Whoa, you guys, butter alert."

"Huh?"

"Blondie's goin' for it."

"Shh!"

Caleb ignored them and pushed a few greasy kernels of popcorn into his mouth, savoring the salty taste and light, crunchy texture. Logan was right. Theater popcorn was way better than the microwave popcorn he sometimes made at home.

"Good, huh?" Logan held out the tub. "What'd I tell ya?"

"Gimme that." Caleb took the whole tub. "I think it's my turn to hold it for a while."

Logan relinquished it with a good-natured smile and tore open their package of Twizzlers.

Behind him, Kelsey was being scolded for texting her boyfriend during the movie, and the third girl, whose name Caleb had learned was Megan, was excitedly drawing everyone's attention to the perfection of Captain America's ass.

"Bet he'd love to get it rubbed down with butter," remarked Anna, and this time when the other girls erupted in laughter, Caleb did too.

Logan turned around in his seat. "Would you guys just let up on this little butter fixation you got going?" he demanded.

"Dude, you started it," said Anna.

The next round of giggling was drowned out by a burst of music that was evidently supposed to be stirring, but as soon as it got a little quieter, the whispering started again. By the time the movie was in the final stretch, Caleb knew that all three girls were out of school on a Friday because it was a teacher institute day, but all three of their moms thought they were studying at Anna's house. He had endured some rather lurid speculation about his and Logan's relationship, heard a few observations about Captain America's pecs and abs with which he heartily agreed, and had accepted a shyly proffered stick of gum from Megan. She had written "U R hot!" on it with a fine black marker.

Logan, upon being shown the wrapper, again turned around to take the girls to task for hitting on his friend.

"'Special' friend, I bet," said Anna.

"Butter friend," Megan added.

"She doesn't mean that!" exclaimed Kelsey, laying a reassuring hand on Caleb's shoulder.

"Now you guys are groping him!" protested Logan. "Paws off!"

"Shh, we're trying to hear this incredibly original dialogue." Anna indicated the movie screen.

Logan scowled and went back to the popcorn.

Finally the closing credits rolled, and people started to get up and file out, leaving wrappers and trash behind them. Anna, Megan, and Kelsey seemed to spend an inordinate amount of time gathering all their belongings, dropping things, and bumping against Caleb's and Logan's seats.

Caleb's anxiety started to rise. As much as he wanted to return to his quiet, familiar apartment, he didn't want to have to deal with any crowds out there in the cineplex lobby. There was also the trip home to be endured. He felt his hand creep into Logan's, seeking support.

Logan squeezed his fingers and said, "I hope you don't wanna jump up right away. Let's just relax a little longer. I'm dying to find out who the 'key grip' was on this movie."

Anna stepped out into the aisle and snorted. "That's code for 'I'm dying to make out with you.'"

"Have fun." Kelsey waved cheerfully and left with her two friends.

"You," Logan said to Caleb, "are quite the chick magnet today. I'm almost jealous."

"Well, I'm jealous that you got called the Incredible Hulk and Shrek, whereas all I scored was 'Blondie'." Caleb could hear the slight tremor in his own voice.

"You're forgetting the gum," said Logan.

"Oh yeah."

"Not gonna switch teams, are ya?"

"Not if this team has butter."

Logan leaned back and grinned at the ceiling. "Can't wait to get you home."

CHAPTER
EIGHT

CALEB entered the bathroom and pulled off his clothes. Reaching around the shower curtain, he adjusted the spray to hot. After six weeks, it was such a relief to wash without having to worry about getting his cast wet. Removing the cast yesterday had been stressful for everyone. When the doctor insisted he take a sedative rather than risk a panic attack while the cast was being sawed off, Logan looked on the verge of swooning, likely infected by Caleb's amputation fears. It was sort of nice to be the one patting Logan's hand and reminding him to breathe.

Tonight, they were going out. Logan had insisted on being responsible for purchasing tickets for the Cubs versus the Marlins, refusing to let Caleb help pay for them. Caleb stepped into the shower, letting the heat relax the tense muscles in his back and neck. He hadn't slept well last night, his brain refusing to quiet. He had longed for the feel of Logan pressed against him, the heat of his body warm and welcome. A game was three hours long and until now, they had only managed two hours, and that was to a matinee movie, where less than a dozen people attended. Not like Wrigley Field, where there would likely be over forty thousand fans packed into the old ballpark. *God, what if I have an attack during the game? How will we get out?*

"Stop!" Even after over a month of successfully working with his therapist, it still felt weird to talk to himself aloud, but he couldn't argue with the results. He had managed two brief trips out on his own. Dr. Ryan apparently knew what she was talking about. "Logan got us aisle seats. He'll be able to haul me out of there if I freak out." He squirted a dab of shampoo on to his hand and started lathering his hair.

"No one will notice if I end up racing out of the stadium. They'll just think it's the nachos making me sprint to the nearest bathroom."

Leaning back his head, he rinsed off the soap. Regaining control was harder since he had reduced the dosage of the anti-anxiety medication, but it needed to be done. He didn't want to depend on the highly addictive pills as a long-term solution. He finished washing and got out of the shower.

Wiping off the mirror, he looked at his reflection. His most recent trip out had been to a hair salon to get his mop of hair cut short. Logan had goaded him into getting the cut by buying him a hairnet, claiming it was to keep hair out of the food. Caleb had refused to cook for him for a week, but he still booked an appointment. In revenge, he found the glitziest, most posh place he could find, where the stylists were fab-u-lous and charged more than a month's worth of groceries for a wash and cut. Seeing Logan sit on the trendy leather couch surrounded by the Chicago chic, looking wide-eyed and frantic, had been worth the price.

Caleb made his way into the bedroom and pulled on a pair of sweats and a T-shirt. He had expanded his wardrobe, but he was still more comfortable in his old clothes. He pulled his meditation mat from the closet and placed it on the floor facing the bed. Using a lighter, he lit a large candle in the center of a brass plate. He settled on the mat, legs crossed, hands resting on his knees, and closed his eyes. Breathing slowly and deeply, he let the warm, woodsy scent of sandalwood soothe him. He used the words of his therapist as a focus. *You're not trying to stop being afraid. You're trying to stop fear from controlling you. Embrace the fear and then let it go*. It sounded easier than it was, but he had made progress. He couldn't escape his fears, but he could make peace with them and try to make them useful instead of crippling. He emptied his mind of random thoughts, worries, emotions, and hopes for the future until only the fear remained. He tried to pin down each fear. The embarrassment he felt when others witnessed his panic. The helplessness when he lost control. The feelings of unworthiness. The dread of rejection. He focused on each fear and then tossed it away like a wad of paper.

Taking another deep, cleansing breath, he opened his eyes and rose. He blew out the candle, stashed the mat in the closet, and headed for the main room. He settled behind his desk and booted up his laptop.

He needed a distraction and work was usually good for one. As he opened his e-mail, there was a knock on the door. Frowning, he looked at the time. Logan wouldn't be here for several hours. He hesitated. *Who could it be?*

OUTSIDE in the hall, Logan waited for Caleb to open up. He listened, but he didn't hear any sounds of movement. "It's me," he called through the door. "I'm early."

Quick footsteps sounded and then Caleb was gazing up at him with an expression of such shy happiness on his face that it made Logan feel warm all over.

Logan grinned at him. "Surprise." He stepped into the apartment and secured the door before dragging Caleb close for a brief kiss. When he pulled back, he asked, "You're not wearing that, are you?"

Caleb looked down at himself. "Have you gotten over your sweatpants obsession?"

"Hell, no." They shared another brief kiss. "But that don't mean I want anybody else seeing you in them." His hand wandered to Caleb's ass, giving it a possessive squeeze. "You need to buy some that don't threaten to cut off your circulation."

Caleb wrapped his arms around Logan, hugging him close. "They'll be too busy staring at you to notice my wardrobe deficiencies."

"You go right ahead and keep being clueless about how hot you are." He ran his hand through Caleb's damp hair. "Much less likely to replace me with Randy the Beautician that way." Caleb's hands were caressing his muscles in a very distracting way.

Caleb rolled his eyes. "You're the one who had half the staff begging to rub oil on your bald head."

"Hey!" Logan said, lifting a hand to his head. "Shaved, not bald."

Caleb looked at his forehead dubiously. "If you say so."

Logan grabbed Caleb around the waist and threw him over his shoulder. "Be nice to me, you little shit," he said, smacking Caleb's tempting ass. "I got off of work early just to see you before the game."

Caleb made a strangled sound. "Let's sit on the couch."

Logan complied, sitting on the dark leather couch and hauling Caleb onto his lap. Caleb's face was a bit flushed, likely from the head rush, as he leaned in for a kiss. He tasted like the chamomile tea he favored, buttery and floral with a hint of honey. Logan liked that he had time to savor the taste of him. Far too often, their encounters were rushed since he had begun working full-time and he still needed to get home for his 8:00 p.m. curfew. He hated crawling out of bed and leaving, but he refused to have Caleb at his rathole. Caleb was reintroducing himself to the world he'd hidden from for years. He didn't need reminders for why it was safer to stay at home than venture into Logan's neighborhood.

Logan noticed Caleb's normally neat desk was covered in papers and brightly colored Post-it notes. "You working?"

"Oh, that. I'm presenting to Daniel's class next week, so I need to figure out what I'm going to say."

"You going in person or using that web thingy?"

"I haven't decided. It would be easier to interact with the class and answer questions if I'm there in person."

Caleb didn't need to voice the downside to that scenario. Going back to the school where the panic attacks had started was bad enough. But standing in front of a lecture hall full of over-caffeinated and bored college students would give anyone pause. *Yeah, until they got a look at their guest speaker. Then every girl and gay guy would be paying attention like an eager puppy.* "Do you want me to go with you?" *And smack the puppies with a newspaper when they jump all over you?* he added silently.

"I can't keep relying on you, and Daniel will be there."

Sometimes the whole business of being supportive really sucked. Logan was glad Caleb had found a new friend, but why couldn't it be the "I'm a dyke and proud of it" chick from the first floor? Instead of a hot professor with wide, blue eyes and tousled curls. *Who's everything I'm not. Smart and educated and not an ex-con.* The kind of person Caleb should be with.

Logan kneaded Caleb's shoulders. As his fingers worked to ease the tight muscles, Logan could see the tension growing in Caleb's shoulders. Leaning forward, he buried his face against Caleb's neck.

Caleb's skin had that freshly scrubbed scent with a whiff of candle smoke. Kissing the side of his neck, he asked, "What's your number?"

Caleb huffed. "My ass is pressed against your dick and you want to know *that*?"

He nuzzled Caleb's neck, silently urging him to continue. He knew Caleb hated admitting his level of anxiety, but the therapist insisted it was important, especially if Caleb was going to get further than two blocks from home on his own. Logan tried very hard to keep his own fears hidden. He didn't want to stilt Caleb's confidence by admitting he didn't want Caleb going anywhere alone.

Logan hadn't seen much of Foster since yelling at her on the floor of the warehouse, but that didn't make him any less wary of his supervisor. Michael said there wasn't much else he could do without bringing Klass on board. Logan wasn't sure if he should approach Klass or not. Something was going on with his boss. Last week, he observed a guy in a slick suit and with carefully coifed hair walking on the floor with a flustered-looking Klass trailing behind him. Toward the end of his shift, Logan spotted the same man exiting the break room, face flushed and styled locks in disarray. When Logan entered the break room, he found Foster applying lipstick in the dingy mirror above the utility sink. From the smirk she directed at him, Logan had no doubt she'd offered herself up to Mr. Slick Suit like a vagina vending machine.

Sighing, Caleb leaned forward, resting his chin on Logan's shoulder. "I talked myself down from a six in the shower."

Logan wrapped his arms around Caleb. A six was high, but not the crippling panic of a ten. "How about now?"

"I was really low after meditation, maybe a two…." He trailed off and Logan told himself to be patient. Running his hands over Caleb's back, he could feel the muscles twitch and tense.

"Seeing you makes what we're planning to do more real… so I'm at a three." The strain in his voice meant it was likely closer to a four, but Logan didn't contradict him. He knew Caleb felt guilty when something Logan said or did triggered anxiety. He wanted the day to go well. They had been slowly increasing the time away from the apartment, but this wasn't a test and he refused to let Caleb tear himself apart if it didn't work out.

"Would you dump me if I relapsed and got drunk?"

"Of course, not!" Caleb said, leaning backward.

Feeling his chest ease from a fear he hadn't had the courage to acknowledge, Logan leaned forward in the seat, swallowing against a suddenly dry throat.

Caleb brought their foreheads together for a moment before kissing him gently. "But I'd want you to get back on the wagon and try again. I wouldn't accept you just giving up."

"So stop being so damn hard on yourself," Logan said, his voice hoarse. "If it doesn't work out today, there'll be another nine innings to try again."

Logan had been saving for first and last month's rent for somewhere nice enough for Caleb to visit when the thought of buying tickets came to him. Hope had power, and he'd give anything to give it to Caleb. It had come as a big surprise that the tickets were so expensive this time of year. It wasn't like the Cubs were going to make it into post season, but he'd had to go to a ticket broker to ensure he got aisle seats in an area close to an exit. Money was tighter than he liked since he'd stopped letting Caleb pay him. "You mostly have your uncle to thank for today." He gritted his teeth. He'd barely managed to cover half of the cost, and Klass had been the one to find the tickets online.

"No," Caleb said, brushing a hand across Logan's cheek. "He might've helped, but the tickets were all you." He kissed Logan sweetly. "Thank you." He kissed him again, a little whisper of a kiss. "What should I do to thank you?" Rotating his hips, he ground his ass onto Logan's lap.

Logan knew what he wanted, but hesitated to ask. He didn't want to make Caleb self-conscious or think he was obligated to comply. Caleb could be painfully shy at times and incredibly clueless about his own appeal. But ever since that first phone call when he'd listened to Caleb come, he'd yearned to see the show in person. Even knowing the call had led to Caleb's panic attack hadn't burned the desire from him.

Caleb grinned as if he could see the dirty thoughts in Logan's head. "Tell me." Leaning forward, he nibbled on Logan's earlobe. "Is it kinky?" He pulled back and stared at him appraisingly as if he could pry the fantasy from Logan's head. "I have a very unsanitary one involving pancake batter and a frilly apron."

Even though it was likely his ass in that girly apron, Logan couldn't keep from groaning. "Yeah, let's do that."

Wagging a finger at him, Caleb said, "I want to know what's in *your* pervy head."

Logan gnawed on his lower lip. "We don't have to do it just 'cause I suggest it."

Caleb grinned and they shared another kiss. "I know."

Feeling his cheeks flush, Logan said, "I want to... uh... watch you touch yourself."

Still smiling, Caleb leaned back so far that Logan had to scramble to grab his waist and prevent him from falling on to the coffee table. Arm stretched, Caleb opened the drawer on the coffee table and pulled out a bottle of lube and a condom. After placing the items on the couch, he stripped off his T-shirt. Logan noticed an angry red line surrounding Caleb's neck like a collar, making him wonder how the man could stand his T-shirts being so suffocatingly tight. Wordlessly, Caleb unzipped Logan's jeans.

Bewildered, Logan took off his pullover and helped Caleb slide off the jeans. Maybe the request had freaked him out and he was pretending it hadn't been made? Logan reached for the lube, but Caleb snatched it from his hand. "Hands at your sides and keep them there." When Logan opened his mouth to protest, he said, "You said you wanted to watch not touch."

Logan groaned, letting his head fall back against the back of the couch. Laughing, Caleb stood long enough to get his sweatpants off before returning to Logan's lap. They both groaned at the first touch of skin against skin. Caleb tore open the condom with his teeth. After only a few strokes, he'd hardened enough for Caleb to slide the condom onto his dick. Logan's mouth watered as Caleb's equally hard cock drew tantalizingly close as he rose up, his knees on either side of Logan's thighs. Another squirt of lube and Caleb reached his long fingers to his entrance. Logan watched with fascination as Caleb began to stretch himself. Caleb held his cock to his stomach, giving a perfect view of him shoving and twisting his way inside his tight hole. Soon Caleb's pale hips were thrusting down upon his own fingers, a few quiet moans escaping as he curled his touch and brushed deep inside. It took every bit of Logan's will to keep from bucking his hips in the air as needy little sounds escaped Caleb's lips.

Caleb sighed heavily and pulled his fingers free, a hungry look in his eyes when he positioned himself over Logan's throbbing cock. Logan concentrated on not coming like a teenager as Caleb slicked him up with lube. Without hesitation, Caleb shoved his way down in one hard motion.

"Oh, fuck!" The sudden heat and tightness was almost more than he could take. When Logan could think again, he said, "You're going to be sore."

Caleb smiled, bright and eager. Logan hadn't thought his dick could get any harder, but he'd been seriously wrong. He sat transfixed as Caleb rubbed his hands across his pale skin, green eyes closed and a deep blush upon his cheeks. He let his eyes follow that blush down to his long neck and over the smooth contours of his chest. A sprinkling of baby-fine blond hair trailed down over his flat stomach to his well-groomed, honey-colored pubes.

"Do you think you can keep still?" Caleb asked, teasing innocence in his voice. He twitched the internal muscles of his passage, sending a bolt of pleasure down Logan's length. Struggling to breathe, Logan could only mutely nod.

Caleb's eyes closed as he stroked himself, slow and lazy at first. Logan groaned and Caleb's eyes fluttered open to lock with his. The flush on Caleb's cheeks darkened. Logan felt his hands curl into fists at his sides as Caleb increased the pace, stroking his cock but somehow keeping his hips still. Caleb's other hand slid up his chest and squeezed a rock-hard nipple, causing them both to hiss. Another twitch from that tight ass, and Logan nearly dislocated his hips to keep from thrusting.

Logan knew the hitch in Caleb's breath meant he was close, which was good because any longer and he'd never be able to walk again. A few more urgent pulls and Caleb came, crying Logan's name as his eyes clenched closed and splattering his seed against his chest. *God, he's beautiful.*

After a deep breath that made Logan grit his teeth to keep from coming, Caleb said, "I want you to fuck me so hard I'll be squirming on the hard plastic seats at Wrigley, still able to feel you inside me."

Logan didn't need to be told twice. He surged forward, ignoring Caleb's yelp of surprise and the squish of sweaty flesh peeling off the leather couch. He pulled out long enough for Caleb to kneel on the couch cushions before shoving back inside. The next few minutes were a blur in Logan's mind. He pounded into Caleb, the other man meeting him thrust for thrust, both filling the room with loud cries and deep moans as the couch squeaked in surrender.

Logan plunged in again, two, three more thrusts, before he felt the tension reach its peak. He bucked into Caleb mindlessly, too focused on feeling his orgasm to control his movements. A distant part of his brain worried he might actually pass out from the pleasure. He wrapped both his hands around Caleb's waist to keep himself upright until the last of the waves had abated; then all the strength ran out of him and he collapsed to his knees on the floor, panting and completely spent.

"Wow," Caleb said, flopping over onto his side on the cushions.

Logan laid his forehead on the couch and reminded his lungs that breathing was a good idea. After a few minutes, he felt Caleb move on the couch.

"Was it okay? I mean... w-what you w-wanted?" Caleb asked, sounding tentative enough to cut into Logan's afterglow.

Logan managed to summon the energy to raise his head a couple of inches. "You're not allowed to be insecure after frying all the brain cells in my head."

When Caleb didn't respond, Logan sighed. *From vixen to blushing virgin.* Hauling himself up, he clambered onto the couch, pinning Caleb beneath him. When Caleb turned his head away, Logan didn't stop him. Instead, he asked, "Did you like what we did?"

Caleb blinked rapidly, his eyes turning wet and glistening, and Logan felt a surge of panic race through his gut. "Shit, did I hurt you?"

"No," Caleb said, wiping an escaping tear from his cheek. "You didn't hurt me. I just...." He rubbed at his eyes. "Why can't I just enjoy the moment? Why do I...." He made a move to slide off the couch, but Logan used his weight to keep Caleb in place.

"Don't run away."

"Let me up."

"Why? So you can go hide in your bedroom?" Leaning down, he kissed Caleb on the forehead, and then each eyelid and each corner of his mouth. "Do you think that little slab of wood can keep me away from you?" He watched Caleb work through whatever shit was going through his head. "I'd say I was sorry for suggesting it, but I'd be lying. Watching you touch yourself was the hottest thing I've ever seen."

Caleb's eyes widened. "Really?"

"I'll be jacking off to the memory from now on when I'm hot and horny at my place, wishing I'm with you."

Caleb sighed, a small smile on his lips.

LOGAN hoped the dark clouds looming overhead weren't a sign for how the day would go. A 3:10 start on a weekday and the threat of rain were enough to keep the fair-weather fans away. Caleb vibrated in his seat, either from anxiety or an attempt to avoid freezing to death in drizzling fifty-degree weather. Logan scrunched in his seat as best he could with the limited space. He'd likely converted the seat behind him to obstructed view, but there wasn't much he could do about it.

Caleb's gaze roamed over the stadium, seeming to take in all the details. "Thank you for this," he said, so sweetly he might as well have shoved his tongue down Logan's throat. The sappy look Logan knew was on his own face probably wasn't helping matters, but he couldn't seem to stop.

He noticed a stocky guy to Caleb's right, dressed in blue and red like nearly everyone else in the stadium, staring. The girl next to him had long, blond hair and was busy bitching about the cold. The man appeared more resigned than hostile as he first glanced at his girlfriend and then back to Caleb. Stuck between a whiney girlfriend and a fag, the look said. As long as the guy didn't give them any trouble, he could think whatever he wanted.

"I still can't believe they traded Zambrano to the Marlins," Caleb said. "I'm going to miss his water cooler hissy fits."

The neighbor snorted. "I swear the man would rather get a homerun than a perfect game."

And then they were off, rambling about stats and future prospects like they were the best of buddies. Logan couldn't follow half of it, so he didn't try. He shared a look with the girlfriend before he said, "I'll hit the concession stand."

Pulling himself away from his new best friend, Caleb asked, "Do you want me to go with you?" *And make sure you stay away from the beer* being the unspoken message.

"Nah, I've got it. Don't want you to miss the opening pitch." He already knew what Caleb wanted. Caleb had described it in such graphic detail last week that Logan had had to jump him. Caleb took food porn to an all new level. Heading down the stairs, a portly guy passed Logan with what had to qualify as a vat of beer, since the guy needed two hands to carry it. He tried and failed to be disgusted by the sight. He weaved through the crowd toward the third base line to the concession stand Caleb had said he preferred. When his turn came, he ordered a foot-long hot dog loaded with onions, peppers, and sauerkraut for Caleb and Bases Loaded nachos for himself.

After making his way back to their seats, he handed Caleb his food and retook his seat. He then avoided looking at Caleb until he was sure the food was devoured. There was no way he could watch Caleb stuff a foot-long hotdog in his mouth and not get arrested.

In the fourth, the dark clouds moved off and the sky brightened. Caleb took one look upward and reached for his backpack. He pulled out two blue, plastic ponchos and handed one to Logan. Caleb quickly donned his poncho and encouraged Logan to do the same.

"I think it's clearing," Logan said, right before the heavens opened up and pissed all over him.

Caleb and his new best friend were rambling away when Logan got back from a trip to the john. Caleb must have seen something in his face, because he smiled sheepishly.

"I realized I never even asked if you're a White Sox or a Cubs fan."

Caleb was so obviously trying to include Logan in the conversation that Logan was tempted to ignore the question just on principle. It didn't help that he had no idea what to say. He doubted Caleb would appreciate the truth. He didn't give a shit about either team and was only indulging Caleb's love of baseball like a good little boyfriend. Come winter, he expected Caleb to park his ass on the couch every Sunday to watch football, preferably naked and draped over Logan's lap. He intended to take full advantage of every commercial and halftime break. Opting for neutral, he said, "I like both, I guess. I've never had a preference."

The entire stadium didn't stop and stare as the words left his mouth, but damned if it didn't feel that way. The look on Caleb's face was less than comforting.

The asshole neighbor nudged Caleb's shoulder and said, "You should dump him," in a tone of absolute seriousness.

Caleb held up a hand as if to say "I can break up with my boyfriend without you." He then spent ten years gathering his thoughts. "You've never mentioned this before," he said, like Logan had neglected to tell him about a wife and two kids in the 'burbs.

They were starting to attract attention without a single voice being raised. An hour-long rain delay and icy winds meant only the diehards remained in the stands. They had to get their entertainment somewhere.

As Caleb appeared to be debating what to say, Logan wondered how he'd missed the fact he was dating a fanatic. His brain gave him a mental slap to the back of his head: *He's an agoraphobic at a baseball game, you moron.* Wide open space. Check. Large, unruly crowd. Check. Uncontrollable conditions. Fucking check.

"Look, I don't have anything against White Sox fans. I mean, it could be worse. They could be Cardinals fans." Caleb's lime-colored eyes narrowed. "You're not a Cardinal fan, right?"

Logan shook his head vigorously. When Caleb gave him a look that could rival Dabb's, he reluctantly added, "I've been to Cardinals games, but it was only a few times. A guy I knew who moved to St. Louis had season tickets and—"

"Do you want to switch seats with me?" The asshole yelped when his girlfriend smacked him in the arm. "What? I was just offering."

Caleb snapped his fingers, ignoring the offer for the moment. "Try to imagine if I said I loved the Chicago Bears *and* the Green Bay Packers."

"Huh." Not liking big-time rivals made sense. Although, it seemed like it should be okay to be a Chicago fan. The Packers and the Bears weren't even in the same state. Something told him he shouldn't voice this opinion if he ever wanted to see Caleb naked again.

Looking ridiculously hopeful, Caleb asked, "Now do you get it?"

"If I say yes, will you promise not to dump me?"

Caleb patted his knee. "Yes." And because he was an evil little shit, he added, "Unless the Cubs lose. Then, I'll totally have to dump you or risk jinxing next season."

Because Mother Nature was a squealing fag-hag, the rain sputtered to a stop and the skies cleared. Logan was working himself up to a full-on sulk when Caleb's cold hand snuck under the poncho to link their fingers. Caleb gave him a gentle squeeze, keeping their hands joined as they watched the ground crew pull the tarp off and prep the field. *I'm in love with him*, Logan realized with terrifying clarity. It wasn't an emotion he'd felt before, and even as a part of him wanted to run screaming for the nearest exit, he knew it was the truth. It felt like his gut had been twisted together with tenderness and longing and caring into one giant knot. He felt like he would do anything to keep it tied. It wasn't a love of equals that was for sure. He had a long road ahead to becoming the man who deserved to be sitting here, holding Caleb's hand. That wouldn't keep him from growling at anyone who dared to take his place.

As they moved with the crowd out of the stadium, Caleb kept himself plastered to Logan's side. Glancing at his watch, Logan read the time: 7:30 p.m. There was barely enough time to get home before curfew if he left straight from the stadium and hit nothing but green lights. He'd never make it if he took Caleb home first. With the game being so close, he couldn't have asked Caleb to bail early. Zambrano got a double in the sixth inning, but Logan wasn't sure whether that was a good thing or not, considering Caleb and his buddy had debated it until the final pitch. Zambrano walked away with a no decision, but his former team took the win.

Caleb pulled away from him and walked to the curb. Looking over his shoulder he said, "You're going to need your own cab."

"I've got time to take you home first."

"I'll be fine," Caleb said, sounding braver than he looked. He clutched a bag of cotton candy like it was a teddy bear. "You're wasting time. Now go."

Logan didn't have time to argue even if he thought it would work. Caleb had a stubborn streak a mile wide if he thought someone needed him. He settled for hailing a cab and discreetly speaking to the driver, slipping him an extra ten dollars to wait until Caleb got inside the building. Confident the driver would make damn sure Caleb got home safely, he stepped back and said, "Call me when you get home." He forced his knees to unlock and walked away.

CHAPTER
NINE

CALEB took a deep calming breath that ended in a coughing fit. The air in the cab was thick with a spicy scent that made the inside of his nostrils burn. Leaning forward, Caleb asked the driver, "Do you have the time?"

"Quarter to eight, sir," the man said in a thickly accented voice.

There was no way Logan would make it back to his apartment by the eight o'clock curfew. *What if Dabb is waiting for him? And he ends up arresting Logan?*

"Stop," Caleb said, his cheeks flushing when the cabbie responded to the command.

"We are not there yet, sir." The cabbie looked over his shoulder, sweat beading above his lip. "And your friend was most insistent I get you home safely."

"Most insistent" being code for Logan scared him shitless by growling and deliberately staring at his ID card. If Caleb didn't calm down, the guy would insist on escorting him to his apartment door like a prom date.

"You're right. I wasn't thinking." Caleb tried to keep composed for the rest of the trip home, focusing on his annoyance with Logan. He knew he had a spotty track record, but he wasn't a child. He'd managed to go to Meng's by himself. He could handle walking from the cab to his building without Logan intimidating the driver. He was still brooding when the car veered sharply and pulled to the curb. When he tried to pay for the cab, the driver wouldn't take it, claiming Logan had covered the fare. He exited the cab rather than argue with the agitated man.

After keying the front entrance, Caleb entered the building and made his way to his floor. To his surprise, someone stood beside his door. "Karen? What are you doing here?"

"I need to talk to you about Logan," she said, sounding earnest.

Wary of her motivations, he said, "What about?"

Karen looked at her hands as if debating what to say. "I think Logan needs help and I know you're his... friend."

Flabbergasted, Caleb stared at her as she continued. She bit her lip. "I think he's been drinking on the job."

An immediate denial died on Caleb's lips before he could voice it. He had seen the longing in Logan's eyes when he looked at the patrons drinking beer at the game. *What if he's drinking at home when there's no one there to see? What if that's the real reason he doesn't want me to visit?* Caleb's knees began to shake at the thought. When he had met Logan's AA sponsor, Stacy, she had said relationship and money troubles were the top stressors for recovering alcoholics. *What if the expensive tickets and my near meltdown sent him straight into a bottle of booze?*

Karen gave an indelicate snort. "You should see your face."

With a conscious effort, Caleb tried to focus on her. *Was she joking?* It seemed impossible that even she could be so cruel. "What are you talking about?"

She gave Caleb a hard smile. "Imagine how easy it would be for someone to convince Logan's PO that he's back to being an alky. Especially when Dabb finds out that Logan violated his parole a month ago by meeting me at a bar."

Caleb felt a stab of irritation as he realized when she was talking about. Logan hadn't mentioned it would violate his probation to meet her at a bar. *Why did he agree to meet her there?* Focusing on the here and now, he said, "Dabb's too smart. He won't believe you."

"You did," she said ruthlessly.

The truth in the words made the hot dog in his gut threaten to make a reappearance. He should have known better than to believe anything that came out of her mouth.

Likely sensing his distress, she went for the kill. "Could you live with yourself if you were the reason Logan got sent back to prison?"

Caleb sighed and rubbed his forehead. "What do you want, Karen?"

"Your uncle is retiring and his replacement officially takes over on Monday. I want you to convince Logan to leave with your uncle."

Caleb gaped. He hadn't known his uncle was thinking of retiring, let alone this week. Was the corporate head office forcing him out for someone younger and cheaper? It might explain why his uncle hadn't mentioned it.

"Why do you need Logan to quit?" With a flash of understanding, Caleb understood why. Dabb. Dabb had permission from corporate to access the warehouse in order to check on Logan. And Logan had mentioned that Dabb had helped him get the job as a package handler. *Maybe he knows someone at corporate.* Dabb must scare someone like Karen shitless. But that still didn't explain why the sudden rush to get rid of Logan's PO.

"I could go to Dabb and tell him what you're doing."

She shook her head derisively. "You're in love with Logan. You'd say anything to keep him out of jail and more importantly, you have no proof."

The latter was certainly true. All those years ago at the warehouse, he had seen what? A Latino package handler he didn't recognize stuffing something that looked like a stack of package labels under his shirt as he exited the bathroom stall. And he had seen Karen follow him out of the same stall. Suspicious, but no real proof of anything. Even tonight, she hadn't admitted to committing a crime.

Holding up the phone, Karen said, "Time to call lover boy."

Caleb raked a hand through his hair. "You expect me to convince him to quit his job over the phone? He needs Dabb's permission to change jobs." Trying another tactic, he asked, "Why call him now? He's coming by after his shift tomorrow."

"He had to agree to work a triple shift tomorrow to get off early today."

Jesus. Fifteen hours? How could he survive that? Another thought trickled in. *He did it for me.* Caleb's eyes burned and his throat thickened. He took the phone from her.

LOGAN didn't look at his watch until he'd reached his apartment building. The lit screen revealed the time: 8:09. He opted to sprint up to the stairs rather than wait for the elevator.

Dabb was leaning against his apartment door eating from a package of M&M's. Logan wasn't even surprised. He felt oddly deflated. He hadn't been late to curfew once and the one time he was, of course, Dabb was waiting for him. Dabb must have a hundred ex-cons assigned to him, and he couldn't be everywhere. Logan didn't know why he'd told Dabb about the game, except maybe wanting his PO to know he wasn't a completely useless boyfriend.

Dabb wasn't dressed to blend in to this neighborhood with his khaki pants, sandals, and fanny pack. But Logan doubted anybody gave his PO a hard time, and it wasn't because his untucked shirt bulged slightly at the hip. Dabb didn't need a gun to be a badass. He just was. Logan wasn't looking forward to this conversation.

Unzipping the pack, Dabb ordered Logan to step closer. He held up the breathalyzer and gave Logan the order to blow. When the beep sounded, he looked at the display and said, "Glad to see you resisted the lure of ballpark Budweiser." He put the tester away and pulled out a mininotebook. "Now let's talk about the curfew violation," he said while scribbling on the pad.

Logan sighed. "Shit weather and a rain delay made us late getting out of the game."

Without looking away from his notebook, Dabb said, "Let's go inside."

"Fine, but I need to call Caleb and make sure he got home okay." Logan unlocked the door and entered, pulling out his cell phone and dialing Caleb's number. The phone rang before he could punch the Send button.

"Hey, baby." Logan wanted to ask how the ride home had gone. Instead, he settled for asking, "How you doing?"

Dabb started searching the apartment, opening drawers and sifting through stuff, no doubt looking for booze or drugs. Logan moved as far away from his PO as possible in the 350-square-foot apartment.

"F-fine."

Wanting to keep this conversation short with Dabb listening, Logan said, "Let me call you back. Dabb is busy sniffing through my dirty drawers."

"No!"

Logan heard what sounded like a muffled argument. "Caleb?"

For a blinding moment, Logan knew what real panic felt like. A barrage of worst-case scenarios exploded in his brain like a triggered minefield. The force of it sent him reeling against the wall. At the sound of the dial tone, reason punched through and reminded him he'd seen Caleb's home phone number on the cell display. *He made it home, but who the fuck is with him?* He doubted Caleb was arguing with Mrs. Simon. Six rings later, the voice mail kicked in. Logan stared at the phone, trying not to lose it.

Raising a brow, Dabb asked, "What's up?"

Logan's phone rang before he could respond. In lieu of a greeting he asked, "Who were you talking to?"

"Uh, n-no one. I accidentally turned on the television."

Logan frowned at the phone. It hadn't sounded like the TV, but Caleb didn't sound panicked. Tired and a little rattled, yes, but that was expected after a trip to the ballpark.

"Tell Dabb it was my fault you were late."

"Don't worry about it, baby. I'll talk to you tomorrow. Get some sleep." Logan ended the call and turned to find Dabb wearing an amused smirk.

"Do you want me to go over there and tuck him into bed?"

Logan scowled at him.

Dabb put up his hands. "Hey, don't get grumpy with me. You're the one who sent him home by his lonesome instead of bringing him back here. You could've been braiding each other's hair and painting each other's toenails tonight. Sleepovers are allowed provided the person has their own permanent residence."

Logan looked away. "I don't want him coming over here. Nothing but former drunks, druggies, and wackos live here." Many of which weren't very former.

"Newsflash, Logan. You're one of them." An uncomfortable expression crossed Dabb's face as he shifted from one foot to the other. "Did Caleb tell you I showed him the crime photos?"

Logan stared at him. Caleb hadn't said a word. He'd assumed Dabb had told him about the fight, but learning the details wasn't the same as seeing the gory pictures of his crime. He brought a hand to rub at his forehead. He wanted to ask Dabb why he'd done it, but he was afraid of the answer he'd hear. Complete strangers went out of their way to help Caleb. He couldn't be angry with Dabb for trying to protect him.

"You know what he said after I got done trying to scare him off?" Dabb said, pulling Logan back from his thoughts. "You deserve a second chance. He's right. But you've got to let yourself have that chance. Pretending the past didn't happen is a surefire way of reliving it."

"What if I fuck it up?" Logan asked, hearing the desperate edge in his own voice, the way the words came out frayed around the edges. "What if I go back to being that man and I drag him down with me?"

"Being that man is a choice, not a foregone conclusion. Ask for help before you get to that point." Dabb's eyes turned cold and hard. "If you can't, then you don't deserve to be with him." Logan wondered if the glint in his PO's eyes meant he was ready to pinch hit if Logan couldn't get his shit together.

"I'm not going to report the curfew violation, just don't let it become a habit."

"I won't," Logan said, opening the door for Dabb. "Thanks."

Dabb looked like he had something more to say, but then he shook his head and headed out.

CHAPTER
TEN

THE fog rising off the lake was still thick at 8:00 a.m. The billowing mists seemed to highlight the city grime by forcing people to focus on the clear pockets in front of them. Caleb shivered in the back of the cab, wishing he had put a jacket on over his sweats and long-sleeved T-shirt. The cold wasn't the only thing making him shake, but he needed to stay focused in order to help Logan.

Arriving at his destination, Caleb paid the fare with a trembling hand, exited the cab at the corner of Monroe and Wabash, and entered the Office of Parole. In his last session, his therapist, Dr. Ryan, had made him create a list of triggers for his panic attacks. The emotional ones had been easier than the physical triggers. How could he describe that prickly feeling he got when someone was staring at him? Watching and waiting for him to fall apart. Caleb could feel it now. He zeroed in on the main desk and focused on it as he moved through the lobby, trying to ignore the way his skin twitched with each step.

A dark-skinned woman in her forties with close-cropped hair talked on the phone while typing into her computer rapidly. Her eyes narrowed as he approached. "Hold on," she said, before covering the receiver. "Do you have an appointment?" Tilting her head to look around Caleb, she barked, "Why are you still loitering in my lobby, Carlos?"

Caleb looked over his shoulder and saw an attractive Latino man with warm, brown eyes and slicked back hair.

"I'm waiting on my ride," Carlos said, before pressing his lips together as if to keep another word from escaping. He turned his attention to Caleb. "You an ex-con, pretty? Did some pig catch you on your knees?" He looked Caleb over, slow and deliberate.

The woman snapped her fingers. "What do you need, blondie?"

Caleb whipped his head toward her. "I'm here to see John Dabb."

"Do you have an appointment?"

"No," he said, realizing he had been stupid not to call first. He'd been too focused on psyching himself up to leave the apartment.

"He won't see you without an appointment. I can call him and try and schedule one for ya, but that's it."

"Okay."

This response seemed to throw her momentarily. Like maybe she expected Caleb to argue. Handing him a notepad, she said, "Write down your contact information and when you'd be available."

When Caleb completed the task, the woman directed him to take a seat on a long, wooden bench.

Watching Caleb's approach, Carlos asked, "Why don't you come closer and keep me company until Big D gets here."

Caleb took a seat on the bench. "She said he won't see me without an appointment."

"You watch." Carlos pointed to the woman as she dialed a number. "Big D won't send you away." He clicked his tongue against his teeth. "He'll give you hell for breaking the rules, but he won't send you away."

Caleb smiled. It was good to hear his impression of Dabb confirmed. Tough but fair. "Is Mr. Dabb your PO?" He flushed as he realized he had assumed the man was an ex-con, but Carlos didn't seem bothered by it.

Carlos slid over the bench until their thighs pressed together uncomfortably close. "Yeah, they give all the faggots to Big D. Let the fag deal with the faggots." He rolled his eyes. "Better we have him than some of those other *culos*. But if you get caught trickin', he'll nail your ass and not in the fun way, *bebe*." Carlos licked his full bottom lip slowly. "A damn shame. I'll bet your mouth would be worth it."

Caleb snapped his gaping mouth shut when Carlos winked at him. "I'm not… a prostitute," he whispered. The ding of the elevator compelled Caleb to stand, ignoring Carlos's murmurs of appreciation.

Scanning the lobby, Dabb asked Caleb, "Did you come here by yourself?"

"Yes. I took a cab."

Dabb studied Caleb's face for a moment before tilting his head toward Carlos. "Was he behaving himself?"

Carlos gave Dabb a cocky grin, but his shoulders hunched just a bit. "Was only being friendly, Big D."

Drawing Dabb's attention back to him, Caleb said, "I'm sorry I didn't think to call first. I can come back later."

Dabb shook off the offer and ushered Caleb toward the waiting elevator. Leaning against the wall, Dabb demonstrated his tenaciousness. "You want to tell me what Carlos said to get you redder than a lobster?"

"He said a lot of your parolees are gay."

"And no doubt me being gay was the reason they were assigned to me."

Caleb nodded, embarrassed all over again.

"That's not the official reason." The tone of Dabb's voice made it clear that the reverse was true.

"If it's any consolation, Carlos would rather have you for a PO."

Dabb's lips twitched, but he didn't comment.

The elevator arrived at the third floor and they exited the car. At the opposite end of the hallway, an emaciated man with straggly brown hair looked to be arguing with an older man with a thick, black mustache and a fresh-faced police officer with curly brown hair.

The older man—Caleb guessed he was a PO—said, "You need to calm down, Pauley."

"The test is wrong, man. I'm clean. Clean as a fucking whistle."

The officer rolled his eyes and put a hand on the ex-con's shoulder. The touch seemed to ignite the growing tension. Pauley made an inarticulate noise and shoved the officer's hand off him. When his PO grabbed his arm, Pauley kicked him in the balls. The PO made a squeaky grunt and collapsed to his knees.

Putting a hand on Caleb's chest, Dabb said, "Stay here," before sprinting toward the men.

Pauley made it halfway down the hallway before the officer tackled him around the waist and drove him to the floor. Dabb quickly joined him, pushing Pauley's shoulders down. It wasn't until the cuffs clinked in place that Pauley began to cry. Great, big sobbing breaths that made his slight frame shake. He repeated "I'm sorry" over and over as the officer drew him to his feet and read him his rights.

Dabb returned and unlocked his door, dragging a stunned Caleb inside, away from Pauley's desperate pleading.

Dabb seemed unfazed by the altercation in the hallway. Unable to resist, Caleb asked, "Will Pauley be sent back to prison?"

"One dirty drop likely wouldn't have got him sent back, but assaulting his PO and resisting arrest all but guarantees it."

Caleb puzzled over the phrasing—not wanting to ask—until he remembered Pauley's claims he wasn't using drugs. He blinked several times as he took notice of his surroundings. Even though Logan had described his PO's unusual décor, Caleb wasn't prepared for the explosion of color clogging the small space. Taking a seat in front of Dabb's desk, he tried not to gawk, focusing instead on Logan's PO.

Dabb leaned back on his chair and cranked up his stare like the dial on a stereo. His drawl slow and ragged, he asked, "What can I do for you, Caleb?" Flushing as if realizing how suggestive his tone sounded, he clarified, "Why are you here?"

When Caleb tried to speak, his voice wavered. "I need your help, but I don't know how to convince you I'm telling the truth. And I'm afraid I'll make things worse if you don't believe me."

"I can't give you any guarantees, but I'll listen to what you have to say."

Caleb's mind congested with doubts and fears. *I should leave now before Logan ends up on the ground with handcuffs tight around his wrists like Pauley.* Sleep hadn't come easy last night, and when it had, it was filled with disturbing dreams. A litany of worst-case scenarios. But he didn't see any other solution. Logan would never let Karen dictate his life, no matter how serious the threat. "About four years ago,

I was working as a package handler at my uncle's company. My shift was the Night Sort and Karen Foster was the supervisor."

Dabb grunted. "A real peach, that one."

And rotten to the core, Caleb thought. He went on to explain the suspicious behavior he had observed in the bathroom. "The guy took off, but Karen stayed." He swallowed hard, his heartbeat fluttering in his throat. "She told me just how bad it would be for me if I accused her of stealing and I ended up having a panic attack."

"Did she admit to stealing?"

"Never."

Dabb seemed pleased by this answer for some reason. "What happened afterward?"

"I stopped working there."

Dabb squinted. "Why?"

"I couldn't…." Caleb raked a hand through his hair. "I couldn't handle the idea of going back there. I was having a hard enough time leaving my dorm room to go to my classes."

Dabb looked thoughtful. "You've been dealing with the agoraphobia a long time."

Caleb ducked his head. "Too long."

"But you're making progress, right?"

"More like two steps forward, one step back."

"That's still progress. It may take you longer, but you'll still get to where you're going." Dabb didn't push further. Instead he asked, "Are you afraid Foster will try to drag Logan into her theft ring? Four years is a long time to keep a scam like that going."

"I hadn't realized Karen still was… or maybe I didn't let myself believe it. But last night she was waiting for me when I got home from the game. She wanted me to convince Logan to quit his job. She implied she could make life difficult for Logan if I didn't."

Dabb's salt and pepper beard twitched. "I'll bet she implied with the subtlety of a sledgehammer she could get Logan's parole revoked if you didn't go along with her." He pulled off his glasses. "You took a big risk coming here. Have you told Harry about all this?"

Caleb stared at him blankly. "Harry? Do you mean my uncle?"

"Uh, right." Cool, collected Dabb tore into a bag of M&M's like a starving man. He shoved a handful into his mouth and chewed. After swallowing, he asked, "Have you talked about your suspicions with your uncle?"

A disturbing thought occurred to Caleb. "Do you know my uncle? Is that why he picked Logan? So you and he could report back to my uncle."

"What? I had no idea Harry picked Logan until I called him. I tried to talk him out of it."

"But you vouched for Logan and my uncle trusted your judgment. That's why he was willing to hire an ex-con with a history of alcohol abuse and violence to work at the warehouse and to help me."

"It wasn't a setup, Caleb. We both know Logan well enough to know he'd never spy on you for Harry."

"You must've known him a long time if he lets you call him Harry." His mother called him Harry, but Caleb couldn't remember anyone else being allowed to use the nickname. He shivered as he remembered the last time he had heard her use it. "His heart, Harry." The hysteria in her voice had sliced through him, but it hadn't been sharp enough to separate him from the panic. It wasn't until his uncle cried out to him that the panic released its hold. With effort, Caleb pulled back and focused on what Dabb was saying.

"It wasn't anything serious and it was nearly twenty years ago. We've stayed… friendly."

Caleb tried to mask his surprise as he realized what Dabb had said. The look on Dabb's face said he had failed miserably. *Dabb and Uncle Harrison?*

Dabb closed his eyes and rubbed the bridge of his nose. "Please tell me I didn't just out your uncle."

Caleb didn't bother lying. His mind was too busy reeling.

Dabb swore under his breath. "Why wouldn't he tell you? Or at least tell me he hadn't told you. You're gay and from what I've seen not the self-loathing type." He added another layer of shock. "Your mother knew he was gay."

Caleb answered him honestly. "I don't know why he didn't tell me. Maybe because he made me promise not to tell my mom I was gay."

Dabb darted a glance at Caleb before looking away. "I'm sorry."

Caleb shook off the apology. Dabb wasn't to blame. "I need to talk to my uncle and Logan about Karen. But I won't mention anything about you and him if you don't want me to."

Sounding concerned, Dabb asked, "Have you done that before?" At Caleb's confused expression, he clarified. "Gone back to a place where you had a panic attack?"

Caleb fiddled with the sleeves of his shirt. "Not since they first started happening."

"If you can face that, I figure I can handle old Harry being pissed at me."

Caleb attempted a smile and rose to leave.

CALEB knocked on his uncle's office door. Directing his attention to his uncle's secretary, he said, "Thanks for letting me see him, Sally."

Sally was short and had her gray hair in a bowl cut so precise she was probably wearing one when it was cut. "Welcome, sweetheart," she said, looking like she wanted to ruffle his hair, or worse, pinch his cheeks.

He escaped into the office when his uncle bade him to enter.

His uncle's eyes widened. "Did you come here by yourself?"

The question of the day. Caleb didn't blame him for being surprised. For nearly a month after he had panicked here, the mere mention of the warehouse sent his heart into overdrive.

"I'm sorry to just show up, but I need to talk to you."

"What's wrong?"

Caleb had intended to question his uncle about Karen, but his brain had other ideas. "You and John Dabb... *know* each other," he said, feeling his cheeks warm.

"How very indiscreet of John," Uncle Harrison said primly, lacing his hands together on the mahogany desk.

Caleb bit his lip, his need to understand overpowering his mortification. "Mom's been gone for years. Why keep it a secret from me?"

"I suppose, I lived the lie so long, it felt more real than the truth."

Something told Caleb they still weren't even in the same ballpark as the truth. "Do you wish you weren't gay or that I wasn't? Is that why you didn't tell me?"

"There was no such thing as out and proud forty years ago, and there was still so much fear twenty years ago when I met John."

The more his uncle prevaricated the clearer it became the man wanted the truth to stay buried. In the past, Caleb would have let the matter drop, but not anymore. It was time to get out a shovel and dig. "Wearing a rainbow T-shirt isn't the same thing as telling your gay nephew you're also gay."

His uncle closed his eyes and slumped forward. In a voice barely audible he said, "I was afraid you would hate me for being a hypocrite. Your mother was worried but supportive when she found out about me in the eighties. I convinced myself she wouldn't react the same with you, or she would think I'd turned you gay."

Not understanding, Caleb said, "You might have convinced me not to tell my mom, but you never made me feel ashamed or that I needed to hide it from other people."

"But you did hide. Literally instead of figuratively. You were isolating yourself long before you stopped going out. And it was my fault."

Caleb shook his head. "You didn't cause my panic attacks."

He continued as if Caleb hadn't spoken, the words pouring out in a rush like a broken dam. "You've always been so smart, but I had no idea how determined you could be. I convinced myself your startup business would fail and then I would be able to convince you to get professional help and enter a treatment facility. Instead, you were making a profit in six months without leaving the apartment. I knew you were punishing yourself for your mother's death and I let you do it."

Caleb swallowed hard. "Because you blamed me too."

"No more than I blamed myself."

Uncle Harrison opened a desk drawer and took out a Polaroid photograph. Rising, he walked around the desk and handed it to Caleb. It was a faded picture of his mother, looking flushed and sweaty. She smiled at a wrinkled infant in her arms.

"It was the happiest moment of her life. I saw her leave this world with the same love in her eyes. It shames me more than I can say that I let you spend one moment, let alone years, thinking you were to blame for her death."

"It wasn't your fault either. She'd been on the transplant list for nearly a year. We might have avoided it happening that night, but it would have happened soon. She wouldn't have wanted either one of us to feel guilty."

Uncle Harrison reached around Caleb in a brief, comforting hug. Caleb's surprise made his attempt to reciprocate awkward at best. His uncle had never been particularly affectionate, but Caleb had always felt loved. "Even if fear was what motivated me, I don't regret starting my business, because I really enjoy it and I'm proud of what I've been able to accomplish. You gave me that chance regardless of your reasons."

"Thank you," his uncle said, before pulling away with a single pat.

Caleb rubbed the bridge of his nose. He doubted his uncle would ever get over his guilt. The feeling was mutual, but they could focus on rebuilding their relationship. "I was also hoping to talk to you and Logan. Would it be possible to page him… discreetly?"

"What is this all about?"

"It'll be easier to explain it once."

Not looking pleased, his uncle took out his cell phone and typed out a message. After a few minutes of strained silence, Logan arrived, looking a little sweaty and very confused by the summons. Caleb had a nearly irresistible urge to attach himself to Logan's broad chest like a barnacle. *Sheesh.* As if the situation wasn't awkward enough.

His uncle directed them to sit in the black chairs in front of the desk, but Caleb felt the need to remain standing.

Caleb took a moment to gather his thoughts before he asked his uncle, "Did you tell Karen Foster about my panic attacks when I worked here?"

"I wanted her to know in case something… happened so no one would overreact."

Caleb nodded. He'd assumed as much. "Karen was with me when I had the attack here. I walked into the bathroom and saw her with a package handler and it looked like they had shipping labels. As soon as the guy left, she started in on me."

His uncle and Logan spoke simultaneously.

"Did she threaten you?" Logan asked, his voice low and angry.

"Why didn't you tell me?" his uncle asked.

Choosing to answer the easier question, Caleb said, "Never directly. Only implied. But I started to fall apart and then she dragged in guys from the floor to gawk at me while I cowered in a corner."

Something dark and dangerous slithered across Logan's eyes, and he started walking toward to the door, fists balled. Alarmed, Caleb scrambled over to him and took hold of his hand. He tried dragging Logan back toward his uncle's desk, but it was like yanking on a concrete block. Unmovable. Feeling desperate, he did the only thing he could think of. Kissed him. On the chin, because Logan was seriously tall and it was the only spot Caleb could reach without some cooperation or a stepladder.

Logan blinked several times and the tension left his body. He allowed Caleb to bring him back over to the desk. Caleb linked their hands together. Just in case.

"The day the smoke bomb went off at my apartment complex. Was there anything special about that day? Any reason why someone would want you out of the building?"

Uncle Harrison looked at his hands. "Nothing I can think of."

"You're lying." Caleb knew he needed to have this conversation in person, because his uncle's voice was calm, but his eyes and hands telegraphed the deception. "Stop trying to protect me and tell me the truth."

His uncle blew out a slow breath. "A team from corporate, including my boss, Mr. Brady, was doing a walkthrough of the warehouse to review the changes we had made based on recommendations from a security firm we hired. We were shorthanded that morning to begin with. Mr. Percy, the operational manager, stalled on the way to work. When the team and Mr. Franklin came by, a floor supervisor was the only one to greet them."

"Karen Foster," Caleb murmured, wondering if she had somehow been responsible for the car breaking down too. He wouldn't put it past her.

His uncle opened and closed his mouth several times. "Yes."

"And now they're forcing you to retire."

His uncle shook his head. "I'm sixty-five years old. It was inevitable. They're not having me retire because I left early to make sure my nephew hadn't suffocated in his apartment."

Logan put his arm around Caleb's shoulders and drew him close, kissing the top of his head.

Uncle Harrison looked almost wistful for a moment before he continued. "My replacement had already been chosen. He was a part of the walkthrough."

Caleb paused, wanting to put all the pieces together. "What if I told you I don't think it was a coincidence that the smoke bomb went off that day?"

"Son of a bitch," Logan muttered.

"A couple of weeks before the smoke bomb, someone knocked on my door. By the time I looked through the peephole, they were gone, but they left a note behind. It was a printout of an article." Caleb took a deep breath and felt Logan squeeze his shoulder reassuringly. "It was about a woman who starved to death in her apartment because she was too afraid to leave. All total I got half a dozen different articles."

"Fucking Foster," Logan spat. "Marco was right about her being behind the smoke bomb and the letters."

Caleb nodded. "I wasn't sure at the time, but I am now. I went to see John Dabb this morning at his office."

"Dressed like that," Logan squawked, picking a strange time to be style conscious. He muttered something that sounded disturbingly like "burn them all."

"I went there because Karen threatened to get Logan in trouble with Dabb if I didn't convince him to quit his job."

"Why on earth would she do that?" his uncle asked weakly, as if the idea on top of everything else was too much to process. Caleb could relate.

"I think she picked that day for a reason," Caleb said. "She wanted the opportunity to make you look bad."

"This is ridiculous," his uncle sputtered, bristling with indignation. "I'm to believe she terrorized you, conspired to get me fired, and Logan's parole revoked in order to hide a petty theft ring. If the losses had been significant, the Loss Prevention Division would've flagged it years ago."

Logan chimed in. "My guess is the thefts before were little more than power trips. She gets off on manipulating guys into doing her bidding and pulling one over on her boss. One of Marco's pals told me that she latches on to new guys to the warehouse and they don't end up working here long after she's gotten a hold of them. They quit or she gets them fired."

Picking up that train of thought, Caleb asked, "What's changed?"

"My friend, Michael Miller, works for the security firm that was hired. According to him, six months ago, she was arrested for public drunkenness at a casino and she is swamped with debt." Logan snorted. "Probably even more so recently since someone called the construction company working on her house and told them she's jerking them around. I heard they're threatening to take her to court."

Caleb narrowed his eyes. They would be talking about Logan's failure to share important information later. Logan had the decency to look chagrined.

"So she's hard up for cash and looking for a way to get her hands on a bigger score." Caleb remembered one of Marco's many rants about Karen. "Logan wouldn't play ball and she's probably got someone lined up to take his place. But how does my uncle fit into all this?"

Logan turned toward Uncle Harrison. "Who's replacing you?"

His uncle blinked several times. "Martin Randal. It's an internal promotion."

"He that slick-looking guy that toured the warehouse a few weeks back?"

"Yes," Uncle Harrison said, clearly confused by the change in conversation.

Logan smiled smugly. "Foster is fucking him."

His uncle's face flushed so red Caleb worried about his blood pressure. They both listened in stunned silence as Logan relayed what he had seen in the break room. Randal had emerged from the break room still tucking his shirttails in. Logan didn't doubt for a moment that Foster was responsible for his disheveled state.

His uncle rose abruptly. "I need to speak to my supervisor, Mr. Brady." He hurried out of the office.

"She was at the apartment when you called, right?" Logan asked. "How did you get her to leave?"

Putting a hand to his chest dramatically, Caleb said, "C-can't t-talk with you h-here."

Logan snorted.

Caleb smiled sheepishly. "There's at least one benefit for having a history of mental instability."

Logan hauled Caleb over for a bone-crushing hug. Logan's warmth seemed to fill his whole being. It felt so damn good to be in his arms. Running a hand over the damp T-shirt covering Logan's back, Caleb breathed in Logan's sweet musk, thinking that it wasn't fair that the man could look and smell this good. He knew there were things they should be talking about, but he didn't want to move. For now, he just wanted this moment. His uncle's return ten minutes later had them separating like a pair of teens caught necking on the porch.

His uncle hovered in the doorway. "Martin is writing his resignation as we speak. And I've agreed to delay retirement for six months to aid in finding and training a suitable replacement."

"Do you think he knew what she was planning to do?" Logan asked.

Sounding weary, his uncle said, "I don't know. He admits to having an inappropriate relationship with a subordinate. He also said that he and Ms. Foster had talked about how they could rearrange personnel and schedules to make the warehouse more efficient, but he denies any knowledge of wrongdoing. I think he's probably telling the truth. He seems more like a man of poor judgment than a criminal."

Logan whistled. "I'm surprised he confessed so easily."

"Martin's ambitious. He'll walk away with a letter of recommendation and no official company sanction. And when people ask him why he left the company, he can tell them I changed my mind about playing shuffleboard full time."

Logan snorted, finally understanding. Randal had sold out Foster before she could pin it on him.

"What about Karen?" Caleb asked.

"She's left for the day and is not answering her cell phone. She'll be given the same offer or fired for violating company policy if she refuses."

"That's it?" Caleb's voice sounded raspy even to himself, which wasn't surprising because his throat had become a desert.

"It's the best solution for the company," his uncle said. He was still committed to the people who were ready to toss him out the door after thirty-plus years of service. His uncle could pretend all he wanted, but Caleb still believed Karen had had a hand in the *request* to retire. The idea of Karen not only walking away from this unscathed but with a glowing recommendation made Caleb physically ill.

"I need to go back upstairs and talk to Mr. Forrester about possible damage control if Ms. Foster chooses to sue civilly or file sexual harassment charges."

Caleb swallowed his first response and then changed his mind. "You mean hush money, right? Give her a wad of cash to go away and be someone else's problem."

His uncle gave him a pained expression before leaving the office once again.

Logan didn't seem surprised by the turn of events, and for some reason that pissed Caleb off even more. Where the hell was his righteous indignation? "None of this bothers you? She threatened to get you sent back to prison."

Logan wrapped a strong arm around Caleb's waist, dragging him close. "Baby, people like Foster don't need nobody to take them down. They do the job all by themselves."

Caleb understood what Logan was trying to tell him, and it pained him to think of *any* similarities between Logan and Karen. It did nothing to suppress the growing fire in his belly.

The buzzing sound of a phone set to vibrate filled the office. Logan pulled out his phone and answered it. "What's up?"

Caleb listened to the one-sided conversation with growing interest when Logan said, "You're shitting me?"

At Caleb's silent inquiry, Logan mouthed the name "Dabb."

"Why? Oh, come on, man. You gotta tell me," Logan said, sounding like an enormous five-year-old. His eyes locked with Caleb's, and he said to Dabb, "I'll tell him," before ending the call.

There could only be one reason for Dabb to call Logan. Karen must have gone straight to see him after her shift had ended. *What if Dabb didn't believe me? What if he believes her story? What if he's on the way to arrest Logan right now?*

Caleb's heart rate picked up, the panic gaining strength as if it had been waiting all day for an opportunity to strike. He hadn't realized he was stepping backward until his back slapped against the wall, sending one of his uncle's awards crashing to the floor. The office seemed to shrink around him as if someone were pushing in the walls, closing him in.

"You don't have to do it, baby."

"Do what?"

"Are you back with me?"

When Caleb nodded, he continued. "I've never seen you pull back like that in the middle of a full-on attack."

Caleb was embarrassed to admit the reason had something to do with the sight of Logan on his knees in front of him. "What did Dabb have to say?"

"We can talk about it later," Logan said, rising to his feet.

Caleb let Logan hug him close for a few blissful moments, luxuriating in the warm smell of his body. Burying his face against Logan's chest, he said, "Tell me what he said."

Logan muttered, "Stubborn little shit," before he continued. "Foster's been arrested for assaulting a police officer. She hauled off and slapped Dabb in front of a witness."

Stunned, Caleb asked, "Why did she do it?"

"Bastard wouldn't tell me what he said to her, but a breathalyzer test showed she was totally trashed." Logan looked reluctant to continue, so Caleb gave him a "get on with it" look. "Dabb's working with the theft division detectives to get a warrant to search her house. He needs you to come down to the station and make a statement about what happened last night and what you witnessed in the warehouse."

"She never admitted to anything and it's been too long. They can't hope to prosecute her for what happened four years ago."

Sounding far too patient, Logan said, "They just need to convince a judge to let them search and hopefully they'll find evidence of stolen goods."

Caleb was ashamed to admit he wouldn't have cared if Karen continued to rip off the company if she hadn't targeted Logan. Not very civic minded of him but true. Karen had made it personal, and he had no choice but to act. "Call him and let him know I'm on the way."

CHAPTER
ELEVEN

WHILE Logan had been in with Klass and Caleb, the flow of deliveries seemed to have quieted down somewhat, and from then on, the remaining hours dragged by. He worked out his shift hoping to be the guy to get sent home if the supervisor decided there were too many workers on the floor. Much as he needed the money, he wanted to get out of work.

Exhaustion pulled at Logan as he stared at Caleb's apartment building, but he couldn't go home without checking on Caleb first. John Dabb had insisted on taking Caleb to the police station, and Logan had been grateful for it. He couldn't stand the idea of Caleb sitting alone in an interview room and having to explain about his panic attacks to two detectives that would likely look at him like he was a freak. They wouldn't understand how brave Caleb was. He trusted Dabb to make sure they treated Caleb right.

After making his way upstairs, Logan rapped his knuckles against Caleb's door. He heard the squeak of the floorboards under the thin carpet, but the door didn't open. Placing his palm against the wood he said, "Caleb?" More squeaking. As he was digging his cell phone out of his pocket, he heard the scraping sound of the chain being unlocked. The door creaked open by itself, eerily similar to a horror movie. He half expected a monstrous cat to come flying at his head as he pushed the door open and entered.

"What the...?" At first glance, the living room looked like it had been ransacked. Couch cushions tossed on the floor. Books pulled from the bookcases and dumped in piles on the cream carpet. DVDs were stacked precariously on the coffee table in a crooked column. There seemed to be stuff heaped on every available surface. Looking carefully, he noticed that nothing appeared to be broken or damaged. It likely wasn't vandalism then since the TV wasn't smashed and they hadn't made off with the stereo. It looked more as if someone had been searching for something. He spotted Caleb standing in the kitchen. A wave of déjà vu moved through him at the sight. Caleb's arms were wrapped around himself as if his grip was the only thing holding him together. After everything that had happened today, Logan wouldn't be surprised for it to end in a panic attack. He'd witnessed three attacks since Caleb had been getting treatment, and had read the literature the therapist gave him. But none of that explained the state of the apartment.

"What's going on, Caleb?" Logan asked softly. The kitchen was in worse shape than the living room. Dishes, food storage containers, pots, and cooking paraphernalia he couldn't begin to identify were stacked haphazardly on the countertop and floor. What looked like the contents of the pantry were in and around the sink.

Caleb looked at the clock on the stove that read 6:02 p.m. "You're off work early," he said, his voice sounding flat.

"Klass let me go home early," Logan said, leaving the "so I could check on you" left unspoken. "Did you lose something?" he asked, gesturing to the chaos around them.

Caleb's green eyes studied him for what seemed like hours, and then to Logan's surprise his expression shifted, shedding the assessing gaze and edging into something that looked astonishingly like grief. "No, but I found something."

"What di—" Logan started to say before his brain snatched the words from his mouth and smacked him over the head with them. He hadn't thought about that bottle in weeks since he'd shoved it in the bathroom cabinet. He'd meant to go back and get rid of it once he had better control of himself. *How could I have forgotten?*

Caleb threw his arms up, fists balled. "Have you been drinking this whole time? Is that why you got together with me?" He grabbed the minibottle of scotch off the counter that Logan hadn't noticed amongst all the other stuff. "So you'd have a convenient place to stash your booze that your PO can't search?"

"You know that ain't true." Logan pointed at the bottle. "Check the seal. I never drank from that bottle or any other bottle."

"I don't know what to think, Logan." Leaning against the fridge, he slid down until he was sitting on the linoleum floor. "Whether you drank it or not doesn't change the fact that you've been hiding it from me. That you didn't trust me enough to tell me what you were going through."

Logan followed Caleb's lead and sat on the floor. A wall of Tupperware and cooking pots stood between them. "I shoved the bottle in the cabinet to get it away from me because I didn't trust myself not to drink it. And then I just put it out of my head."

"Why not ask me to throw it out for you? Or talk to me about what you were going through?"

Caleb made a frustrated noise when Logan offered no explanation. "You know every humiliating detail about my panic attacks and you've shared almost nothing about your struggles with alcohol now or in the past. I've meet with your sponsor, Stacy, but she can only give me general information about alcoholics, nothing specific to you. And today was the first time I'd heard Michael's name, let alone that you apparently have him investigating Karen."

"It's not the same damn thing," Logan said. "You have trouble leaving your apartment and I nearly beat a man to death with my bare hands." He paused, taking a deep breath. He'd seen the similarities between addiction and agoraphobia right from the beginning. On the surface, Caleb was more likely to hurt himself than others, but there were more ways to hurt than physical. Seeing Caleb look so still and lifeless on the bed had taken ten years off Logan's life, bringing back memories he'd just as soon forget. He could remember hesitating before walking into his father's bedroom each morning, wondering if today would be the day he'd find a corpse buried under the covers. Caleb had thrust him straight back to that hell by disabling the phone instead of calling for help. But that was a long way from the damage Logan could do to Caleb if he went back to drinking.

"I walked into this relationship with my eyes wide open. John Dabb made sure of that." Dropping the bottle, he drew his knees tight against his chest. "So either you don't think I could handle hearing about it or you don't think I could help."

Even though he knew it was true, Logan still couldn't believe Caleb had seen the crime photos. How could he see those and not be afraid? Michael hadn't been afraid to love him even when he should have been. Logan didn't remember fracturing Michael's wrist, but he'd heard the snap in his dreams too many times to count. "If you were smart, you'd have nothing to do with me, but that don't stop me from lo… wanting you. I want to become the kind of man you deserve, but I'm not there yet." He felt something in his jaw start to throb. "I don't like reminding you of that."

"I love you," Caleb said, proving again how fucking brave he was. "But I've spent too much time feeling helpless, and I won't go back to that life. You have to be able to talk to me and to let me help you. If you can't, then there's no point in us being together."

Logan realized he'd asked the same thing of Caleb. It couldn't have been easy for Caleb to talk about the panic attacks. Hell, Caleb had confessed to pissing in the kitchen sink the first day of his accident, because he was too afraid to go back into the bathroom. For a neat freak, that was right up there with causing an apocalypse. He'd solved the problem by not eating or drinking anything the rest of the weekend, adding dehydration and low blood sugar to his broken wrist and concussion. He'd trusted Logan not to mock or judge him when he talked about it.

"Michael has been my best friend since we were in the sixth grade. He and me always looked after each other, because our parents sure as hell weren't going to do it. But the booze twisted that and made things worse. I'd blow my grocery money at the liquor store and he'd sneak food into my fridge or offer to pay for pizza. I'd call him up too drunk to remember my own address and he'd crawl out of bed to come pick me up. He'd threaten to never speak to me again if I didn't get help, but in a couple of days he'd be back to sitting on that barstool next to me, feeling completely helpless. I hurt him in every way possible."

"Do you regret hurting him?"

"Now? Hell, yes. But back then… I didn't care, Caleb. The only thing I cared about was getting my next drink. He'd been like a brother to me for so long, but none of that mattered. If I go back to drinking, you won't matter either."

Caleb shook his head. "I don't believe that. You're not the same man you were a year ago. That man didn't know what it felt like to lose everything and have to start over."

Caleb looked at the single-serving bottle of scotch whiskey on the floor, forcing Logan to remember that his idea of a serving of booze used to be about the equivalent of ten of those minibottles.

"When did you buy it?"

"Weeks ago from a guy selling on the street."

"You mean six weeks ago, right? When I broke my wrist?"

"I didn't lie to you, Caleb. I didn't get drunk because you didn't answer the door or answer the phone when I called."

Caleb nodded. "It's one of the things I've been working on with my therapist. I can feel bad about making you worry or upsetting you, but I'm not responsible for how you choose to react to those emotions." He shrugged. "It's still a work in progress." Uncurling his body, he crawled over the items on the floor and sat cross-legged in front of Logan. "Tell me what you were thinking when you bought it."

Logan paused, trying to remember what was going through his head at the time. "Whenever I used to try and quit drinking, I'd do okay for a while. But then something would happen and I'd end up bingeing, drinking twice as much as I usually did. I hadn't had a drink in three days when I walked into the bar the night of the fight. As I was sitting in the holding cell, I remember thinking I should've had some booze on hand, just in case things got too bad. I wouldn't have gone out to the bar that night if I had."

Caleb traced the side of Logan's face, the skin of his fingers impossibly soft against Logan's stubbled jaw. "Do you still believe that?"

Logan sighed, leaning into the touch. "No, I woulda drunk it and then gone looking for more. The booze makes you a liar and the lies you tell yourself are the biggest."

Caleb could be naive about a lot of things, but he knew too much about denial and the damage it could wreak. He wouldn't be fooled by Logan's attempts to avoid the problem if he started drinking again, if he learned about the signs. "Michael has been going to Al-Anon meetings, for friends and family of alcoholics. Would you…." He swallowed the baseball lodged in his throat. "Would you go with him sometime? You don't have to keep going if—"

Caleb scrambled on top of his lap until they were face to face, peppering Logan with kisses. "Yes, yes, yes."

Logan wrapped his arms around Caleb, burying his face against his neck. "Love you too," he whispered against his cheek. Hearing a hitch in Caleb's breathing, Logan tightened his hold.

After a few minutes, they untangled and Logan's eyes were drawn to the clock. "I'm not working tomorrow. Why don't you put off cleaning this place until tomorrow morning and I'll come by and help you?"

"I could make bacon pancakes," Caleb said, smiling so sweetly Logan nearly missed the evasion.

Caleb had to have been searching for hours, and Logan didn't doubt he'd spend all night cleaning it. He could understand the impulse, not wanting to wake up with the apartment still torn apart. Taking out his cell phone, Logan punched in Dabb's number. Dabb picked up after only one ring as if he'd been expecting the call.

"I'm at Caleb's and I was hoping to stay," Logan said, only just then realizing it sounded like he was asking for permission for a booty call.

"Is he okay?"

Logan took a deep breath, not realizing until now what he intended to do. "I fucked up," he said, and Caleb gripped his bicep hard enough to bruise. "I stashed a minibottle of booze here weeks ago and Caleb found it."

The silence that followed was deafening, but the warmth of Caleb's body pressed close was comforting.

"You didn't have to tell me that," Dabb said, sounding both in awe and annoyed at the same time.

"You said being that man was a choice. I'm making mine. I don't want to be that man again."

"Let me talk to Caleb."

Reluctantly, Logan held out the phone to Caleb. "He wants to talk to you."

Logan moved into the living room and started replacing the books on the shelves. He tried not to listen to the conversation, but it was pretty obvious Dabb was making sure Caleb wasn't traumatized by going to the PO office alone, being interviewed by detectives, and finding alcohol hidden in his apartment. Jesus, it had been a long fucking day. Logan put another dust-free (how is that even possible?) book on the shelf. After a few minutes, Caleb gave him back the cell phone.

"Here's what we're going to do," Dabb said. "You will go back to contacting me weekly instead of once every three weeks. And you will talk to your sponsor and share at your next AA meeting about what happened."

Logan winced. Stacy was going to be pissed that he hadn't told her about buying the booze. "I didn't drink it."

"You don't need to drink to act like a drunk."

Logan rubbed his forehead. A dry drunk. That was what they called it in AA, and Stacy had alluded to it when they'd talked in the cafe. It wasn't enough to be sober. You'd end up right back where you started if you didn't deal with the shit that had you picking up the bottle in the first place.

"Are we clear?"

"Yeah." Logan ended the call. "It'll be okay," he told Caleb, towing him forward and wrapping his arms around him. Caleb relaxed into the embrace with a weary sigh, and Logan kissed the top of his head. "Let's put this place back together."

Logan finished replacing the books on the shelves and moved on to the TV cabinet. Caleb likely had some system for sorting the DVDs like alphabetical by genre or something, but at least Logan could give him the appearance of order. After replacing the couch cushions, he entered the bedroom. It wasn't in bad shape. Not surprising considering how few clothes Caleb seemed to own. It only took a few minutes to clean up, leaving the scene of the crime remaining.

The bathroom looked like it had exploded. Packages of soap, cleaning products, toilet paper, and an assortment of grooming products littered the floor and filled the sink. The toilet tank cover was balanced on the seat. Caleb could give Dabb a few pointers. He'd thought to look in places Logan had never even considered. And he'd had plenty of experience hiding booze from Michael. Caleb had unscrewed the grid panel on the air vents and even taken apart the wall sconces. Thinking about what Caleb must have been going through as he searched made the muscles under Logan's skin jump.

CALEB took a seat on an island stool, exhaustion battling with his jangled nerves. The kitchen was restored. His hands were red and wrinkled from scrubbing. That he had been rattled enough to put dishes on the *floor* unnerved him. Slumping forward, he propped his head up with his elbow. The frantic searching had seemed eerily similar to a panic attack. His mind had felt thick and disjointed, unable to focus on anything but the search.

Logan exited the bedroom, eyes on his cell phone. "Dabb says to tell you they got approval to offer Foster a deal. What's he talking about?" Putting the phone away, he approached a bit tentatively as if not sure of his reception.

Caleb barely resisted the urge to smack his forehead against the countertop. Sitting up, he summoned a smile. It must have looked hideous, given Logan's expression.

Moving behind him, Logan placed his hands on the back of Caleb's shoulders. His fingers began to rub and soothe the muscles of his neck, easing the tension Caleb hadn't realized was there until it faded.

"When the police showed up at Karen's house, they found her boyfriend shoving boxes into their SUV," Caleb said. "They brought him down to the station and it only took ten minutes for him to call his lawyer and demand a plea deal in exchange for implicating Karen." The detectives had been courteous when he gave his statement but somewhat jumpy. They kept shooting little glances at Dabb before they asked their questions, making Caleb think it had been a waste of time to come down to the station. He should have felt vindicated when John told him what they had discovered, but mostly he felt numb. "They're holding her on the assault charge for hitting John for the time being. But John said she'll probably accept a deal to avoid standing trial for larceny. Likely, she'll serve six months in prison and be required to seek help for gambling and alcohol addiction."

Logan slid his arms around Caleb and held him tight. "There's a chance it'll help her," he said, the skepticism clear in his voice. "It'll be her choice."

Caleb broke the embrace and turned to look at him. "She doesn't deserve it. You would've spent two more years in prison if she'd gotten your parole revoked." Just saying the words made his heart lurch.

Logan's mouth spread into a thin-lipped smile. "From what I'm told, the guy in the bar fight was an asshole who probably deserved to get hit for throwing the first punch. But he didn't deserve what I done to him. Michael and those two other patrons didn't deserve to be hurt. My second chance came at their expense."

"Are you saying we should forgive Karen for everything she did?"

"I won't forgive her for hurting you," Logan said, shaking his head. "But for what she tried to do to me?" He shrugged. "She likely wouldn't have targeted me if I didn't have a record."

Caleb cocked his head. "She didn't factor in John. My uncle told him about the thefts and it was the reason John kept showing up at the warehouse even when he didn't need to check on you."

Logan frowned. "Why did your uncle tell Dabb about the thefts while talking about my parole conditions?"

Ducking his head, Caleb said, "They... uh... have apparently known each other for years. I think that's why my uncle picked you to work for me, but John claims he didn't know anything about it."

"John claims, huh?" Logan mimicked, his jet-black eyes narrowing. "When the hell did you and *John* become best friends?"

"He asked me to call him John and he's been a great help to both of us. He stayed with me when the detectives interviewed me and I don't think I could've gotten through it without him. We talked for a while before he drove me home."

"You know Dabb wants you, right?"

"God, don't ever say that!"

Logan raised his eyebrows. "Not that I'm not thrilled by the reaction, but I am wondering why. You got something against May-December romances or Dabb in particular?"

"John and Uncle Harrison met twenty years ago and they were... friends with benefits for like ten years before John got married. They've kept in touch ever since."

"Are you shitting me?"

Caleb shook his head. "John accidentally let it slip when I figured out they knew each other. He was pretty distressed when he realized I didn't even know my uncle was gay."

Logan snorted. "I coulda told you that. No straight man is gonna pick out guys he thinks his nephew will find attractive just to deliver the mail even if he's trying to goad him into leaving the apartment."

Caleb heard the whistle of the teapot, pushed to a standing position, and went to the stove. Turning off the burner he said, "I guess I should've known. Especially since I've never known him to date anyone, but I assumed he was too busy helping my mom and me." He held up a mug. "Hot chocolate?"

When Logan gave his assent, Caleb filled the mugs with his special blend of spicy cocoa powder and added the boiling water. While blending the mixture he said, "When I came out to him my junior year of high school, he let me know he was okay with me being gay, but he didn't want me to tell my mom." He handed Logan a mug and then picked up his own. "Apparently, she knew about him, but he was afraid she would react badly to finding out about me."

"Knowing about a brother and a son isn't always the same," Logan said softly. He took a sip of the hot chocolate, groaning at the first taste.

Caleb took a deep swallow from the rich drink, letting its warmth soothe him. "It doesn't matter, not anymore. We both need to move forward and try to be better about supporting each other." He wrinkled his nose. "I'm just having a little trouble processing my uncle being gay and having a former relationship with John."

Logan laughed so hard he spilled hot chocolate all over the counter. "Who do you think topped? Or maybe they switched?"

Caleb threw a tea towel at him. "Stop! I don't ever, ever want to think about that."

Logan's grin said that was fantastic news, and Caleb couldn't help rolling his eyes. He set his mug in the sink. Still snickering, Logan brought him the other mug and the dirty towel.

Wrapping his arms around Logan's neck, Caleb said, "I don't want Dabb. Or Daniel." He laughed. "Or the tranny on the second floor." He kissed Logan. "Not even the very hot Carlos. You're who I want. Let me have you." They kissed again.

Pulling back Logan asked, "Who's Carlos?"

Caleb snorted. "An ex-con I met today at the PO office who thought I was a hooker."

"Hoped you were is more like it," Logan grumbled, putting his hands on Caleb's hips. "And it's no wonder with these clothes."

Caleb looked down at his sweats and long-sleeved Cubs T-shirt. "Okay, I get they're a little tight, but they're old and ratty not sexy."

"They're sexy on you. Trust me, baby. I whacked off the first day we met thinking of you in those sweats."

"Really?"

"Oh, yeah," Logan said, lifting him effortlessly and depositing him on the granite counter top. "Don't go nowhere."

Caleb felt a little ridiculous sitting here with his feet dangling, especially when Logan left the kitchen. It reminded him of sitting on an examination table, waiting for the doctor to show up and start poking him. All that was missing was thin white paper under his ass. "What are you doing?"

Retrieving a pair of scissors out of the desk drawer, Logan said, "We need to have a wardrobe intervention for your own good."

Caleb nibbled at his bottom lip. "They're comfortable."

Logan shook his head. "You don't wear them because they're comfortable. You wear them because they comfort you." He walked back into the kitchen and placed the scissors on the counter.

Covering Logan's hand with his own, Caleb asked, "What if I promise not to wear them out?" He rubbed a thumb over Logan's knuckles.

"We'll get you some that fit instead of ones that cut into your skin and leave bruises." Logan grabbed a chunk of Caleb's Cubs T-shirt on his upper chest and snipped.

Looking down at the hole, Caleb said, "Were you lying about not being a Cardinal fan?"

Grinning, Logan pushed Caleb's thighs apart and stood between them. "I'll buy you a new one." He blew on the exposed skin, his breath warm and sweet. Caleb's nipple shot to attention, eager to please in spite of its owner's objections.

Logan circled the skin around the puckered bud with his calloused fingers. "You don't need them anymore."

"I don't want to do this right now. Let's just go to bed."

Logan watched him closely. "Tell me why."

"It's been a long day and I'm tired."

"Try again," Logan said, shaking his head.

Caleb felt his eyes well and he rubbed them, mortified to be near tears over a stupid T-shirt. "I know it's ridiculous to want to keep them. I'm not ready to give them up, but I can put them away and start wearing the new stuff."

"If you shove the clothes away in your closet…." Logan shook his head and grumbled something that sounded like "or the bathroom cabinet." Looking sheepish, he continued, "Then they'll always be there if things get too bad and you need them again."

As he fingered the worn fabric of his gray sweats, Caleb's thoughts unwillingly traveled back to the past several years. When he had first stopped going out, it had been easy to convince the package handlers his uncle hired just to knock and leave the items outside the door. Weeks would go by when he didn't speak directly to anyone. Until his uncle got wind of it. Caleb suspected it was Mrs. Simon who ratted him out. Then his uncle hired Marco, the incorruptible. There was a reason Marco never ate Caleb's cooking. All attempts to bribe, badger, or beg the stubborn man failed. Marco refused to make it easier for Caleb to hide. His kindness and friendship had started Caleb on the journey that Logan helped him complete. It would be wrong to let all that effort go to waste. Lifting his lashes, he met Logan's piercing stare, giving a small nod.

Logan smile looked like it might split his face in half. He laid the scissors on the top of Caleb's thigh.

Looking down, Caleb asked, "Do I have to actually be wearing the sweats when we cut them up?"

"No, but it's better this way."

"Why is it better to a have a sharp pointy object near my groin?"

Logan gave him another toothy grin. "Positive association is what I think your shrink called it. Whenever you think about getting rid of the rest of your old clothes, you'll associate it with me sucking your cock."

Caleb's mouth dried. "That could work."

"Hmm, time for some active participation." Logan slid his fingers under the collar of the T-shirt and cut through the fabric. "Give it a yank, baby."

After a moment's hesitation, Caleb grabbed his collar with both hands and pulled, his cheeks warming as the shirt ripped to just below his collarbone. Tilting Caleb's neck back, Logan rubbed his thumb over the red marks from the too-tight collar, making Caleb shiver. Leaning over, he used his tongue to trace down to the collarbone, and Caleb massaged the back of Logan's neck, encouraging the contact. Logan continued to remove chunks of material—tasting and nibbling the exposed skin—until Caleb's T-shirt resembled Swiss cheese.

"God, baby, you're so beautiful." Cupping Caleb's face in his big hands, he leaned forward for a deep kiss. His tongue tasted sweet and spicy, like the hot chocolate.

Logan pinched the fabric on Caleb's inner thigh and snipped it. Putting the shears aside, he took hold of the fabric and pulled, the material ripping in protest. He yanked on the sweats repeatedly until he had created a hole big enough to fit his hand inside. Massaging the sensitive skin of Caleb's inner thigh, Logan kissed him. Caleb made an abortive moan as his tongue was sucked slowly and thoroughly.

Caleb canted his hips when Logan pressed his other hand against the tented fabric of his sweats. Breathing deeply, he smelled the odd combination of musk and kitchen cleaner. With great care, Logan made a hole in the straining fabric. Caleb's cock poked through the opening.

Caleb groaned as his cock was swallowed down to the root. Using his thumb and forefinger to loop around Caleb's length tightly, Logan slid his lips back up again, playing his tongue over the soft ridge of Caleb's dick, tasting and teasing him before plunging forward again. Caleb's fingers slid along the cool surface of the granite as he leaned back. Logan's bristled chin and the slick heat of his tongue created a delicious contrast as he sucked hard.

Caleb shuddered and he cried out, "Close," wanting to give Logan a chance to pull back.

Logan growled, the vibration sending a jolt through Caleb's whole body. Caleb cried out wordlessly, thrusting his hips with abandon and shooting come on Logan's tongue. Watching the rapid rise and fall of Logan's chest, Caleb willed his sated body to move.

Caleb yanked at Logan's T-shirt, the need to touch his skin still strong in the hazy afterglow of his orgasm. He unbuckled the fly and unzipped Logan's jeans. "Do you want me to—"

"Use your hand," Logan demanded, grabbing the sides of Caleb's face. "I want your lips. They drive me insane," he said, before attacking Caleb's mouth. His tongue seemed to probe every inch of Caleb's mouth, and Caleb tasted the saltiness of his own release and his lover's growing desperation. Caleb moved his hands over the contours of Logan's defined chest, the skin warm and damp under his fingers.

Groping blindly, Caleb found Logan's cock and began pumping it. Logan's knees knocked against the island, and he let out a frustrated grunt. The angle wasn't right for someone over six and half feet tall. Caleb pushed on his chest to get enough room to kneel, wishing there was a towel to spare his knees. Logan had other plans. He snatched Caleb around the waist and hauled him up. One hand planted under Caleb's ass and the other keeping his undone jeans from falling, he walked into the living room.

"Show off," Caleb accused, wrapping his arms around Logan's neck.

"Midget," Logan countered, dropping Caleb from high enough to make the leather couch squeak when he landed. Caleb gave a momentary thanks that it was late enough that Mrs. Simon would be asleep with her hearing aid turned off.

Logan shucked his jeans and boxers in one fluid movement. Caleb wanted to follow suit and get out of what remained of his clothes, but Logan didn't give him a chance before he pounced. His lips found Caleb's again in a breath-stealing kiss.

Scrambling to his knees, Caleb took hold of Logan's pulsing cock. Logan jerked his hips, pressing his stiff length into Caleb's hand harder, faster. The strength of his movements shoved Caleb backward until his back nearly bowed over the top of the couch. The leather felt cool and slick on his skin. A wall of hard muscle pressing against him should have felt stifling, but instead it felt right. Even though there was no way he could get hard again so soon. His dick twitched as if accepting the challenge.

Gasping for breath, Caleb angled his body to suckle Logan's hard nipple. Logan growled low and grabbed a fistful of Caleb's blond hair, yanking their mouths together again. Another bruising kiss and he pressed their foreheads together, their panted breaths mingling. "Every day I want to drink," Logan whispered hoarsely. "But I want you more."

Caleb's eyes burned as he kissed Logan softly. "You have me."

A shudder ran through Logan's body, and he released his hold on Caleb's hair. Snaking a hand between them, he fisted Caleb's cock. One stroke from his strong fingers nearly sent Caleb over the edge for the second time. Seeing as how Logan hadn't gotten off once yet, Caleb figured he should do something about that. If only his spine hadn't turned to jelly.

Logan's smug grin said he knew the effect he was having and loved it. Angling to the side, he wrapped both their cocks in one tight fist. All Caleb could do was sink his fingers into the corded muscles of Logan's biceps and hold on. A few strokes later, he peaked, a wordless noise forcing its way out of his throat. He sprayed spurt after spurt of his sticky seed between their tightly pressed bodies.

Caleb leaned forward, burying his face against Logan's neck. "I want you to come all over my clothes," he said, and Logan shot his load, covering the tattered remains of Caleb's T-shirt and sweats with threads of warm come.

LOGAN hadn't realized how tired he was until he climbed into the bed. The mattress was much more comfortable than his single bed. His feet didn't even hang off the end. He shifted onto his back, drawing Caleb to his chest before pulling the covers over both of them. Caleb's skin felt incredible underneath his palm: soft, supple, and slightly damp with sweat. It felt so right to be lying here with Caleb draped across his chest, the heat of their bodies mingling. There was no way he could wait until his parole ended to sleep with Caleb in his arms again. He had no illusions that tonight was anything other than a onetime concession from Dabb. He needed to get out of the rathole and into somewhere decent. He wouldn't care if it was small so long as he could call it home without shame.

"What's wrong," Caleb asked, sounding on the verge of sleep.

"I was thinking I should pick up a newspaper on Sunday and check out the classifieds."

Caleb kissed his chest softly. "Most of the apartment listings are online nowadays. I could help you look if you want."

"I'd like that, but it might be a couple of months 'til I can save up enough for a deposit."

Sounding more awake, Caleb said, "According to my last bank statement, you haven't cashed the five hundred dollar severance check I gave you. It won't be enough for a deposit, but it would be a start."

Logan had been annoyed to find the check stuffed in with his paycheck. Klass was a sneaky as his nephew. "I don't want to be paid for helping you."

Caleb lifted his head and turned to look at Logan. "I'm not suggesting it. The conditions of your employment clearly stated you would be given four weeks' notice or pay in lieu of notice unless being dismissed for just cause." He poked Logan in the stomach. "Did you not read the employment letter I gave you and Dabb?"

Logan remembered it looked real official. "I thought it was cute how the *C* in CK Web Solutions looked a little like the Cubs' logo."

"It's a legitimate business expense. I would never submit a fraudulent cla—"

"Okay, okay," Logan said, pulling Caleb down for a kiss. "I believe you." When Caleb grumbled, Logan kissed his forehead. "Didn't read it 'cause I knew it would be fair if you wrote it."

"You still should have read it," Caleb said, sounding marginally mollified.

Logan chuckled. "Sleep now, because you're not leaving this bed tomorrow."

Caleb settled into place. "Not even for bacon-filled pancakes and real maple syrup?"

Logan's resolve crumbled under the weight of starchy delights. "To cook, but we eat in bed." He held his breath, wondering if the request would be too much for Caleb's inner neat freak.

"Sounds like a plan," Caleb said, sounding far too pleased with himself.

Logan groaned. "I'm going to end up in a frilly apron, aren't I?"

Caleb patted his chest. "And nothing else."

JD RUSKIN writes character-driven romance stories about complicated and a little screwed-up men. She believes in happily ever after endings, but she's not afraid to make the boys work for it. She enjoys writing and reading stories with juicy plots, memorable characters, and smoking hot encounters. When not writing, she has a passion for traveling, photography, and graphic design.

Visit her website at www.jdruskin.com or contact her at jdruskin1184@gmail.com. You can also find her online at www.facebook.com/#!/JDRuskin1184.

Also from DREAMSPINNER PRESS

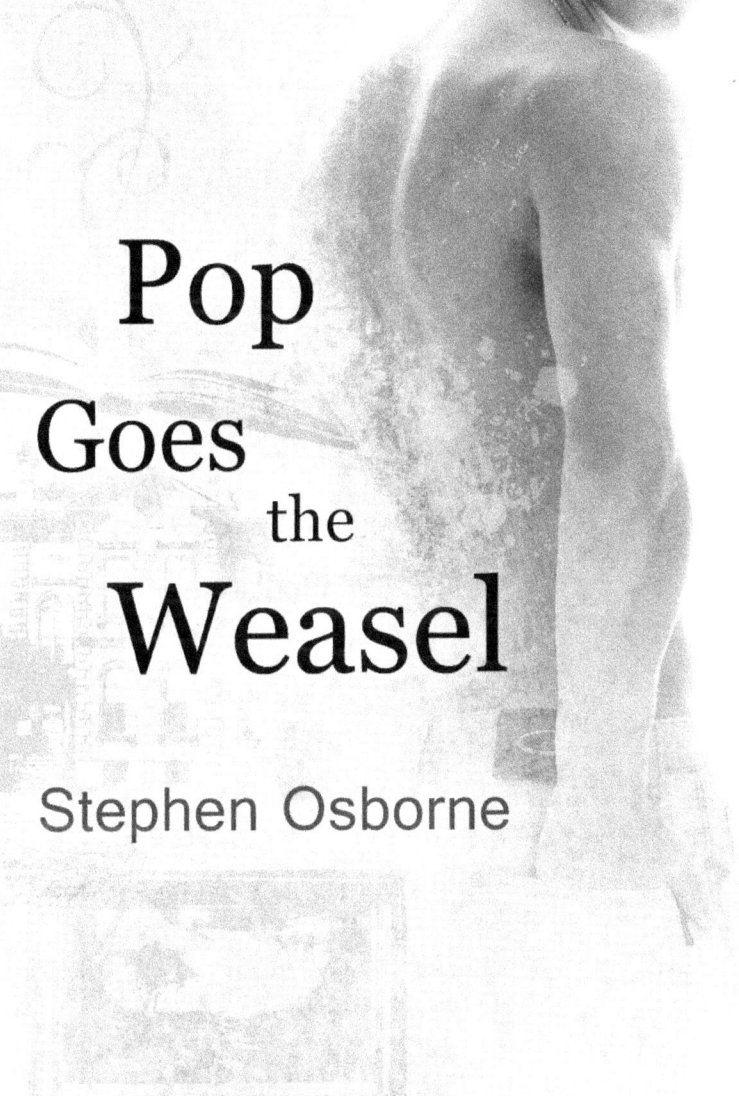

Pop
Goes
the
Weasel

Stephen Osborne